Smoky Darling

A Darling Lake Novel

S. J. Tilly

Smoky Darling
Darling Series Book One

Cover: Lori Jackson Designs
Editor: Brittni Van, Overbooked PA Services

This book is dedicated to my Banshees.
You know who you are.
And you make my life better.

Heads up...

Chapter 1

Elouise: Age 7

"Move in, Lou's up!" Brandon's sneer goes straight into my chest, but I'm not gonna let him scare me away. Not today.

Clenching my fists at my sides, I step up to the chalk outline of home plate.

The other kids chuckle as they all take a few large steps forward.

Kick the ball. Just kick the stinkin' ball and pretend it's Brandon's stupid face.

Pulling in a deep breath, I poof out my cheeks as I exhale.
Focus.

Brandon laughs as he shares a look with the kid guarding first base.

I squeeze my fists tighter. *I'm making it to that freaking base.*

"Just pitch the damn ball!" I shout the words, surprising us both.

His eyes narrow, "Whatever you say."

Brandon spins the kickball one more time before he cradles

it in his right hand, pulls his arm back, then sends the ball flying across the blacktop towards me.

I take a couple stutter steps forward, trying to time my strides perfectly.

Closer.

Closer.

One more step and I kick out with all my might, my toe connecting with the rounded rubber surface.

Except the ball doesn't rise off the ground. Instead it skids across the blacktop, straight towards Brandon.

Crap!

Kids are already yelling about me being *Out*, but there's no quitting. Not today. Not for me. So, I run.

My legs pump, moving as fast as I can towards the manhole cover marking first base.

Brandon shouts something, but I don't listen. I just keep running.

Footsteps sound behind me, and I know Brandon's chasing me so he can tag me out. But he hasn't thrown the ball to the kid on first base so I have a chance.

The distance between me and my goal is shortening.

I'm going to make it!

A sudden shove to my back sends me flying forward.

The tips of my shoes scrape against the road as I try - and fail - to catch my balance. Instead of screaming, I feel the air freeze in my lungs as I brace for impact.

I have just enough time to extend my arms and close my eyes before my palms, then knees, slam into the unforgiving street. There's a second of shock before the stinging pain hits my system.

Don't cry. Don't you dare cry!

I'm surrounded by silence. Everyone waiting to see what I'll do.

"Hey, Asshole!" My brother's angry shout breaks the quiet.

My eyes are still pinched closed, but I can hear the sound of footsteps scattering in every direction. Everyone running for their lives.

Brandon might think he's cool, because he's a 5th grader, but my brother is in middle school.

I want to watch them all flee like the cowards they are, but I'm afraid to move. If I don't move, maybe the pain will go away.

Still trying to catch my breath, I focus my attention on the soft *bounce bounce bounce* of the dropped ball.

James crouches down next to me, "You okay, Lou?"

Opening my eyes, I nod, not sure I won't cry if I try to talk out loud.

I hear more steps approach and I'm sure it's Tony, my brother's best friend. They're always together.

"James, toss me that ball."

Still on my hands and knees, my spine stiffens. That's not Tony's voice. It's too deep. It's... Ohmygod, it's Beckett. Tony's older brother.

Carefully, I turn my head to watch James scoop up the ball and underhand it towards the voice.

A shadow passes over me, and I have to keep turning my head to see all the way up to the person's face.

My heart rate starts to beat wildly all over again. It's definitely Beckett.

Except he's not looking at me. No, he's looking down the street.

"Brandon!" he booms.

His shout is so loud, I swear it echoes off the houses lining the street.

Another voice whispers an "oh shit" and I know Tony's joined the group too.

Following Beckett's line of sight, I see Brandon running through a yard two houses down.

Beckett lets out a grunt of effort, a moment before Brandon slows to look back at whoever called his name.

The kickball is already whistling through the air and my mouth drops open.

No way.

No way is that gonna hit him from this far away!

The timing is perfect. Freaking. Per. Fect.

Brandon's just turned around when the ball hits him square in the face. He didn't even have time to flinch.

And the sound of rubber meeting person is the most satisfying thing I've ever heard.

Brandon's arms fly out to his sides, and he falls flat on his back, landing like a knocked over tree.

James and Tony both let out loud whoops of laughter but I'm still staring in stunned silence. Not believing what just happened.

When another moment passes, and Brandon doesn't move, I hear myself whisper, "Is he dead?"

Beckett snorts then shakes his head, "Nah, just got the wind knocked out of him. Serves the fucker right."

Then Beckett looks down at me, and I forget how to breathe.

He's so dreamy. His chocolate brown hair, his golden eyes, his-

Wait! He's getting closer!

"Come on, let's get you up."

Beckett's big hands slide under the armpits, and he lifts me off the ground like I'm some sort of doll. His tone is so kind, I almost forget that I just saw him smash another kid in the face with a kickball.

He waits until my feet are firmly planted beneath me before he lets go.

By now James and Tony are standing in front of me, checking out the torn knees of my jeans and the few spots of blood on my hands.

"It's not so bad," James smiles. But I know he's just trying to make me feel better, because I saw his wince.

I nod at my brother, then muster up the rest of my courage to look Beckett in the eye. "Thank you."

My voice is quiet and wobbly, but Beckett just shrugs. "No problem, Elouise." Then he turns to our brothers. "You guys got it from here?"

The boys say something in reply, but I don't hear it.

Elouise. He said my name. My full name!

Sure, our brothers have been best friends forever - and I've seen him a few times over the years - but I didn't know he knew my name. My real name too, not just Lou, like most people call me.

And that night, lying in bed, with neon green Band-Aids on both my knees, I decide that I'm in love with Beckett Stoleman.

Chapter 2

Elouise

"Hey!" Maddie drops down next to me on the ground, her black curls bouncing with the movement.

I wave a greeting with my free hand, while the other continues to trace the letters in the dirt with a stick.

"Did you see Brandon's face this morning?" She asks.

But it's not really a question, since we ride the same bus and it's hard to miss his two black eyes and swollen nose.

Maddie and I have been best friends since we sat next to each other in First Grade last year. I wish we were in the same class again this year, but we ended up with different teachers so now we only see each other over lunch and recess. It totally sucks.

"He's been telling everyone that he got into a fight and that they should *see the other guy*," Maddie rolls her eyes, "But Samantha J. heard from her brother, who heard from his neighbor, that Brandon got creamed by a ball, and that's why his face is all messed up today."

Honestly, I was a little surprised he didn't come up to me this morning, demanding that I keep my mouth shut. But it's

6

not like I was the only witness. And maybe the threat of Beckett is enough to keep him away from me for good.

Beckett.

I sigh his name in my mind and trace the letter B again, making it more pronounced.

Maddie leans against my shoulder to see what I'm doing. "E plus B? Ooooo! You have a crush!" She shimmies her shoulders and claps her hands like she always does when she's excited. "What is the B for?"

"Beckett." I tell her because I tell her everything.

"Beckett?" Her face scrunches up. "Who's Beckett?" Maddie turns her head and scans the playground on the other side of the small field.

"He doesn't go here."

"You mean he goes to a different school?" She turns back to me. "How'd you meet him?"

It's a fair question, considering we sat right here the day before and I didn't say anything about him. But in my defense, I didn't know that I was going to fall in love with Beckett Stoleman yesterday.

"He isn't from another town or anything." I switch my focus from the B and drag the end of my stick over the E. "He's just older than us."

"How much older?" Maddie asks slowly.

My cheeks heat because I had the same question last night.

I've always just known him as Tony's older brother but the sudden need for me to know more was overwhelming. So, I waited until James went to his room after dinner then approached my mom.

I hadn't told her about Brandon knocking me down, I just said I tripped during kickball. I didn't want her to freak out and make it a whole big thing.

Sitting next to Mom on the couch, I did my best to act as

casually as possible. "Do you know how old Tony's brother is?" She looked at me over the top of her book and I started to panic so I added, "He was around after school and one of the kids asked me but I didn't know the answer."

I felt bad lying, but I didn't want her asking me a bunch of questions.

She answered me but said it in a way that told me she was suspicious of my motives. Thankfully, before she could interrogate me, the phone rang. She held up a finger as she went to the kitchen to answer it. But two seconds of listening and I knew it was my aunt on the other end of the line, and that they'd be on the phone for the rest of the evening. Which they were.

So, by the time Mom came to tuck me into bed she'd forgotten I'd asked about Beckett.

Scratching at the plus sign, I respond to Maddie's question. "Fifteen."

"Fifteen!?" She shrieks, then doubles over laughing.

"What? It's not that old!" I argue. Even though it is *that* old. He's practically an adult compared to us.

"He's a freaking high schooler?!" Maddie shakes her head and sits up again. "Is he cute?"

I nod and bite my lip.

She nudges me with her shoulder. "Come on! What does he look like?"

Using the tip of the stick, I draw a big heart around the initials. The dirt is hard, so the outline is hard to see, but I keep tracing it over and over.

"He's *so* cute. And tall. He's gotta be the tallest kid in high school." I have no idea if that's true, but it feels true. "And his hair is this perfect shade of brown. Like... I dunno. Like that hot chocolate your mom always gets. And his voice." I drop the stick and fall back onto the ground. "Maddie, you just have to see him."

She lays back next to me. "How'd you meet him?"

I sigh. Then, laying side-by-side, I tell my best friend the whole story. When I get to the part about the ball hitting Brandon in the face, I worry that Maddie might laugh herself to death, but she pulls through.

When I'm finished, she nudges me with her elbow. "Well, what now?"

"What do you mean?" We turn our faces towards each other.

She lifts a hand to gesture wildly. "I mean, what are you going to do about it?"

"Nothing," I grumble.

"What?!"

"Maddie, he's fifteen. I'm not even gonna be eight for another month and seven days."

She huffs, "So what? According to my cousin, older men are better. Something about them being *more experienced*."

"In what?"

She shrugs, "I dunno. But she makes it sound like a good thing. So, I think it's okay that he's..." she pauses, and I see her lips moving as she counts, "...eight years older than you."

"Hmm." I haven't heard anything about *older men* before but her cousin has had lots of boyfriends so she must know what she's talking about. "Alright. Then I guess I gotta find a way to make him like me back."

"How you gonna do that?"

"I have no idea," I turn my gaze back to the sky, "but I'll think of something."

Chapter 3

Elouise: 1 month and 7 days later

"Lou, go make sure your dad didn't forget to put the root beer in the fridge!" Mom yells down the hall.

"Okay!" I yell back, then start searching the house for Dad.

I find him in the garage, bent over the lawnmower, muttering to himself.

Stopping at his side, I look down to see what the problem is, but it just looks like a lawnmower to me. "Whacha doing?"

Dad groans as he straightens up and drops a heavy arm around my shoulders, "I'm getting my butt kicked by a yard tool."

I giggle. Dad always acts like he doesn't know what he's doing, but he'll have it fixed by tomorrow.

"Did you need something? Or are you hiding from Mom's pre-party madness?" He raises his eyebrows because we both know how Mom gets when we have company coming over.

"Mom wanted me to see if you put the pop in the fridge."

Dad tips his head back and slaps a palm to his forehead, making me grin.

"It's still in the car," he admits. "Wanna be a doll and move it for me?"

I roll my eyes. Of course I don't want to do it. I'm the one with the birthday today and therefore I shouldn't have to do any manual labor. But it'll keep me out of the house for a few minutes, so I don't bother pointing that out.

Dad's car is still parked in the driveway but the garage door is open so I walk the few steps over and open the trunk. The cases have slid forward – away from the opening of the trunk – meaning I have to reach so far to grab them that my feet leave the ground.

After a lot of wiggling, I get all the cases moved back to where I can reach them, and haul the first one up and into my arms. I can feel that they're still cold, so this weird fall heat-wave hasn't gotten to them yet.

I shift the weight and trudge around the car back up the driveway. A gust of wind rolls through, making the balloons tied to the front porch bounce all over the place.

On my third trip back to the car, I'm tempted to tell Dad he bought way too much pop, since there's only four people coming over. But it is a sleepover, so maybe Mom will let us drink as much as we want.

Hoisting out the last case, I set it on the ground and reach up to close the trunk when a car pulls up, stopping in the road at the bottom of the driveway.

Tony climbs out of the passenger side, and I remember that Mom told James he could have a friend stay over tonight, too.

"Hi, Lou. Happy Birthday!" Tony calls out, walking up the driveway.

I'm about to respond, when my eyes move back to the car, and my whole body freezes.

Beckett. Beckett is driving the car.

My mouth goes dry, and my palms start to sweat. And *ohmygod I can't believe it's him!*

As hard as I've tried, I haven't even seen a glimpse of him since that day when he defended my honor, helped me up, and called me by name.

Forcing myself out of my daze I lift a hand in a shaky wave. But he's busy doing something with his radio, so he doesn't see me.

"Uh, how's the party planning going?"

The question snaps my attention away from Beckett's profile and I find Tony looking at me with a really weird expression.

"Huh. Oh, um, good." Okay, this is my chance. "You know... Um, if you wanted, I mean if *he* wanted, Beckett could stay for the party."

Tony opens his mouth, but he closes it again without saying anything. Then his eyes dart to something over my shoulder.

"Uh, Lou, did you just invite Beckett to your birthday party?" James' voice sounds from right behind me. And from his tone, I can tell I gave myself away.

I square my shoulders, "It's the nice thing to do."

He steps up next to me. "Since when have you ever been nice?" he teases.

"Shut up." I cross my arms.

"So..." he grins like an idiot, "you want to celebrate your birthday with Beckett, huh?"

"What? It's not that crazy."

"Oh sure, I'm sure 16-year-olds go to birthday sleepovers with 8-year-olds all the time."

I purse my lips, trying to force away my embarrassment. It's not like I don't know how ridiculous my crush is. But it was worth a shot to ask.

James leans back against the car. "Actually, I think this is a great idea. I mean, just think," he smacks Tony on the arm, "if my sister and your brother got married then we would be brothers."

My eyes dart back and forth between James and Tony. I'm pretty sure he's making fun of me, but they are best friends so maybe he really does like the idea.

Wait.

"Sixteen?" I ask, glancing back at the road, only to see Beckett driving away.

My arms uncross and I take a step forward. His birthday must be near mine if he's sixteen now.

I let out a big breath. Beckett can drive now, which makes him a million times cooler. And it makes it that much more obvious that he's out of my league.

A hand lands on top of my head.

"I can tell you're *in love*, but you're too young for a tattoo. So, if you want me to write his name across your forehead in Sharpie, all you have to do is ask." James musses up my hair while Tony laughs.

I shove his arm away. "I'm not in love, dummy." I recross my arms and start walking towards the house. "Mom wants you to bring that pop in." I call over my shoulder, realizing I left the last one on the ground but not wanting to face James and Tony again. Not right now.

I knew my brother would give me crap if he found out about my feelings for Beckett. Which is why I've been careful to not even mention it around James. And I mean, Tony's only ever been nice to me, but I don't know if he'll tell Beckett about this.

Please, pretty please, don't let Tony tell Beckett that I love him.

Chapter 4

Elouise: Age 15

Washing my hands, I inhale the peppermint scented soap. Mrs. Stoleman really went all out with her Christmas decorations, even the hand soap in the little bathroom is themed to the season.

Letting out a sigh, I turn off the water and dry my hands, staring into the mirror.

My reflection stares back at me. Judging me.

I don't know why I tried so hard. I spent hours getting ready today. Hours planning my red velvet dress. My white tights. My shimmery eye shadow. My glossy red and white butterfly clips holding each small braid in place for my half ponytail. When I left the house, I thought I looked amazing. Mature. Adult.

But my lip gloss has worn off. My hair is starting to frizz – despite the layers of hair spray – and the damn crotch of these tights are sagging to my knees.

Growling, I yank my tights up one more time before giving up completely.

This was supposed to be my big debut in front of Beckett.

My reveal.

My *moment.*

But instead of blowing him away with how grown up I've become; he's barely spared me a glance.

Of course, there's like a million freaking people here. I hadn't expected that. I'd wrongly assumed that it was just going to be my family and his. A sort of reunion for James and Tony after their first year of college in separate schools.

Oh, how wrong I was.

Beckett did say hello when we first got here.

But that's it. *Hello.*

No double take. No wide-eyed appreciation. Just *Hello.*

I brush my hands down the front of my dress, smoothing the wrinkles out of the fabric.

I won't be discouraged now. Not after all this time. Not after filling notebook after notebook with our initials. Not after all the tears I cried when he left for college five years ago. Not after the tears I cried all over again when James left for college last year. My parents thought I was distraught about losing my brother, and I mean, I was sad he'd be gone, but really I was sad because with James and Tony out of town I would never get the chance to see Beckett. Maybe ever.

So when my parents told me we'd be coming to this Christmas party at the Stoleman's, I knew this was my chance.

Squaring my shoulders, I pull open the door and step out into the noisy house.

I got this!

Except ten minutes later, here I am, sitting alone at the small breakfast nook in the corner of the kitchen.

Clunking my forehead down on the table, I accept defeat.

How am I the youngest person in this entire house? Seriously, doesn't anyone have nieces or nephews anymore? Or is the whole night a conspiracy to make it obvious that I'm still a baby?

James is busy with Tony and their group of friends from high school. Mom and Dad are chatting it up with the other parents of the neighborhood. And last time I saw Beckett he was deep in conversation with someone's dad.

I lift my head and let it thud back down on the tabletop.

Why does Beckett have to look so freaking handsome? So freaking grownup?

His hair is shorter than the last time I saw him, and his face is showing signs of a beard. I don't really know what a 5 o'clock shadow is, but I think what he has might qualify. And his outfit. *Gah!* He's wearing these khaki pants that make his butt look super cute and this dark red button up shirt that brings out the golden color in his eyes. And if I squeeze my eyes shut really tight, I can pretend that we are dressed to match each other.

Topping off the look, and the absolute worst part, is the glass of wine in his hand. It makes him look that much more sophisticated, and is a stark reminder that he's 23-years-old and that much further out of my league.

"Not having a good time?"

The deep voice startles me so bad, I let out a small scream as I jolt into an upright position.

To my absolute horror, I find Beckett standing two feet away, laughing.

My mouth opens, but my heart is racing and I can't think of anything clever to say.

He makes an apologetic look while pulling out the chair opposite me. "Sorry for scaring you."

I open my mouth again, but... words... what are words?

The lopsided smile he gives me makes it feel like there's a pile of grasshoppers in my stomach. Then he points to himself and says, "I'm Beckett."

Before I can stop it, a small snort comes out and I say, "I know who you are."

My eyes widen. *Oh my god, why did I say it like that!?*

He shrugs, "It looked like maybe you were drawing a blank."

Trying for nonchalant, I shrug back. Then immediately regret the decision. I don't want to look like I'm copying him.

Beckett takes a sip of his wine, his eyes staying on me, and I want to scream. The whole point of me being here tonight was to impress him. But instead, he finds me sitting here like a loser, startling at everything he says.

Get this back on track, Lou!

"So," I start, "How's Chicago?"

His eyebrows raise in surprise, like maybe I wouldn't know what town he went to for school and that he stayed after. But our brothers are friends, so it's not completely unlikely that I'd have heard through them. He doesn't need to know that I've spent the last several years trying to learn everything I could about him.

"It's good. Busy. How's high school?"

He knows that I'm in high school now!

Heat. So much heat fills my chest.

"It's fine," I work to keep my voice level. "Same old, ya know."

He hums, "Do you like school?"

His question catches me off guard. Do I tell him that I love school? Do I try to play coy?

Deciding that I want him to fall in love with the real me, I give him an honest answer. "I do. I'm not like amazing at it, but I want to be a teacher one day."

He makes a thoughtful face and a sound of approval. "I think you'd be good at that."

He thinks I'd be good at teaching!!!

17

He nods, as if reconfirming what he just said, "Good for you, knowing what you want to do when you grow up." *When I grow up. Ouch.* "Most people don't figure that out until they're halfway through college studying under the wrong major. Some never figure it out."

Brushing off the *grow up* comment, I focus on what he just said.

"Did you?" I ask. "Figure it out, I mean."

"I hope so." He smiles.

His smile is so comforting, I feel myself relaxing into the conversation. It's the sort of smile you give a friend. Or someone you like.

"Beck Baby," my body jumps at the sudden grating voice, "there you are!"

If I were a dog, my ears would've laid flat at the sound of someone calling Beckett something so stupid.

I swear I see something like annoyance flicker over his face, but before I can blink, it's gone.

"Kira?" Beckett's tone shows his confusion.

Already feeling sick to my stomach, I turn my head to watch a skinny girl – sorry, woman – in a tight red dress approach us. Her dress is the shorter grownup version of mine. Her hair is bright blonde, curled in big ringlets around her face. She has a pretty black choker around her neck and sparkly heeled shoes. Complete with bare legs.

Beckett slides his chair back, like he's going to get up, but before he can, she lowers herself onto his lap.

That sick feeling inside me grows. Twisting and turning. Coiling up from my stomach and sliding straight to my heart.

"I didn't think you were coming until tomorrow." Beckett says to the woman, perched on his thighs.

"I just couldn't wait that long." She replies, in a voice that sounds like something I'd hear in drama class.

Her eyes dart over to me before she grabs his face in her hands and lowers her mouth to his.

Hot tears fill my eyes as I shove away from the table.

No one tries to stop me.

No one says my name.

No one says anything.

Running in my bare, nylon covered feet, I flee the kitchen.

How could he? How dare he! Right in front of me!?

Humiliation and sadness slam against each other inside my chest.

I push through clusters of bodies until I reach the entryway.

Dropping to my knees, I dig around in the pile of footwear until I find my shoes. Not *shoes*. Not sparkly sexy heels. Big snow boots. Big ugly black snow boots because it's winter outside and because my mom made me wear them. Because I'm still just a kid playing dress up. Because no one will ever see me as anything other than a kid.

Violently shoving my feet into the boots, I find my puffy bright purple jacket that clashes with my dress, and I yank it on over my carefully crafted Christmas outfit.

I'm not being careful or quiet or subtle, but no one notices. Everyone is having way too much fun with all their friends to notice the one child throwing a fit.

I jerk open the door and step out into the cold night.

My breath clouds before me, blurring my view of the sky.

The air is still, the cold hanging all around me, chilling the tears as they slide down my cheeks.

Beckett didn't care.

One deep inhale.

Beckett doesn't love me.

I watch my exhale thicken the air.

Beckett loves someone else.

Another deep inhale.

Beckett won't ever think of me like that.

I blink away more tears as I let my breath out.

I need to stop loving Beckett.

One final inhale.

I can't keep loving Beckett.

One last breath out.

I watch it float up towards the twinkling stars.

I'm going to forget all about Beckett Stoleman.

And I do.

For another three years.

Chapter 5

Elouise: Age 18

"Holy shit, have you seriously gotten that far?"

Maddie's question breaks my concentration. I look up to find her trying to peek over my shoulder, but she's too short to see anything.

Joking, I slap my hand down over the assignment I have on the counter in front of me. "No cheating, you... cheater!"

"Good one," she rolls her eyes, "But for real, how are you almost done?"

I shrug, "It's not like we've been busy."

We both glance around the empty coffee shop, as if to confirm that things haven't suddenly changed.

Maddie sighs, "Yeah, what a boring ass day. I thought people would be out shopping today."

It's my turn to roll my eyes, "That's the day after Thanksgiving, not the day before. Plus it's not like people will come out to Darling Lake to shop. Even the people that live here go into The Cities." I pause, gesturing to the empty street outside the shop. "And I doubt the antique shops around here do Black Friday sales."

"Touché," she snorts, before letting out an exaggerated groan. "Fine. If you're going to be all productive and shit I guess I'll do my Psych homework, too." Maddie backs away from the counter with a smirk and a nod toward the door. "Guess that means you'll have to help the hottie that's about to walk in."

My cheeks start to heat just at the mention of *hottie*.

We're halfway through our senior year and I'm still awkward as hell when it comes to guys. At this rate I'll die a virgin. Thankfully, Maddie's just as bad, if not worse, so I won't die alone.

I'm sliding my homework down to the shelf below when the front door opens and the attached rain stick flips over, filling the space with the soft sound of coffee beans tumbling through a wooden tube.

"Wel-" I start to form the standard greeting – my lungs full of the air needed to form the words – but my eyes lock on the face approaching me and my brain skids to a stop.

The early evening sun is streaming in through the wall of windows across from me, framing the guy – the man – like an angel walking out of the clouds.

Tall. Broad. Unruly locks of hair. Penetrating gaze.

Oh.

Oh, holy shit!

Beckett.

In all his adult glory.

His chin dips down, just an inch, in the coolest gesture I've ever seen.

"Hey," his voice is... deep.

Is it possible that it's gotten even deeper? Does that happen?

There's a sparkle in his eyes and I know it's recognition.

"Hi!" my word cracks halfway through, sounding more like a squeak than English.

He stops directly across the counter from me, a smile tugging at his perfect lips.

I can't keep my eyes on his. It's too much. Too direct. So I let them jump around, taking in his height and the shape of his shoulders.

How many muscles does he have? Did he get taller?

I stopped growing when I was like 14 but maybe guys are different.

Remembering that I'm the one who actually works here, I clear my throat and try again.

"Hi there, um, can I, I mean, what can I get you?"

Ohmygod, I sound ridiculous.

I force my eyes back up and catch him staring at my face. Which of course makes my cheeks darken even more.

This is too close.

I haven't checked my makeup in hours! And I have that pimple. *Oh shit the pimple!*

My smile starts to falter, but I will it to stay in place.

I look good. Okay, I at least look decent. It's been three years since he's seen me, and I know I look older. I've learned how to tame my hair. I've toned down the body shimmer. I've... well I still have that adolescent weight around my hips. And thighs. And ass. And it's probably not even adolescent weight, just regular weight, but I look okay. At least BeanBag doesn't make us wear uniforms. And I'm wearing my good jeans today.

Beckett shifts his weight, pulling his wallet free from his jeans. "I'll take a large black coffee."

Ugh, even his drink order is cool.

"Sounds good!" I tap the correct keys on the register and tell him the total, but he's already holding out a Five.

My fingers tremble a little and I have to make two attempts before I get the cash register open.

Get it together, Lou. I scold myself, before reaching out, handing him back his change. Proud that the paper doesn't flutter in my grip. "Just one sec while I get that for you."

He makes a sound that I take to be understanding and I catch a glimpse of him putting the change into the tip jar as I spin away.

Out of the corner of my eye I see Maddie creeping at the doorway to the backroom, no doubt enjoying the show I've been putting on so far. I can't even look at her when I grab the wrong size cup and have to put it back then pick up the Large one.

Reaching for the coffee spout, I realize I didn't ask him which type of coffee he wanted. There's a moment of paralysis before I decide to just pick for him.

I know Beckett. I used to be in love with him.

Used to. Not anymore. That'd be crazy.

My eyes move between the options before I settle on the dark roast. Rich, bold, robust. The perfect blend for Beckett.

I pull the lever down and watch the dark liquid pour into the cup.

"Hey, you around for dinner tonight?" Beckett's voice vibrates the air and time slows while his question wraps around me like magic from a Fairy Godmother's wand.

After all this time...

Spinning to face him, I breathe out the only answer I could ever give. "Yes!" My voice is full of breathy excitement and my mouth is pulled in the widest smile.

He asked me! Beckett just asked-

The spell pops as several things happen at once.

My spin comes to a stop with me facing Beckett. Beckett, who has a small silver cell phone pressed to his ear.

My heart also stops.

But what doesn't stop – the hot as hell coffee inside the unlidded cup in my hand.

Hot liquid splashes over my knuckles.

My mouth drops open in shock. Whether from the burning of my skin or the scorching embarrassment, I'll never know.

With a small noise of pain, I hurriedly switch hands and set the coffee on the counter, shaking out my right hand.

Maddie's feet slap against the floor as she rushes out towards me, "Elouise!"

Beckett flips his phone shut and is shoving it back in his pocket when Maddie says my name. And right when I thought my life couldn't get any worse, I watch his eyes widen before they drop to the name tag affixed to my shirt.

My hand throbs as my heart deflates.

He doesn't remember me.

"Elouise?" he asks, understanding dawning in his expression. Then he looks back down to the hand I'm clutching to my chest, "Are you alright?"

Laugh or cry, bitch. Time to laugh or cry.

A slightly manic laugh bubbles out of me, "I'm fine. Not the first time I've spilled on myself."

"She's not lying," Maddie agrees, handing me a cold wet towel to wrap around my fingers.

I'm sure she's ready to laugh her ass off at me, but being a true best friend, she waits.

Maddie makes quick work pouring Beckett's coffee into a clean cup and putting a lid on it before handing it to him.

Beckett takes it but keeps his worried gaze on me. "You sure you're alright?"

I bite my lip and nod, because that line between laugh and cry is still *very* thin.

"Thanks so much for coming!" Maddie chirps, moving slightly in front of me.

And the bestest best friend award goes to...

Beckett looks like he wants to say more but thinks better of it and takes a step back. Then with another dip of his chin, he's gone.

I wait until the door closes behind him, then I let out a muffled scream and sink to the floor.

My head drops back against the cupboards and I close my eyes.

I can feel Maddie slide down to sit next to me. "So..." she starts, "is your hand really okay?"

"Feels better already." I hold it up. "Thanks for the towel."

"Good." Humor enters her tone, "Umm, want to tell me why you thought that grown ass man was asking you out?!" She barely gets the question out before she's bent over her knees in hysterics.

Slitting my eyes open, I squeeze the towel above the back of her neck, letting cold water droplets fall onto her exposed skin.

She shrieks but keeps laughing. "Seriously Lou, that guy was so old. I mean he was hot. But *old*."

"He's only 26."

She cocks an eyebrow at me. "One, that's basically 30 and everyone knows your life is pretty much over by then. And two, how do you know his exact age?"

When I sigh, Maddie sits up straighter.

"Wait... do you know that guy?" She pries.

I slowly nod.

Maddie glances back over her shoulder, like she can see through the counter to where he'd been standing just minutes ago.

"That was Beckett."

"Beckett?" her head snaps back to look at me. "THE BECKETT?!" she shouts. "As in the man you've been planning to marry since the second grade?"

This over-the-top reaction is exactly what I need to tip me back towards laughter.

Shaking my head at myself, I confirm, "The one and only."

Maddie fans herself. "Okay, I get it now. The obsession makes total sense."

Chuckling I give her a shove. "I'm not obsessed." She scoffs. "Okay, fine. I'm not obsessed anymore."

Maddie picks up the wet towel from where I set it on the floor and tosses it towards the sink, missing it completely. "Well... you're 18 now. Technically, you could date him if you wanted to."

I close my eyes, settling my head back against the hard surface. "Never gonna happen."

Chapter 6

Elouise: Age 30

"REMIND me again why I agreed to do this?" I ask Maddie.

"Well, for one, you're a total sucker."

A laugh bursts out of me, echoing in the small space. "Fair."

"And two," her voice comes in clearly through my car's speakers, "You love nature."

I groan, and flip my turn signal on, spotting the sign for the state park up ahead. "I love gardening. And sitting on my porch watching birds. I'm beginning to think that I might not love camping."

"Fair. But didn't you go all the time when we were kids?"

"Yeah," I agree, "but that's half the problem. Most of my shit is from when we were kids."

Maddie chuckles, "Don't tell me that you brought your My Little Pony sleeping bag."

"No, that was too small. I brought my brother's old bag."

"Pray do tell, what theme did James's have?"

I can't help but laugh at myself. "Teenage Mutant Ninja Turtles."

She snorts, "Those poor kids won't even know what to do with you."

Even though she can't see me, I shrug, "They're used to my bullshit."

"Well that's the truth."

It really is true. A portion of the kids that are coming on this Camping Trip From Hell are students in my fourth grade class. But I'm not the only teacher here. There's Mr. Olson, who teaches the other 4th grade class. Mr. Bob, the gym teacher. And then a bunch of parent volunteers. I didn't read the email closely, but if memory serves the students are all 3rd, 4th and 5th graders.

As if she can hear my thoughts, Maddie asks, "Is Mr. Olson still trying to be besties with you?"

"Kinda, he asked me to call him Richard again, but I just can't," I sigh, and follow the signs toward the campsite we have reserved. "I feel like I'm being a bitch, but when he asked if I'd be willing to help out with this Spring Break Nature Weekend crap, I thought it was a *he's asking everyone because no one wants to do it* sorta thing. But when I said yes, he acted way too happy. Like I'd said yes to a date. Not a weekend of dirt sleeping while chaperoning a herd of kids."

"Yeah, that's awkward," Maddie commiserates. "What would you say if he ever did try to ask you out?"

"Ugh, I hope that never happens," spotting the group of cars, I slow down even more, delaying the inevitable. "I mean he's nice. And he's cute enough. I just don't feel that spark, ya know? There's no excitement when I see him. Plus, I heard he's the one that fucked up our reservation." Maddie laughs. "I'm serious! When I agreed to this, I was told we'd be sleeping in cabins! But no, now I have to sleep my 30-year-old ass on the hard ground. In March. In fucking Minnesota." Her laughter increases. "This isn't funny!" I shout, knowing damn well that it is funny. "Do you have any idea how cold it's supposed to be over the next three days?"

Maddie stops laughing long enough to answer, "Pretty damn cold."

"Pretty damn cold," I grumble out loud, pulling my car into an open parking spot.

"Please tell me you packed more than your brother's sleeping bag from the 90's."

"I brought a whole pile of blankets that I plan to use as a mattress."

"That's something," her voice is filled with fake cheer.

"Oh, fuck off." I drop my head against the steering wheel. "I'm here."

"You got this! It's just three nights. And you said you're bunking with that one mom you like."

"Yeah, yeah."

She chuckles again, "Alright, I'll let you go make your burrow. Text me tomorrow to let me know how it's going!"

"If you don't hear from me by dinner time, send a rescue party," I hang up and force myself to get out of the car.

I open the trunk and start to load up my arms with an assortment of bags. One duffle filled with clothes and toiletries. One backpack filled with snacks and a small bottle of vodka. One overflowing beach bag stuffed with half a dozen throw blankets. And lastly my sad little sleeping bag wrapped around a pillow.

Loaded up like a damn donkey, I trudge down the path, following the handmade signs directing me to the Darling Elementary Group site.

Fifteen minutes later, I've finally made it to my destination.

My arms are trembling and I'm sweating my ass off despite the nearly freezing temperatures. Pretty sure that isn't a good sign for how the next few days are gonna go.

Out of fucks, I drop my arms and let everything fall to the ground around me. I need to find Rebecca and find out which tent is ours so I know where to put my stuff.

Hands on my hips, I catch my breath while taking in the camp site. It's not really what I'd been expecting. I'd pictured it as one big clearing, maybe near the woods, with all the tents in a circle. But that's not what this is.

Dense forest has surrounded me since I pulled off the highway and the trees have only gotten larger the deeper I got into the park. And standing here, looking up, it feels like the center of nowhere, rather than an hour outside of The Cities.

The forest is blocking any wind that might be blowing, and the still air carries the voices of the people who are already here setting up.

Instead of one large clearing, there's a couple dozen small ones. In each little circle of packed earth, a tent has been erected, forming a community of campers. Each tent is a different color and size, creating a sort of mismatched circus feel. And in the center of the cluster of camp sites is one large fire pit, circled by felled tree trunks that I'm assuming will be used as seating. There's also a dozen or so picnic tables that have already been covered with coolers, sealed plastic tubs, and small camping stoves.

"Huh," I say to myself. My dread lessens by a degree as I soak it all in. Then my eyes are drawn to the gravel path that winds away from the site. My gaze follows the trail up to a squat brick building and the large sign reading "Rest Rooms" above the pair of doors.

Damnit. I forgot about the communal toilets and showers.

Silver lining, there's plumbing. And there's a separate side for the men so I don't have to worry about running into Mr. Olson, or any of the other men, in the showers.

31

I blow out a breath and focus back on the search for my tent mate.

It only takes me a moment before I spot her on the far side of the site. Her blond hair standing out against her bright red puffer jacket

Leaving all my stuff where it is, I head her way, waving at the other parents and students milling about.

"Elouise!" Rebecca greets me when she sees me approaching. "Oh, sorry, *Miss Hall*."

I roll my eyes, "Hey, Rebecca. Or should I call you Cody's Mom."

She laughs, then looks down at my person, "Where's all your stuff?"

"I left it over there." I gesture behind me. "I didn't want to carry it any further than I had to."

"That's what all these men are for," she bats her eyes, and I snort.

I met Rebecca at the beginning of the school year when she brought her son in for the Meet the Teacher night before classes began. She's single. A great mom. And always on the prowl for her next husband. *Her words, not mine.*

"I suppose I can help you carry your crap," she sighs dramatically. "This is us by the way."

My eyes move to the cute grey tent she's pointing to. "Wow," I pause to take it in. "It looks pretty nice."

"My ex insisted on spending a small fortune on it. So, I insisted on keeping it in the divorce." She shrugs, "But let's be real, it's still sleeping in a fucking tent."

I laugh but can't argue - because she's not wrong.

I'm not a tall person, and I can see straight across the top of the tent, so there won't be any standing up straight once inside. But it looks brand new, which hopefully means waterproof. And I like the teal-colored zippers.

There's even a small overhang jutting out above the entrance, giving the few feet of dirt in front of the tent an almost porch-like feel.

"Welp," I lift my arms then let them slap down against my sides, "shall we?"

True to her word, Rebecca helps me carry my crap over to the tent. But then she disappears, saying something about hunting down the gym teacher. Now, an hour later, my snacks are organized in the corner, my blankets are laid out – making up the saddest mattress in the history of mattresses – and my bag of clothing is half exploded in the corner.

Rebecca's half of the tent is much more put together than mine. She has a thin inflatable mat under an expensive looking sleeping bag, with a faux fur blanket folded nicely across the top. Reaching over I poke at her pillow, and yep, it's memory foam.

Sitting cross-legged on my lumpy getup, with my winter jacket zipped all the way up, I curse my lack of preparedness. Spring Break my ass. This fucking sucks.

I'm eyeing the bag hiding my vodka when a whistle sounds somewhere outside the tent.

Crawling, I unzip the flap and stick my head out.

Mr. Olson is standing near the main fire pit, whistle dangling from a string around his neck and a clipboard in his hand. He's dressed in an outdoor version of his usual outfit. Tan cargo pants instead of khakis, winter jacket over his Darling Elementary polo and green tennis shoes rather than loafers. I think he's close to my age, but he's always dressed a decade or two older.

He raises a hand, "Gather round, everyone."

"Gather round," I repeat, shifting so my feet are sticking out of the tent and I can pull my boots on. I don't remember a lot about camping but I do remember that shoes stay outside.

The only way to make sleeping in a tent worse is to sleep in a muddy tent.

With more struggle than I'd care to reflect on, I get to my feet and head toward Mr. Olson.

"Hey, Miss Hall!" a trio of my students skip past and I feel the first real smile on my face since I got here.

I might be a touch salty about this whole experience, but I love my kids and it'll be fun to spend time with them outside the constraints of the classroom.

Joining the crowd, I listen to Mr. Olson as he explains the outline for the next few days. Tonight is a dinner of sub sandwiches, brought by one of the parents, but the rest of the evening is just for us to settle in and get comfortable.

I almost snort at that comment.

Comfortable indeed.

Tomorrow we'll loosely gather for breakfast, then an outdoors expert is coming to teach us about different survival techniques. Clearly I'm the only one who didn't read the itinerary because no one else seems surprised by this. I'm not sure what an *Outdoors Expert* is, but that might be interesting. Then we'll have dinner around a bonfire... And - wash, rinse, repeat - the same plan for the next day.

And then, god willing, we leave here alive.

I didn't prepare properly for most of this, but I did bring a phone backup charger, so I might freeze to death at night, but I'll still be able to text Maddie to tell her to wipe the browser history on my laptop.

"Hi."

The deep voice startles me so bad I jump.

Trying to keep my heart inside my rib cage, my hand presses against my chest. Turning my head in the direction of the voice, and I find a man standing way too close.

He takes a small step back and puts his hands up, "Sorry, didn't mean to scare you."

I vaguely recognize him. He's a few inches taller than me. Black hair cut short. Clean shaven face. And blue eyes that are just a little bit... wild.

His smile is friendly, but a prickle of something runs up my arms.

I shake my head at myself. I can't be acting this jumpy, or I'll give myself a heart attack before the trip is over. "It's okay, I was just zoned out there."

"I noticed." He holds his hand out, "I'm Adam, Ross's dad."

"Oh, right!" I shake his hand, my memory coming back. "Nice to see you again."

Ross was a student in my class last year. He was a good kid - a little quiet, and very bright.

Adam's grip tightens around my fingers for a half second before he lets go, "So, how've you been?"

"Oh, um... good." I resist the sudden urge to wipe my palm off and tuck my hands into my coat pockets. The only thing that could make me enjoy tonight less, is small talk. But I still force out, "Yourself?"

I'm sure he's a fine person, but I don't really care. What I do care about is crawling headfirst into my sleeping bag and pretending I'm not here.

"Good. Good," He hooks his thumbs in his belt loops and rocks back on his heels. "I'm doing alright. Got a divorce last summer."

My mouth opens, then closes.

What the hell am I supposed to say to that?

"Oh, um, sorry to hear that," I glance around, hoping for a rescue.

"No need, it was for the best," the smile hasn't left his face and it's making me feel all sorts of weird.

"Okay, well..." I plaster on my best smile, "I'll see you tomorrow!"

My exit is awkward as fuck, but I'm not in the right head space right now to talk to some guy about his divorce.

Not waiting for a reply, I turn and head to the path that leads to the bathrooms. I don't really need to go, but I did need to get away from whatever-the-hell that was.

I'm stopped by three more people before I make it out of the camp site. Then I make a quick stop back at my tent to grab my toothbrush and run through my ablutions as quickly as possible.

Thankfully, by the time I find myself zipped into my tent, I'm yawning and ready to pass out. I don't typically have trouble sleeping, but I was worried that the drastic change in setting would keep me wide awake.

I haven't seen Rebecca since Mr. Olson called us all together, but she definitely made a pit-stop here because she left a battery-operated lantern on, filling the tent with light.

It's a little weird not having a way to lock the entrance flap, but the thin tent walls make it easy to hear if anyone is approaching. Not hearing any footsteps nearby, I quickly strip down and change into my sweatpants, fuzzy socks, and a soft cotton long-sleeved shirt that'll be serving as my pajamas for the next few nights.

Once I've shimmied myself into my sleeping bag, I reach out and turn off the lamp.

Darkness consumes the space around me.

Blinking into the dark, I force my body to relax.

Ten minutes later, I pry an arm free from my too small sleeping bag and reach across the tent for Rebecca's furry throw blanket.

With as few movements as possible, I get it laid out over

me. The extra layer immediately adds a little warmth and I already don't want to give it back.

I try to roll my shoulders. My sad little blanket mattress does nothing to soften the nearly frozen ground beneath me.

Okay, go to sleep.

I close my eyes and focus on my breathing.

An hour of shivering later, when it's clear that Rebecca's spending the night elsewhere, I snag her empty sleeping bag, unzip it and drape it over my prone form, pulling the edge all the way up and over my nose.

I wait for two seconds, then I slip my arm out from under the pile, dig my bottle of vodka out of my bag, and sit up just enough to take the world's quickest drink.

Grimacing, I screw the top back on, shove it back in the bag, then pull the blankets back up to my face.

Fuck this hard ground.

Fuck this cold.

Fuck everything about this trip.

Squeezing my eyes shut, I will myself to sleep.

Chapter 7

Elouise

I JOLT INTO CONSCIOUSNESS, my phone alarm blaring two inches from my ear.

Blindly, I reach up to turn off the awful noise, but my arm halts, hitting a barrier.

My body flips into panic mode, the trapped feeling suddenly overwhelming. But flailing only serves to make me feel more enclosed. My brain takes way too long to remember that I'm cocooned in a too small sleeping bag.

The material twists and tightens around me as I try to roll over, and the little reason I have left flees.

Oh my god! Get me out of this cotton coffin!

My phone alarm is getting louder.

Make it stop!

The closest tent is more than twenty feet away, but I don't want to be the asshole that wakes up a bunch of kids earlier than necessary on what's supposed to be a fun Spring Break trip.

Biting back a curse, I roll onto my back and try to force myself to calm down.

Wishing I'd stuck with those damn ab workout videos I promised myself I'd do, I use every scrap of core strength that I have, I sit up.

The sleeping bag sits up with me, and the sound of the alarm becomes muffled as the phone slips down the makeshift slide I just created.

"Seriously?!"

Pulling the top edge of the sleeping bag away from my chest, I look down to see a dull glow coming from somewhere near my knees.

I can't reach it.

I bend my knees – hoping to make the phone slide back towards my butt – just to feel the phone thud against my feet, in the Very Fucking Bottom of the sleeping bag.

It's like I can feel my blood pressure rising. A combination of rage, annoyance, and sleepiness bubbling in my veins.

I take a slow breath to calm down.

The phone volume ticks up a notch, and it takes every ounce of my control to keep from screaming.

Slowly, I reach for the zipper on my claustrophobic, 25-year-old sleeping bag.

Keeping my calm, I drag it down.

I will not let this day defeat me before 7am.

The zipper jams.

If this were a cartoon, my face would turn bright red and clouds of steam would be whistling from my ears.

I take another slow breath.

"You've got to be kidding me."

I jiggle the zipper.

Nothing.

I try pulling it back up.

Nothing.

I try to yank it down as hard as I can, but the stupid little metal tab just digs into my fingers.

"You piece of shit!" I growl at the turtle grinning up at me.

Not caring about the consequences, I grip the two sides just above the jammed zipper and tear the sides apart like Hulk.

Except the fabric holds. Not a single thread tears.

"What?!"

I yank harder, hunching into it.

But it doesn't fucking rip!

Rolling onto my stomach, the sleeping bag twisting around my body, I press my face firmly into my pillow and let out a shrill scream while kicking my feet.

My bare toe collides with a cool hard surface, and the alarm goes silent.

I lift my head from the pillow.

Did I really just snooze the alarm with my tantrum?

The silence brings a level of calm back to my little polyester room.

After one more inhale, I put my weight onto my elbows and army crawl forward, worming myself out of the sleeping bag.

Finally free, I ignore the loss of warmth and pull my sleeping bag out of the tangle of blankets. Holding it upside down, I shake it, and my phone finally slides out, screen showing the countdown until the alarm will sound again.

There will be no snoozing for me. One, because I want to hurry up and snag a shower before everyone else is in there. And two, because there's no amount of money that would get me back into that Teenage Mutant deathtrap right now.

I shift into a sitting position and let out a small groan of pain. My entire body aches. It feels like I slept on a bed of nails.

What adult chooses to vacation like this?!

I rub at a particularly sore spot on my hip.

Two more nights. Just two more nights.

I already sorted out my clothes for today and put them into my backpack. All of my outfits are going to be pretty much the same. A pair of black leggings. Thick socks. A thong. A full coverage sports bra. A tank top. A long-sleeved shirt. And a zip-up hoodie. Not very stylish, but functional. And that's the important part.

Pulling my jacket over my pajamas, I make sure my shower stuff is in the bag too and unzip the tent.

A handful of other adults are already milling around, but everyone looks just as exhausted as I feel, so we all just nod our greetings and leave it at that.

Entering the restroom, I hear water running but find that only one of the four shower stalls are in use.

Picking one, I push into the small space and lock the door behind me.

It's been a long time since I've been in a campground shower, but this seems about on par with my memory. Maybe even a little nicer than I was expecting. The shower stall is divided up into two sections. The first is about half the size of a typical toilet stall. With the door at my back, there's a small bench on my left and a couple of towel hooks on my right. Then right in front of me is a thin white shower curtain that stops about a foot above the floor.

With more acrobatics than I'm interested in doing this morning, I eventually strip naked and slip on a pair of cheap flip flops. Under no circumstances am I standing here barefoot.

Shivering, I yank the shower curtain back and step in.

Doing my best to run through my shower routine quickly. I keep the water temperature just above lukewarm. I don't know how the pipes work in this building, but I don't want to be the person who uses up all the hot water. Although, after the start of my day, I'm not willing to martyr myself under completely freezing water.

41

When I'm done rinsing, I turn the handle, stopping the stream of water. I squeeze the excess water out of my hair, pull the curtain open, and stare at the empty towel hooks.

"Oh, fuck me."

The urge to scream again is back.

"Everything okay in there?" a voice asks from somewhere in the bathroom.

"All good!" I call back, hoping I sound like a sane person. "I'll be out in a few if you're waiting."

Standing naked, the air quickly cooling the water dripping from my body, I look at my backpack, knowing it doesn't have what I need in it.

I didn't pack a towel. I know I didn't. I didn't even pack a washcloth. I had to use my bare hands to lather the soap on my body.

Shiiiiit!

Not seeing another choice, I pull my sleep-shirt free from my pile of discarded clothes and use it as a makeshift towel. Makeshift is the keyword, because all fabrics are not created equal. I don't know what this shirt is made of, but it appears to stop absorbing when my body is only about 80% dry.

Giving up, I drop the wet shirt onto the bench and start to get dressed.

I get my thong on. No problem. Then I start on the leggings.

Leggings are great, because when they're made correctly, they can keep everything in place. I've never had a small stature, and my extra rounded curves need all the added control they can get. But pulling on skintight leggings when your body is still 20% damp is tantamount to being forced to watch your parent's sex tape. Something no human should have to endure.

I yank. And tug. And shimmy. And feel everything jiggle.

I jump and silently curse while I pull some more.

Inch by inch, they creep up my thighs.

The room is still cold, but now it's mixed with an uncomfortable level of humidity, and all this struggling is making me start to sweat. Which *ohmygod* only adds to the problem!

Clenching my teeth, screaming in my head, I give one final jerk, at the same time that I jump, and my leggings slide into place.

I make a silent promise to myself that I won't drink anything today, so I won't have to pee and therefore won't have to take these off.

Then I reach for my sports bra and almost cry.

"I'm fine." I whisper the mantra to myself, as I put my arms through and pull the bra over my head.

The material does that special Sports Bra Trick where the material rolls into a tight twist, wedging itself into my armpits and above my boobs.

"I'm fine. I'm fine. I'm fine."

More sweat forms on my back and I contort myself, bending my arms in ways they don't want to bend, grasping for the bottom band stuck high across my back.

"I'm fine." I'm not as quiet this time, but I don't even care anymore if someone overhears me.

My fingertips catch the band, and ignoring the spasm that's starting in my arm, I get a hold of the material and tug.

I twist and bend and clench my teeth.

An eternity later, with a final snap of elastic, it's in place.

Reaching a hand down the front of the bra, I pull each boob up so they're nestled nicely in their spandex cage.

Feeling like an overstuffed sausage, I slap on some deodorant, tug on my layers of shirts and escape the shower stall.

Beelining it back to my tent, I'm able to avoid eye contact and make it inside without incident.

S. J. Tilly

Happy that Rebecca is still nowhere to be seen, I collapse onto the floor. I need a moment alone to work on finding my Zen.

I allow myself two minutes of wallowing, then I comb through my hair and fashion it into two long braids, draping one over each shoulder. Knowing I can't walk around in this weather with uncovered damp hair, I find my purple knit hat and put it on.

Using my phone in place of a mirror, I smooth some concealer over the dark stains under my eyes. I'm not trying to impress anyone; I just don't want to look like a total hot mess. Swiping on a little mascara, I decide that's as good as it's gonna get.

I'm tempted to lay down, but I know if I fall back asleep, I'll just hate myself for it when I'm forced awake by Mr. Olson's freaking whistle.

Back outside, I make my way towards the fire pit. There's no bonfire going, but...

Oh sweet baby Jesus, do I smell coffee?

Following my nose, I find one of the dads with a pot of hot water, metal cups, and instant coffee.

With blessedly few words, he pours me a cup of life-juice and I take it over to an empty picnic table.

Sipping the coffee, I feel the stress of my morning slip away.

This is pretty okay.

The sun is out and already making me warm enough I can leave my jacket open. There are birds chirping in the trees around us and the kids all look wide-eyed and bushy-tailed, ready to see what today will bring.

I smile into my cup. This might not be so bad actually.

A body sits down next to me. "Hey, roomie."

I grin over at Rebecca, "Well, good morning. Did you have a nice night?"

She smirks, "Oh, I had a *very nice* night. He might not look like much, but Coach has hidden talents."

I choke. First, I've never heard anyone refer to Gym Teacher Bob as Coach before. Second, that's about the last person I would have assumed she'd be with.

"But enough about me," Rebecca tips her head, indicating for me to look across the way. "Have you seen the survivalist guy yet?"

I shake my head, fine with the change of topic, "Why, is he hot?"

She lets out a groan, "So fucking hot. That man could survival me any day of the week."

"What does that even mean?" I laugh, surreptitiously look around for this mystery man. "Do you know where they found him?"

She shrugs, "I heard someone say he's from Darling Lake. But who knows if that's true."

Between two clusters of people, I catch a glimpse of a tall figure wearing a backpack, but I can't tell if it's the newcomer Rebecca's talking about or just one of the dads.

The sound of a whistle announces the start of the day, and we get up to gather round the empty firepit where Mr. Olson is standing.

He waits for us all to settle, hushing a few of the kids, before he starts, "Good morning!"

There's a mumbled chorus of "good morning" in response.

"So glad we all survived our first night in the woods," he chuckles, and I've never wanted to throat punch someone more in my life. "If you didn't have breakfast already, we have granola bars over there," he points to a table, "you can eat while our special guest tells us what he has in store for us today." Mr.

Olson clasps his hands. "So, without further ado, allow me to introduce you to Mr. Stoleman."

Stoleman?

The collective gaze of the crowd turns my way, and a prickle of unease crawls up my neck.

Slowly, I turn around, gaze locking on a man's profile as he walks past me, towards the front of the group.

No.

The sun sneaks through the trees, highlighting the chocolaty brown locks mussed around the man's head.

It can't be.

His facial hair is the same rich color as his hair, and it's almost thick enough to be considered a beard. Like maybe he shaved it yesterday. Or the day before.

Reaching Mr. Olson's side, the man stops and turns to face everyone.

"Please," his voice is clear, and deep, and I feel it resonate in my bones, "call me Beckett."

Chapter 8

Elouise

No WAY.

Absolutely no fucking way.

I... I don't even know what to think right now.

Last time I saw Beckett he... *holy hell* he didn't look like this! How is he getting hotter? I do the math in my head, 38, this motherfucker is 38 years old and looking finer than he ever has before.

While I stand gawking at his stupidly handsome face, I catch snippets of what he's saying. "Grew up in Darling Lake... Went to the same school... Loved camping..."

This can't be happening.

Can *not* be happening.

The universe has it out for me when it comes to Beckett Stoleman. Every time I see him, I make a fool of myself. Each time worse than the last.

At least I don't have acne this time, which is the best thing I can say about my current situation.

The crowd laughs at something he says, and I force my ears to listen.

"... because someday you might find yourself in a situation where it's just you and Mother Nature." Beckett's eyes scan the crowd, then stop directly on mine. "And if we take care of her, she just might take care of us."

My pulse spikes and I swear to god my vagina just converted herself from a storeroom into a waterslide. But that's just too bad because I'm not taking these fucking leggings off to change my panties.

When Beckett's gaze travels away from me, I suck in a breath.

Rebecca smothers a chuckle next to me, "You okay?"

I start to nod automatically, but quickly switch to shaking my head, "Not even kinda."

She nudges me with her elbow, "What is it?"

Keeping my eyes on Beckett, I whisper back, "I know him. Or, well, *knew* him."

Rebecca's voice is just as quiet, which is good because she just goes for it, "Did you guys used to bang?"

Her question is so absurd, a laugh jumps up my throat. Slapping my hand over my mouth, I try to catch it, but it just comes out as a loud snort-cough.

Several pairs of eyes turn my way, so I slide my hand down to my chest, like I'm just clearing my throat.

When people's attention moves back to Beckett, I chance a glance at him, hoping he didn't hear me. But he's staring right at me. Or rather, he's staring at the hand I have on my chest.

I drop my hand and he looks away.

"Oh, baby!" Rebecca snickers, "I can feel the sexual tension already. This is gonna be fun to watch."

"Oh my god, shut up!" I hiss as quietly as I can.

"Not until you promise to tell me the whole story."

"Fine. I promise," I toss back the rest of my coffee, wishing it was something stronger.

It'll probably be nice to tell Rebecca about my not so sordid past with Beckett. Talking always helps me sort a situation. And once I walk through it, Rebecca will see she's way off base with her *sexual tension* comment. For that to be possible, both parties need to be interested. This is just a case of teenaged, unrequited love turned adult embarrassment.

Honestly, I'd bet money that he doesn't even recognize me. Let alone think about me *like that*.

Chapter 9

Beckett

Little Elouise Hall. All grown up.

My eyes drink her in for the hundredth time.

Grown all the way up.

I made the mistake of not recognizing her once, but I won't do that again. No, now, I have her outline burned into my brain.

One look, a single glance, was all it took for me to see that this is Adult Elouise.

Even bundled up in layers of clothing, she can't hide the shape of her beautiful body.

With her back turned towards me, my eyes start at her feet and trail their way up. Mud-splattered ankle boots that somehow look cute. Thick, strong thighs, wrapped in tight, black leggings that are a damn gift to mankind. And that ass. Jesus Camping Christ, that fucking ass. I want to get my hands on it. I want to grip it. Lick it. Smack it.

Feeling my blood heat, I drag my eyes up.

Staring at her back means I don't have a view of her chest, but if it matches the rest of her curves, I know where I want to lay my head tonight. And I can't see her eyes, but I can picture them perfectly. Bright, stunned, deep brown orbs, staring at me in shock while I introduced myself earlier. Lips parted... *Fuck.* She's dressed for camping and I'm over here nearly panting. Staring...

I want my hands on her.

She has a hat pulled low over her head, but it doesn't hide her pretty brown braids. And it doesn't stop me from imagining grabbing those braids and showing her just the way I like it. A little rough. A little hard. A little-

"Hey, Mr. Beckett," there's a tug at my sleeve.

I glance down at the kid yanking on my jacket and clear my throat. Nothing in the world kills a boner like a Surprise Kid.

"What's up, Little Man?"

He doesn't blink as he asks, "Have you ever fought a bear?"

I have to bite the inside of my cheek to keep from laughing, because he looks very serious. Instead, I answer just as seriously, "Not yet."

He nods, like this is a perfectly reasonable response. "Okay." Then he seems to think, "Are there bears here?"

"Unlikely."

His brows furrow, "Are there bears anywhere in Minnesota?"

"There are," my whole introduction spiel was about the importance of being educated, so I don't want to lie the first time someone asks me a question, "but most of them are up north."

"But they could walk down here, right?"

"They could, but they don't do it often."

"How often?" This kid's brows keep lowering with each question and I feel like I'm on the wrong side of an interrogation.

"I don't know the exact number of times it's happened. But

if you want to know more, there's a website where you can track bear sightings."

His brows shoot up this time, "Really!?"

"Really," I actually have no fucking clue, but there's a website for everything so there must be.

The kid turns around and takes off at a run, "Mom! Mom, can I use your phone?"

I mentally cross my fingers that my guess was correct.

Distraction gone; my eyes move back to Elouise. She's standing in the same spot, talking to some blonde. She's waving her hands around, animatedly telling her friend a story. Elouise makes another wild gesture, and the friend has to bend over, she's laughing so hard.

I wish I could see Lou's face. She's always been expressive, and I'd give my left nut to know what she's talking about right now.

So, go find out.

I take one step forward when my path is suddenly blocked by Mr. Olson.

His features are pulled tight, and I don't know if he's pissed about me staring at Elouise or if I somehow screwed up his precious timeline. But whatever this look is that he's giving me, it isn't working.

I'm not going to be intimidated by some polo-wearing prick with a clipboard, so I continue to hold his stare until he shifts uncomfortably and glances.

"Everyone is ready, if you are, Mr. Stoleman."

"Alright," I watch as he moves next to me, his eyes going to Elouise's back, same as mine were.

Oh, so that's how it's gonna be?

I stand a little taller. I don't mind a little competition because I never lose.

Chapter 10

Elouise

"So, I spin around, saying *YES*, only to find him talking on his cell phone!"

Rebecca doubles over, laughing so hard tears are rolling down her cheeks. "You did not!" she wheezes.

"I did," it's been long enough that I can laugh about it now, but the next part will always sting my poor teenaged heart. "Then my friend, who witnessed the whole thing, comes running out, yelling my name. And you know what Beckett does?"

She looks up at me, hands still on her knees, "What?"

"He looks down at my name tag."

Her mouth drops open and I can see her features torn between humor and outrage. "He did not?"

"He did."

Straightening, she looks over my shoulder, again. "Well, if the amount of time he's spent staring at you means anything, I'd say that man hasn't forgotten you this time."

My eyes widen and I fight the urge to look behind me, "He has not."

She smirks, "He has."

My brain is trying to make sense of this, when Beckett's voice booms out, "Alright Campers, follow me!"

Composing ourselves, we join the herd following Beckett as he leads us up the path, past the bathrooms and then down a trail I haven't noticed before.

The kids have all migrated to the front of the herd, so they're – for the most part – listening to what Beckett's saying. Whereas I have fallen to the back of the pack, not even attempting to hear what's being said.

Beckett freaking Stoleman.

I just can't even wrap my mind around it. Like... what in the hell is happening?!

I may have lost track of him after I went to college, but Beckett went to school in Chicago, for business – or something like that – so I'm fairly certain he's not some sort of Wildlife Ranger.

And yet, here he is.

The trail crosses over an empty section of paved road and we cross to the other side. My eyes have been down, watching where I step, so when I finally lift them, I almost stumble.

The trees have suddenly dropped away to reveal a beautiful little lake tucked in a patch of evergreens. The water looks still, and there's a sheen of ice in the center of the water.

It's beautiful and peaceful and I may have just found my new Happy Place.

As we all come to a stop, I look around the area surrounding the lake and see a tangle of trails criss-crossing all over the place. Around the lake, through the woods, a series of podium-like stands dotting the gravel paths.

"Alright," Beckett's voice carries over the crowd and everyone falls silent, "one of the most important things to learn for survival, is what's edible. Meaning what plants you can eat, and what you can't. Ideally, I'd help you find living examples of these plants, but since it's still early spring, and things are only just about to sprout, we'll have to discover them in a different way." He bends down to the backpack at his feet, pulls out some worksheets, and hands them to the kid closest to him, "Do me a solid and make sure everyone gets one."

"Even the adults?" the kid asks, clearly doubtful.

Beckett nods, "Yep. Adults get lost in the woods, too."

"Geez, isn't that a lovely thought," I mutter to Rebecca, who has found her way back to my side.

Beckett pulls a clear bag from his pack next, and it only takes me a moment to recognize the yellow color of the classic No. 2 pencils inside. He hands the bag to another student, asking her to pass them out.

Rebecca sighs next to me, "He might be hot, but he's acting like a real buzz kill. This is *Spring Break*." She says the last two words with emphasis.

I roll my eyes, "Yeah, except this spring break doesn't have frozen margaritas in Mexico. It just has a bunch of kids in the frozen tundra."

She snorts, "I should've brought booze."

When a beat passes and I don't respond, she turns to face me fully. "Elouise, are you holding out on me?"

"Well, if you'd actually slept in our tent last night, you'd know the answer to that."

Rebecca grins, "Well look at you, being a rule breaker. But it's all yours, I have Bob to keep me warm."

I try not to pull a face.

Sensing my thoughts, she waggles her brows. "Moves, Elouise. He's got moooooooves."

"Ohmygod." I cover my face with my hands. I don't need that mental image seared into my brain.

"Speaking of," Rebecca whispers, and I drop my hands in time to see Gym Teacher Bob approach.

A gust of wind whips through the small clearing, so I reach up with my free hand and pull my hat down further over my ears.

"Ladies," he greets us both, but only has eyes for Rebecca. "Care to team up?"

Rebecca nods and Bob hands me a worksheet and pencil before walking off with the only friend I have here.

I resist the urge to sigh.

A couple of kids from my class walk past me, so I insert myself into their group and we make our way down the path around the lake. Every couple of minutes we come across one of those mounted placards featuring a photo of a plant, explaining appearance, smell, and where it commonly grows. Then there's a second flap for you to lift that tells you whether or not it's safe to eat, and we mark it off on our worksheets.

So far, I've learned that I'd probably rather starve than chance eating the wrong thing.

The kids are laughing and horsing around when we start down another path, which is why I don't notice Creepy Dad Adam until he's right next to me.

He's just smiling at me, while attempting to match his stride with mine. I lift a hand in the most awkward wave, but keep walking, hoping he can take a hint.

"Sleep well?"

His question is so unexpected that I don't know how to answer.

It feels like an inappropriate thing to ask, but really, it's probably perfectly acceptable considering we're a bunch of adults sleeping on the ground after all. I'm sure sleeping badly was the norm last night.

But there's something about him that puts me on edge, so him asking *how I slept* feels very stalkery.

"I slept okay," I shrug.

He chuckles and bumps his shoulder against mine, causing every hackle I have to rise.

I take a step to the side, putting some distance between us, and if he notices, he pretends not to.

I glance around, looking for his kid, "Where's Ross?"

He waves away the question, "Off with his friends. I didn't want to cramp his style."

Oh, just my style then.

I make a sound of understanding and pick up my pace to stay with the group of kids ahead of us. This impromptu one-on-one time is making me all sorts of uncomfortable.

"So..." he starts.

And his tone has me quickening my pace even more. It sounds like he's about to ask me out and *holy hell* please don't let him do that. The answer would be no. Of-fucking-course it'd be no. But I can't be rude about it. We're here for another two nights!

"I was wondering-"

His words are cut off by a chorus of young voices yelling "Beckett!" and I've never been more thankful for an interruption in my life. Even if it means close proximity to my childhood crush.

"How's it going over here?" he asks the students, and they enthusiastically answer with unintelligible cheers.

He's standing in front of the cluster of the kids, but his eyes are narrowed on Adam.

Weird.

Using the distraction as an opportunity, I take a few more steps over, putting half the kids between me and Adam. And I purposely ignore the fact that it brings me closer to Beckett.

"Mr. Beckett, have you ever eaten something bad when you were in the woods?" a girl asks, and the whole group falls silent.

Beckett smirks as his eyes move over to meet mine, "I have not, but Lou- I mean, Miss Hall has." He waits one beat, "It is *Miss* Hall, correct? Not Mrs."

Oh. My. God.

Ohmygod!

He remembers me.

Heat fills my body, from the tip of my freezing toes to the tip of my blushing nose.

I bite my lip, not sure if I'm about to grin like a fool or puke up my coffee.

"It's Miss," one of the kids calls out helpfully.

"Good." Beckett replies.

Wait. What? Good? What does that mean?!

I feel several pairs of eyes on me, "What'd you eat?" someone asks.

"Um," my brain gives itself a mental jump start, and I force myself to look back up at Beckett. "I, uh, don't actually know what he's talking about."

With his eyes locked on mine, Beckett's mouth forms that adorable, crooked smile, the one I fell in love with decades ago. "Mushrooms, Miss Hall. I'm talking about the time you ate the mushrooms you found in your yard."

My eyes widen, "Wow... I forgot all about that."

"What happened?" someone asks.

"Um..." Trying to recall the memory, I bite the tip of my finger. I glance at Beckett, since he clearly remembers it, but find his attention focused on my mouth.

I drop my hand. My blush deepening.

"I remember my mom freaking out," I admit, still not sure of the details, "and I remember going to the hospital..." I trail off, really having forgotten all about the event.

"After eating a handful of bad mushrooms," Beckett starts, "Miss Hall started throwing up." Every kid makes a sound at that revelation. "Her brother was with her, so he ran and got their mom. And then her mom had to call Poison Control. Since Miss Hall couldn't remember what the mushrooms looked like, her mom brought her to the hospital so they could make sure she was okay."

"And were you?" one of my students asks.

"Duh," a girl replies, "if she died, she wouldn't be here."

"How do you know all of that?" the only other adult asks. His voice sounding way too tense for the conversation.

We all turn to look at Adam, who's standing with his arms crossed and a scowl on his face.

I swear Beckett stands up straighter, "Miss Hall and I go way back."

Adam's jaw clenches, but all I can do is focus on Beckett.

What is going on?

The kids look back and forth between the two posturing males.

"We grew up together," I say, to break up the growing tension. "Kinda."

Technically, we did know each other as kids. But *grew up together* might be a bit of a stretch.

"Cool," one of the younger kids says.

"So, you knew Miss Hall back when she was a kid? Like us?" another asks, sounding absolutely shocked. Like the idea of me having been a child has never occurred to him.

Beckett nods, "Sure did."

This causes a flurry of questions, but Beckett manages to get the group back on task, telling them that he'll share stories tonight after dinner.

I can't imagine what sort of stories he has about me.

He wouldn't... I feel some of the heat drain from my face.

He wouldn't tell them about all the times I embarrassed myself in front of him. Would he?

When the group starts moving, I automatically fall into my previous spot at the back of the pack. I remember that I do not want to end up walking with Adam, so I covertly glance around. And I'm relieved when I spot his back as he strides down the trail at the front of the group.

I don't really know what was going on between him and Beckett, but I'm glad it scared him off.

Half listening as the kids riddle Beckett with questions, I take in the beauty around me.

Yes, it's cold, and my sleeping situation is miserable, but it's impossible to deny the draw of The Great Outdoors.

Life is just starting to shake free from the deep freeze, tiny buds forming on bare tree branches. A juxtaposition to the mighty evergreen trees, boasting their bushy deep green needles. It's not the prettiest time of year, in the traditional sense of the word, but it highlights the change in seasons. A new life cycle. A chance to try again. A fresh start.

We stop at another plaque and after reading the fact card the kids all rush to write their answers.

I hear a quiet snap followed by a gasp, "My pencil broke!"

I'm moving towards the kid to give him mine, but Beckett beats me to him.

He holds out his hand, "Let me see."

The kid places the pencil in his open palm. I can see that the point of lead has snapped off.

Beckett reaches into his pocket, and I expect him to pull out another pencil. But his hand is covering the length of the item but seems too short and wide.

With a flick of his wrist, a blade appears out of nowhere, snapping into place.

It's a knife. A jackknife I think they're called, or something like that.

With way too much fascination, I watch as Beckett makes quick precise swipes with his blade, shaving off the blunt end of the pencil.

I can't look away.

His grip is controlled, hand flexing around the handle. His focus is unwavering. And his stance is slightly hunched over, stretching the material of his jacket tightly over his broad back.

In seconds he has the pencil sharpened to a point. And I'm breathing heavier than I was before.

Chapter 11

Elouise

AFTER THE PENCIL INCIDENT, I managed to avoid Beckett all the way through lunch. Rebecca probably would've given me shit for hiding but she was too busy making goo-goo eyes at Bob.

Finally, for the first time all day, I'm able to relax.

I found a table full of quiet girls and their moms, who happily let me join them for lunch. And they don't seem to mind that I'm sitting with my thoughts rather than joining in conversation.

Double bonus, as lunch wraps up, instead of breaking us up into groups for the next activity, Beckett just had us stay with our tablemates.

So, feeling excited about the reprieve from males, I hang with my girl-group while we learn simple first aid techniques. We wrap fake-sprained fingers. Search for sticks that would make good splints for broken bones. And learn the best ways to treat a burn in the wild.

Beckett keeps a cool head, walking through the groups – praising efforts, giving advice, and melting panties.

I try to focus on our tasks, but it's hard to stop my mind from spiraling around Beckett.

Where did he learn all this stuff?

How did he know about the mushrooms?

Where is he living now?

Is he back? Is that why he's here?

Last I'd heard, he was living in The Windy City, but after that ill-fated Christmas party where my teenaged heart was crushed by the reality of our differences, I stopped asking after him.

And then of course a few years later the Coffee Incident happened. Maddie was witness to that travesty, but I never breathed a word of it to my family.

And less than a year later I left for college.

There were a few times that I thought about googling Beckett's name, looking him up on MySpace, finding him on Facebook, but I always chickened out. I was too worried that he'd somehow find out. And it wasn't like I'd've sent him a friend request.

A small snort escapes me at the memory. What a fool I was.

"Sorry, what was that?" one of the moms asks me.

I wave it off, "Just a cough."

She looks skeptical but Beckett's voice draws her attention. "Alright, everyone, we'll gather together for this last-"

A sharp whistle has the whole camp wincing.

Beckett slowly turns to face Mr. Olson, whose whistle is still pressed to his lips.

"Thanks," Beckett's voice is so dry, I have to slap a hand over my mouth to keep from snorting again.

We've finally made our way back to the main camp, and it looks like Beckett has one more thing planned for us.

Everyone shifts closer, and I surreptitiously keep an eye on Adam, making sure to keep several bodies between us.

"Shorties in front." Beckett gestures for some of the kids to move up. "I'm going to show you what I keep in my emergency kit." He holds up a zippered pack that looks a lot like a soft sided lunch box. "The basics will be the same wherever you go, but depending on your situation you might want to adjust what you keep on hand."

The kids all lean in closer as Beckett opens the kit and takes items out.

I'm amazed that they're this interested in something so mundane, but I'm also leaning closer to the action, too. It's probably just Beckett. His magnetism must work on everyone, not just single horny women.

Pulling out a large Ziplock bag, Beckett addresses the group, "For this next one, I'm going to need a helper for my demonstration."

I squint my eyes, but he's lowered the bag to his waist so I can't see what's in it.

"Miss Hall."

My eyes snap up to meet his, as my cheeks blush. Again.

I'd been trying to see what was in the bag, but it probably looked like I was staring at his junk.

"Yes?" I croak out.

"Come here," his eyes hold mine as he waits a beat, "please."

A shudder rolls through my body.

Beckett Stoleman commanding me around? Yes, fucking please.

"Coming!" I call out, and I swear I hear Rebecca choke on a laugh.

I pick my way through the seated kids, praying that my face doesn't look like a tomato by the time I reach Beckett's side.

"Thank you for volunteering," Beckett jokes, making some of the parents laugh.

Gathering my courage, I step up beside him and give him my best smile. "Happy to help."

"I had a feeling," he smirks.

A heavy arm drapes over my shoulders and I force myself to stay still, rather than lean into his side.

"Miss Hall is gonna help me show you how to properly treat a laceration." When the kids continue to stare, he clarifies, "A cut." Using his grip on my shoulder, he turns me towards him. "Would you please pull up the sleeve of your sweatshirt?"

He lets go of me, then taps my right forearm.

"Oh, um, okay." I stammer, at a loss for something better to say.

The sun came out earlier, warming up the day, so I took off my jacket a while ago.

A moment later I have both layers of shirt sleeves scrunched up around my elbow.

"Perfect."

Beckett leans down to his pack and one of the younger boys lets out a scream. "He's going to cut her!" And I recognize him as one of the kids that witnessed Beckett using the knife on the pencil.

I might not know Beckett well, but I'm quite certain he's not going to slice my arm open.

Beckett holds up a purple marker in his hand, "I promise I'm not going to hurt your Miss Hall." He holds his other hand out to me. "Trust me."

I don't know if it's a question or a statement, but I answer as I place my palm in his. "I do."

It's a simple thing. And easy admission. But something about this moment feels big. Bigger than a first aid demonstration.

It feels like... a new chapter.

Chapter 12

Beckett

AH, hell. I shouldn't have done that.

Feeling Elouise's hand in mine is more than I'd expected.
It's such an innocent act. Hardly even touching. But it feels
incredibly intimate. Like foreplay.

Her palm looks so small against my larger one. And without
thinking, my fingers close tighter around hers. My subconscious
desire to consume her is breaking through the surface and
manifesting itself into action.

Gently, I pull her towards me, and she takes a step closer.

"Like this," I tell her, my voice sounding deeper to my own
ears.

I place my other hand on her elbow, holding it still while I
use my hold on her hand to lower and turn it outward, exposing
her forearm to the campers.

The campers that are watching our every move, I remind
myself.

But even knowing we have an audience; I can't tear my
gaze away from Lou's face. Her cheeks have been a pretty
shade of pink most of the day, and it's fucking adorable.

There's just something about her, about this, that feels like home.

My chest expands.

It's been so long since I've seen her. Over a decade. But the moment I saw her, I knew who she was. Just like how I knew she had a crush on me when we were kids.

She was always a nice girl, friendly and kind. I didn't see any harm in her little childhood infatuation. It was cute. But the age difference between us back then meant I only looked at her as a kid. We were both so young.

But now? *Fuck.* Now I want to throw her soft little body over my shoulder and show her just what I'm capable of doing in these woods.

My fingers flex against the warm skin just below her elbow and I feel the slight shiver that rolls up her arm. A shiver that travels straight up my own arm, down my chest to my-

Shit.

Gritting my teeth, I force my thoughts back to wound care, because popping a boner in front of a group of children is a sure-fire way to kill any chance I might have with this woman.

"Hold still," I command, and she listens.

Lifting the marker to my mouth, I bite down on the cap and pull it free, then let it drop into my palm. The movement draws her gaze, and my tongue swipes across my bottom lip on impulse.

She shifts on her feet and I swallow a growl.

I project my voice for the crowd as I look down at Elouise's bared arm, "I'm going to simulate a large cut."

Pressing the cool tip of the marker to her skin, I draw a bright purple line from the middle of her forearm down to her wrist.

One boy gasps comically and Elouise grins, "Didn't hurt one bit."

She's so good with these kids. Even when she was avoiding me, she was present for the students. She clearly respects them, and they respect her in turn.

A smile pulls at one side of my mouth.

Elouise may have grown up, but she didn't lose who she was. She's still that generous, sweet human. Only now she's all curves, blushing cheeks, and veiled sass.

And goddamn, I want to get her alone so I strip her down and sink my teeth into every soft bit she has.

Fucking Focus, Beckett!

I pull out the different first aid items, demonstrating how to clean and wrap a wound, and I'm brought back to memories of summers in The Boundary Waters.

When I left Minnesota to go to college in Chicago, I didn't expect to spend my summers back in my home state, all the way up at the Canadian border, to work as a camping guide. But I had a friend who had a friend and I found myself making the 9 hour drive every June.

The first few weeks were rough, learning how to navigate the million-plus acres of wilderness. No electricity. No running water. No motors. Just a canoe, a paddle, and a pack.

But I quickly learned how to master my surroundings, and I ended up loving it.

So, I kept going. And once a year, for three months, I'd escape the busy city life and live under the stars.

When I graduated, I stopped going north. Work and life got in the way and not too long after I forgot all about it.

I forgot how much I love being outside. How much I love inhaling that fresh forest air. How much I love being here, in Minnesota.

And dammit, now I owe my dad a thank you. He's the reason I'm here in the first place. Apparently, he's on the same bowling team as the Principal of Darling Elementary, and when the original Survival Guide canceled, my dad volunteered me in his place.

So as I secure the Ace Bandage around Elouise's "cut" I send a silent thanks to Dad. Because if it weren't for him roping me into this, I'm not sure I would've bumped into her at all. And flustering Elouise has become my new favorite hobby.

I give her arm a light squeeze. "Now that we've stopped the bleeding and dressed the wound, she's stable enough for us to get her to a hospital."

The laugh she lets out sounds a little strained, "My lucky day."

"Not just your lucky day," I hide my smirk and gesture down to the Emergency Kit by my feet. "Everyone here will get one of these Emergency Kits to take home," most of the kids cheer, like they just won something way cooler than Band-Aids, "but you won't get them until the last day."

A sea of shoulders slump in defeat.

Sensing the opening, Mr. Olson gives a quick blow of his whistle and starts directing everyone on what's next. My job is over for the day, so as I listen to him go over the dinner cook-out plans, I find my attention moving back to Elouise.

She's still standing close to me and the fact that she hasn't stepped away fills me with an odd sense of accomplishment. Like I've won something.

Her hand brushes against mine. "Um," she whispers, "did you want to take this off me?"

My head turns so fast I startle her.

"What did you say?" I ask.

"I said, do you want to take this off..." her words trail off as her eyes widen, realizing what she'd said.

She looks like she might burst into flames, but instead she slaps a hand over her mouth, trying to muffle her laughter.

"Oh my god," she shakes her head and holds up her bandaged arm. "I meant do you want this stuff back?"

I don't hold my smirk back this time. "Are you sure it's had enough time to heal?"

Elouise rolls her eyes, and I can feel her shyness fall away between us. But that barrier dropping only makes the tension between us feel more alive.

I want to reach out to see what happens when I touch her, so that's exactly what I do.

Chapter 13

Elouise

BECKETT'S HANDS wrap around my wrist, and it's like a live wire.

It's only been minutes since he did this exact same thing to put the wrap on me, but suddenly this feels like a private moment.

Maybe it's because this feels a lot like he's undressing me. Or maybe it's the fact that everyone else has turned away to look at Mr. Olson and we no longer have the audience we did before.

I keep my eyes lowered, watching his long fingers dance over my arm.

Beckett isn't moving quickly, just precisely. Skillfully.

His experience is clear, and I can't help but wonder what else he's experienced at. I bet he'd know just how to touch me. Just how to get me off. I mean his fingers are just so long.

My lungs fill, suddenly starved for air.

God, I need to get laid!

Beckett is demonstrating first aid, and I'm a heartbeat away from humping his leg.

71

Say something, Lou. Anything.

"So..."

Fucking hell, I should've thought this through.

"So?" he echoes, still unwinding the long Ace Bandage.

"Wilderness stuff, huh?"

"Yeah, wilderness stuff." I can hear the smile in his voice, but I'm not brave enough to look up.

I wet my lips, "Not exactly what I thought you'd end up doing."

He lets out this low humming sound that goes straight to my core, making me squeeze my legs together.

"What did you think I'd end up doing, Elouise?" His words are low and another tremor travels up my spine as he calls me by name.

I clear my throat. "I don't really know. I guess I thought you went to school for business. Or something like that."

"I did."

My eyes glance up and lock with Becketts. He's so close. Inches away. "Oh."

Great answer, Lou.

The corners of his eyes tighten, allowing me to sense the smile without looking at his mouth. "I spent my summers working in the Boundary Waters."

My eyes widen. "Huh, well, that explains a lot."

He lifts a brow, "It does?"

"I mean, yeah." I shrug. "Makes sense that you'd learn all this crap - er, stuff – up there. And then you could still do your *business stuff*." I wave my hand around on the last two words because I don't really know what "business" means.

"And what about you? I seem to remember you wanting to be a teacher when we were kids." His fingers brush against my bare skin, making my breath hitch, as he's unwinding the final

72

layer between us. "Did you always plan on working in an elementary school?"

He remembers that?

My head gives a shaky nod. "Pretty much always. I flip-flopped on which grade a few times but I'm happy with my choice."

"And why's that?"

"Well... 4th graders are old enough to follow directions and work independently. But they're still young enough to not be jaded little assholes." I pause, "For the most part."

The loud, deep laugh bursts out of Beckett, and it's the sound wet dreams are made of. But it's also so unexpected that I flinch. The movement throws off my balance and I reach out with my free hand to steady myself on the only thing within reach. Beckett.

My hand is flat against his body, placed firmly against his stomach. Just inches above the top of his jeans.

The muscles clench under my touch.

Ohmygod. Ohmyfuckinggod, he's rock solid.

His laugh cuts off, and I don't know what to do with the look in his eyes. But I can't look away. Both of us trapped in this stasis.

Sensing an added stillness around us, I slowly turn my head and find the whole crowd of campers staring. At us. Beckett's laugh apparently caught the attention of everyone in earshot.

I snatch my hand back from Beckett's stomach, but he still has a hold of my other wrist, and he doesn't let go.

His grip on me tightens for a heartbeat before he loosens it, slowly letting me go.

A shrill whistle has me jumping again.

"Time for dinner!" Mr. Olson addresses the group, shooting a narrowed look our way.

I think I hear Beckett mumble something about "making that asshole eat his whistle" but I can't be sure, because I'm already fleeing across the campsite. Desperate for a few moments alone in my tent. To compose myself, not to rub one out. Definitely not.

Chapter 14

Beckett

"Then we did the Yellowstone River..."

I nod along, like I'm listening, but I'm not.

I don't know why this fuck thinks I give two shits about places he's fished. Just because I know how to fish doesn't mean I want to talk about it for 45 minutes straight. Or ever.

"Oh, we did that one a few years back," one of the other dads chimes in.

I don't need to be here for this conversation. I've shown zero interest, but they continue talking, nonetheless. I shove the last bite of my dinner into my mouth, and continue to ignore them. But at least sitting here gives me an excuse to watch Elouise. The flames of the firepit dance between us, hopefully distorting her view of me so I don't look like a total stalker by staring.

Miss Hall has been surrounded by students since everyone gathered 'round with their skewered hotdogs. It's clear that even the kids who aren't in her class like being around her, and since kids are good judges of character, I'm even more certain that she's the good person I remember.

"Right?" the guy to my left bumps my shoulder.

I nod, pretending to know what he's talking about.

"Beckett, what's your preferred way?" another dad asks.

Aw, fuck.

What's the nice way of saying *I wasn't paying the least bit of attention to your boring ass conversation.*

A feminine shout saves me from answering, and we all turn as one towards the sound.

Amused, I watch Elouise jump back from the bonfire, the hotdog at the end of her skewer completely engulfed in flames.

"Oh no! Oh no!" She tries to blow the fire out, but the roasting stick is too long, and she can't get it close enough to her face. Not that she could blow out that amount of fire. "Shit!" She shouts, making kids laugh. "I mean, crap!" she corrects herself.

I start to rise from my seat, and the dads on either side of me move to get up at the same time. I put my hands on their shoulders, pushing myself up while keeping them seated, "I got this."

"Crap! Crap!" Elouise's chants are getting more frantic, the hotdog clearly doomed with the amount of fire it's still putting off.

As I move around the pit, she starts to wave the flaming wiener around. Probably hoping the wind will help, but it doesn't. Instead, the hotdog – having held on for as long as it could – comes free from the poker. Trailing flames, bits of burnt meat fly from the hotdog as it soars through the air. There's a cacophony of shouts, some from the kids, most from Elouise, and we all watch the poor abused wiener land in a pile of small sticks and dried moss that I collected earlier and stacked off to the side. It's my pile of "fire starters" and it does its job well.

In a woosh, the pile ignites.

This time Elouise skips past cursing and lets out a squeal.

I almost start laughing, but then she starts to hop around.

Elouise is hopping around, and her tits are bouncing, and I no longer care that there's a fire. *What fire?* Tits. All I see are tits.

Her sweatshirt is unzipped, the thin material of her shirt is doing nothing to hide the jiggling with each small jump she makes.

I want to recreate that jiggle, by pounding my cock in her-

Elouise lets out another shriek and I'm snapped back into reality.

Continuing my stride towards her, I see I'm not the only man that has noticed her bouncing around. That motherfucker Adam basically has his tongue on the ground. And Mr. Whistle looks like he's about to have a damn heart attack.

"Lou!" I snap her name more forcefully than I mean to, but it works to get the attention of the other men as well.

She doesn't act offended by my tone, instead, she steps away from the little fire pile and clasps her hands in front of her chest. "Beckett! Oh god... Please!"

I bite back a groan.

Add that phrase to the list of things I want to hear while I'm buried inside her sweet-

"I've got you." My voice comes out like a growl.

Snagging the shovel I left nearby, I scoop up the small fire pile, and with steady hands, I quickly move the few steps to the bonfire. There's a small flare as the twigs get incinerated, but the large fire continues on as it was.

A round of applause goes up around the campsite and I humor the crowd with a little bow, "Thanks to this little reminder, we'll go over fire safety tomorrow."

There's some laughter before everyone goes back to what they were doing before the fiery interruption.

"Thank you," Elouise's voice is full of embarrassment, so

I'm not surprised when I turn around and find her cheeks a bright shade of pink.

"Don't worry, Smoky, I'll take care of you."

It's hard to tell in the flickering firelight, but I swear I see her pulse skip in her throat.

That's right, Babe. I'll take care of you however you need.

Chapter 15

Elouise

HOLDING A HAND OVER MY MOUTH, I try to muffle my cough.

Why did I bring vodka? I should've brought a bottle of wine. Or a few cans of hard cider. Or literally anything other than straight vodka. But it seemed the most compact and discreet option when I was packing.

I plug my nose and take another sip.

"Don't sip it. Gulp it."

Rebecca's voice startles me so bad that I end up inhaling half a mouthful.

"Christ, woman!" I cough out. "What the hell?"

She laughs and crawls over to where I'm sitting, "Gimme."

I hand her the bottle and watch as she takes a pull of the clear liquid like a pro.

"Thanks," she hands it back.

"You're welcome," I screw the cap back on and set it in my bag. "You sick of Bob's moves already?"

Rebecca shakes her head, "Not yet. I just came for my blankets. It was freezing in there last night."

79

"I bet," I grumble.

She eyes me as she bundles up the blankets in her arms, picking up on my displeasure. "You okay in here? Did you want me to stay?"

"No, no." I wave her off. "I'm fine."

"You sure?"

"Totally sure," I nod. "It's just been a day and I'm ready for sleep."

She smirks, "I'll be ready for sleep in about 30 minutes."

I wrinkle my nose, "Ew."

Rebecca laughs and makes her way back out. "You know what they say... If the tent is a rockin'..."

"Ohmygod, get out!" I look for something to throw at her, but she's zipping the tent shut before I can find anything.

As silence settles around me, so does the cold.

I glance at the bag with the vodka, wondering how much I'd need in order to not feel it when I freeze to death tonight. But on the off chance I survive, I don't want to drink so much that I have to get up and pee.

With nothing left to do, I reach over and turn off the lantern, allowing darkness to descend upon me.

I know that I'm not the last one to fall asleep, but the space between the tents must act like a sound buffer because the eerie quiet makes me feel like I'm all alone in these woods.

After trying to get comfortable for several minutes, I finally accept defeat and sit back up.

Since I had to use my normal sleep shirt as a towel this morning, I was left with just my thin tank top to sleep in. So I thought I'd layer on my sweatshirt for warmth, but try as I might, I just feel too restricted to get comfortable. Add that to the small sized sleeping bag and I'm about ready to scream myself to sleep.

With minimal struggling, I get the sweatshirt off, straighten my tank top and shimmy back down into my sleeping bag. Then, feeling like a genius, I lay the sweatshirt over my sleeping bag like a mini blanket.

There. Better.

Silence answers me.

Go to sleep, Lou.

My eyes stay open, staring at the ceiling of the tent.

Sleep. You want to sleep.

Still open. Still staring.

Oh come on, Lou. It's not like anything is going to come get you.

I almost laugh at myself.

Of course nothing is going to get me. This isn't a horror movie. Or any sort of movie. It's just me, alone, but surrounded by dozens of people.

Sleep, Lou.

I'm finally forcing my eyes closed, when a soft sound has them popping back open.

What was that?

The sound comes again and this time it's unmistakable. It's a zipper.

My zipper!

Someone is opening my tent!

I spring up and scramble to reach for the lantern.

"Rebecca?" I whisper, as my fingers brush against the base of the light. "Is that you?"

She doesn't respond.

My fingers tremble, and I tell myself it's from the cold and not fear.

Finally, I find the right button, and I depress it.

Light illuminates the space.

I blink against the sudden change and find bright blue *male* eyes staring back at me.

Not Rebecca.

I pull in a breath to scream.

Chapter 16

Beckett

Shifting my weight, I cross my feet at the ankles and lean back against the tree behind me. The fire is out, and the trees filter out most of the moonlight so I'm shrouded in shadows. Just another shape in the night.

I'm not trying to hide; I'm just trying to stay out of the way. Not everyone is asleep yet. And until that happens, I'll be here. Watching.

I don't know why I feel so unsettled. I've done this campsite dance a hundred times before. It's not the new location, or new people. If I'm being honest with myself, it's her.

Elouise Hall.

I don't know what I expected to happen when I saw her, but this thick layer of sexual tension was not it. And in just one afternoon she's managed to scale all my defenses. Now I can't think of anything *but* Elouise.

I didn't come home to find a woman. But if life has taught me anything, it's that the universe doesn't give two shits what you have planned.

My eyes trail across the sea of tents.

I keep telling myself that I'm looking out for the whole camp, but that's a lie. I'm looking out for her.

I watched Rebecca come and go from their shared tent. I saw the shadows of Elouise dance across the thin wall. I saw her turn the lantern off. And I watched as one-by-one more tents went dark.

But still I stay. Waiting. Needing to reassure myself that everything is fine.

A twig cracks a few paces away.

I don't react. Stillness and silence keeps me invisible.

A body emerges from the woods, walking slowly, head swiveling side to side. Not necessarily bad behavior, but not exactly normal either.

Keeping my body in place, my eyes track the figure. The darkness makes it impossible for me to see who the person is. But when they turn towards Elouise's tent, I stand up straighter.

They get closer to my Elouise, and I step away from the tree.

Whoever this person is, I'm going to have a conversation with them.

The moonlight peeks through some clouds, illuminating their face.

This prick.

The motherfucker stops and drops into a crouch right in front of her tent and I lengthen my stride.

This dead fucking prick.

When I reach him, he's got the tent flap unzipped and half of his body in my girl's tent.

Ducking down, I grip his ankles, and in one violent motion, I yank him backwards.

Resistance gives way as his weight is pulled off his hands, and I hear the satisfying thud of his face hitting the packed earth.

Chapter 17

Elouise

Before my lungs can exhale on a scream, my intruder jerks backwards. His arms grasp for purchase a split second before his face slams into the ground.

My would be scream of fear turns into a squeak of surprise and my hands fly up to press against my heart.

I have no idea what to do. Or say. But before I can decide his whole body disappears, pulled backwards through the opening.

My mouth opens and closes.

What the hell is happening?!

A footstep crunches outside my tent, and then another face is filling the opening.

Beckett's eyes meet mine before flickering across my body. "One moment."

Then he's gone.

Chapter 18

Beckett

I GRIP Adam by the back of his shirt and lift him off the ground. The collar of his jacket pulls tight across his throat, and I revel in the slight gagging sound it causes him to make.

I want to break his legs.

When he gets his feet back underneath him, I let go.

I want to rip his arms off.

He stumbles a moment as his hands reach up to cup his nose.

It's bleeding, but it doesn't look broken. More's the pity.

I want to end this man, but I can't. Not here.

"Sorry man," I tell him in a tone that doesn't sound sorry at all. "Thought you might be a pervert." I slap him on the back. Hard. "You must've gotten turned around. Your tent is over there."

The shove I give him sends him staggering away.

"Yeah, sorry," he doesn't meet my eyes, "I got turned around."

Without another word, he hurries off.

My hands ball into fists.

That prick wasn't lost and the thought of him putting his filthy fucking hands on Elouise has protectiveness pouring through my body. If this camp wasn't filled with kids, I'd tear his fucking head off.

"Beckett?" Elouise's whisper fills my lungs with air.

Crouching down, I look back into her tent.

That first glance I got wasn't enough. Elouise, sitting up, cheeks flushed, hair down, tits on display in her thin, nearly transparent shirt.

I should've gouged Adam's eyes out.

Goddamn she's beautiful. Every last inch of her. And... I can see her nipples. Her perfect nipples are straining against the material, begging for attention.

Arms move to block my view as she crosses them over her chest, and I take my gaze away from her chest to the rest of her. A shiver rolls through her body and I see the small prickles of goosebumps covering her skin.

Shivering.

I take in the full scene in front of me. Freezing air. Tank top. Nipples alert from cold. And a too small, old as hell, sleeping bag.

I tilt my head, like that'll help me make sense of what I'm seeing. "Is that..." I raise a brow, waiting for Elouise to meet my eyes, "Is that your brother's old Turtles sleeping bag?"

Chapter 19

Elouise

I ONLY HAVE time to nod my reply before Beckett is ducking back out of my tent. With a quick pull he closes the zipper, and then he's gone.

Just like that.

Burying my face in my hands I let out a groan. Which is worse, embarrassment or mortification? It's gotta be mortification, right? That's gotta be what I'm feeling.

What in the hell is even happening tonight?!

First, Creepy Dad Adam barges into my tent. I heard what Beckett said to him, but that had to be a load of crap. Right? No one mistakes one tent for another. Not sober.

A shiver runs down my arms and I shoot a glare at my bag with the vodka.

Crossing my arms back over my perky as fuck nipples I silently curse the little bottle of booze.

Weren't you supposed to keep me warm?!

I lift my arms and look down, confirming my current state.

Yep. Nips were on full display for Beckett.

The one bright side is that I think Beckett interrupted

Adam before he got an eyeful of my almost naked breasts. Beckett himself is a different story. He got two eyefuls. And wasn't even being subtle about looking.

But then he took off, and I'm not sure what offended him more, my nipples, or my sleeping bag.

The tent zipper starts to drag up again, but Beckett's voice filters through the fabric before I have time to freak out, "It's me."

"Oh, um, come in." I murmur, unsure why he's back.

When the flap is unzipped, I expect to see Beckett, but instead a pile of blankets gets tossed inside.

"Uh..."

What is happening?

Beckett steps through the opening, ignoring my unasked question, and zipping the tent shut behind him – leaving his boots outside.

He's hunched over in the low space, and I have literally zero intelligent things to say about this new and bizarre development.

Beckett grabs the bottom corner of my sleeping bag. "Out."

"What?"

He tugs it again, "You need to get out of this piece of shit bag, Smoky."

Smoky.

I refuse to overthink the fact that he's given me a nickname.

"Elouise," his look is pure exasperation, "out."

Eyeing the pile of blankets, I figure whatever he has planned will be a lot warmer than my current situation, so I unzip myself and roll out. Taking only a second to think *WTF* at my zipper magically working again.

Maneuvering around each other, I scoot into the corner, and watch with fascination as Beckett creates an honest-to-god bed. I don't know what sort of magic camping store he shops at, but he has a large pad that goes from flat to two inches thick in a blink of an eye. He then layers on a couple of the blankets I'd brought to soften the bed even more. Then with a few quick zips he connects two large sleeping bags to make one giant one, leaving a side open – assumedly for easy entry. And lastly, he spreads two thick wool blankets over the whole pile.

I'm currently shivering, and it looks like heaven.

Sitting back on his heels, Beckett lifts the open corner. "Get in."

Not needing to be told twice, I pretend my boobs aren't jiggling all over the damn place as I crawl past him into the glorious cocoon.

After a few adjustments, I end up on my side, facing him, with the sealed sides at my back and feet. My muscles immediately start to relax, feeling a hundred times warmer already.

"Thanks for..." my words trail off when Beckett shifts back into a crouch and starts to undo his jeans.

Sweet slutty camp dreams, is this really happening?!

"What are you doing?" I ask, my voice up an octave.

"I can't sleep in jeans, Babe."

Babe?

I shake that off.

"But... I mean... you can't..."

He shoves the jeans down his thighs and every synapse in my brain misfires.

Thick, muscular, hairy Man Thighs. Good god. They're perfect.

Ignoring my heart attack, he pushes his jeans off the rest of the way, and... *holy hell*... His... *ohmygod I can't believe I'm seeing this!* His dick is pressing against the front of his dark red boxer briefs, creating the perfect outline.

He's not hard. Not entirely. But it's there. It's right fucking there. And it's... big. It's big and thick and is begging for attention.

The sound of his throat clearing sends my cheeks blazing.

Rolling, I faceplant into my pillow.

Beckett just caught me staring at his... junk.

The cushioned pad shifts beneath me as he climbs into the little bed.

Our bed.

Is this really happening?

Waiting until I know he's covered by the blankets; I roll back onto my side and open an eye to peek at him, "So, you're sleeping here?"

Beckett settles onto his back, turning his head to look at me, "Well it's here or on the bare floor of my tent." His eyes never leave mine, "That okay with you, Lou?"

My chest expands at his use of my childhood nickname. Only family and close friends still call me that.

"I'm okay with it."

He keeps staring, "Nothing's gonna happen."

His statement sounds like nothing but the truth, and it should be reassuring, but it stings. Just a little.

I try to agree, "Oh, I know you'd never..."

"You think I've never?" He quirks a brow.

I have to swallow and look away, forcing myself to not think about all the *things* he's done before.

"I just... I mean, not with me."

"No. I've never with you," his voice is low. Deep.

Is it hot in here? Did something catch fire? Other than my panties?

"Elouise."

"Yeah?" I raise my gaze back up to meet his.

"Go to sleep."

I close my eyes, "Okay."

I don't open my eyes at Beckett's chuckle.

I don't open my eyes when I feel him moving.

I don't even open my eyes when I feel the warmth of his body press against mine.

And I definitely don't open my eyes, when he puts an arm around my shoulders and pulls me firmly into his side.

My body moves into his like this isn't the first time we've been this close.

My breathing slows like every nerve ending I have isn't on fire.

My head nestles into that perfect spot on his shoulder like it's laid there every night.

My eyes don't open until I hear the click of the lantern. Only when darkness fills the tent, do I open my eyes. Just to make sure this is real.

Chapter 20

Beckett

I EXPECT HER TO ARGUE. To resist this pull between us. But without a word she melts into my side.

There's no tenseness.

No awkwardness.

Just... comfort.

Every moment with Elouise feels more and more like I'm home. And I feel like I should be surprised, but there's just something about *us* that makes sense.

Her body softens against me even more, and her breathing changes. And just like that, she's asleep in my arms.

I stare up at the ceiling of the tent, wondering what my next move should be. I didn't really have a plan when I came back to Darling Lake last week. But now... fuck, now I can't tell if I'm thinking with my brain or my dick. Am I just jumping to decisions about my future because I want to be buried into Elouise's sweet little pussy?

My fingers tense around the soft skin of her upper arm and my cock hardens.

I shift. I won't be able to fall asleep with a raging hard-on.

And I can't exactly jerk one off laying right here next to Elouise.

Think unsexy thoughts.

Poison Ivy rashes.

Bear attacks.

First Aid techniques.

Elouise.

My fingers brushing against her soft skin.

Her asking me to "take it off".

"Goddamnit," I grumble into the darkness as Little Beckett strains to punch through the sleeping bag.

When was the last time I was this turned on? This hard over a few innocent touches and glances? Over fucking cuddling?

Probably when I was a fucking teenager. I almost laugh, that's what the little minx in my arms has reduced me to. A hormonal teenager.

Fitting.

I pull her even closer.

Whatever this is, I'm not done yet.

Chapter 21

Elouise

"So..." Rebecca drags out the word as she steps into stride alongside me.

I can feel my cheeks blush and she hasn't even asked a question. "So, what?" I play dumb even though I know what's coming.

"So," she bumps her shoulder into mine, "I woke up super early having to pee."

"That's a little TMI."

She ignores me, "And as I was walking back to Bob's tent, I saw someone crawling out of your tent." She pauses, being dramatic. "But it wasn't you."

I bite my lip.

That answers the question of when Beckett left. All I know is that I slept like the dead and then woke up alone, but surprisingly warm. And I'm not sure if I should attribute that last fact to the expensive sleeping bags, Beckett's body heat or the fact that my blood was sizzling all night from knowing he was there.

Right. Freaking. There.

"Oh come on!" Rebecca hisses at me, "you have *got* to give

me details!" She glances around, making sure that no one is close enough to hear us. "That man is so hot it hurts my eyes. Please tell me his dick is just as good looking."

I can't stop the laugh that spills out of me. It's laced with guilt and embarrassment, even though I only saw the outline.

Rebecca groans, "It is, isn't it?"

I shake my head, "I don't know." I lift my hand to forestall her, "We didn't," I glance around this time, "have sex." The last two words are a whisper.

We're in the middle of a hike, led by Mr. So Hot himself, but thankfully everyone seems to be lost in their own conversations.

After another harrowing shower experience, using that same damn shirt as a towel, I took my coffee to my tent and tried my hardest to make myself presentable. Which makes no sense, since I've spent the entire day avoiding Beckett.

I couldn't even tell you what we were learning about during the first part of the day, because my brain was constantly spiraling back to my night with Beckett.

My night with Beckett. Just thinking about it has me flushing from my face to my toes. Which is ridiculous because all we did was sleep. And I mean, sure, we were cuddled together, but that doesn't necessarily mean anything. You can cuddle with friends. You can cuddle when you're stuck outdoors and you're trying to stay alive through joined body heat. It could've been totally innocent for him.

But... What if I drooled all over him? Or talked in my sleep? Or, oh god, what if I farted in my sleep but he was still awake and heard it?! What if that's why he left without waking me?!

"Elouise," Rebecca jabs me with her elbow, "spill."

Now I can't stop worrying about it!

I keep my voice low and lean closer to Rebecca, "Do guys care if women fart?"

The laugh that bursts out of her is so loud I nearly trip over my next step.

Everyone, and I mean *everyone*, turns to look at us.

I plaster on my biggest smile, "It's fine! Nothing to see here! Keep on going!" I don't dare look Beckett's way because I'm positive he's staring along with everybody else.

Rebecca's stopped – hunched over, hands on her knees, gasping for breath – so I wave for the campers behind us to pass, "Go ahead, we'll catch up!"

I keep the fake smile pasted on my face until the last person passes.

My cheeks are burning when I poke Rebecca in the side, "You done?"

She looks up at me and falls into laughter all over again. It's annoying, but infectious, and I feel myself smiling for real this time.

"Sorry, sorry." Rebecca wipes the tears off her face, "Okay, give me context. Was it when he was going down on you or was it during sex?"

It takes me a second to realize what she's asking. "What?! Oh my god!" I start to laugh- she thinks I farted on him during sex. "That's not-" realizing how bad it could've been I crack up even harder.

It feels like several minutes later when we catch our breath.

Rebecca grins at me, "Girl, I needed that."

I roll my eyes with a snort, "Glad I could be of service."

"But seriously, why would you have asked me... *that*?" she widens her eyes.

"I don't know," I let out a big exhale. "You mentioned seeing him sneaking out of the tent and so my brain started going over all the possible things that I could've done in my sleep to scare him off."

"And sleep farting was the best you could come up with?" Rebecca chuckles again, "It's the morning after, of course he snuck out. That's what you do after... whatever it is that you guys did."

"It was nothing." When she lifts a brow, I hold my hands up, "I'm serious. We didn't do anything."

"But he did spend the night with you, right?"

"He did."

She lifts a brow, "And he just knocked on the tent flap and asked if he could come in to talk all night?"

"Uh, no. He..." All the sudden the first part of the night slams back into my brain. I can't believe I forgot all about that part! "He caught Adam, one of the dads, trying to get into our tent?"

She rears back, "What?"

"Yeah..." I tell her the whole story. About thinking it was her coming back. About Adam opening the tent, and Beckett dragging him out. About Beckett coming back with all the blankets. And making the bed. And making me get into the bed. And taking his jeans off and me staring at the outline of his dick in his underwear.

"I knew it!" Rebecca pumps a fist.

"I didn't see it," I argue, "and it's not like it was erect."

We stare at each other for a moment before we both snicker. I can't believe I just used that word.

"And you're seriously telling me that you didn't do anything? That you had Big Beckett in the same sleeping bag with you and you didn't even kiss him?"

I shrug, "We cuddled."

Her brows shoot up, disappearing under the edge of her hat, "That stud cuddles?"

Biting my lip, I nod.

"Well, I'll be damned."

"But he was gone when I woke up," I reminded her.

She waves that off, "Don't read into that. He probably had to get up early to get the fire going and prep for the day."

"I suppose." I mull it over and realize she's probably right.

"Or..." her head tilts, "maybe- you gassed him out of the tent."

She's cackling when she jumps out of my reach and races up the trail.

Chapter 22

Beckett

THE SOUND of Elouise's laughter vibrates down my spine and it takes all of my will power to pretend that I'm listening to the guy beside me. He probably introduced himself at some point, but my brain has been consumed by Elouise all day.

When I woke up hard as hell in the early hours of the morning, I knew I had to extricate myself from the situation. Because if I didn't, I'd be waking her up with my tongue between her thighs. And even though I'm reasonably sure she'd be okay with that; I didn't want to push my luck.

The man next to me pauses in his rambling, so I nod my head and make a sound of agreement. It must be what he was looking for because he starts talking again.

I should probably thank him. Because if I wasn't in the middle of feigning interest in this conversation I'd walk back to where Elouise and Rebecca are, demanding to know what they're talking about. But chances are high they're talking about me, so it's for the better that I stay up here.

I saw Rebecca when I left Elouise's tent this morning, so

S. J. Tilly

I'm sure she's grilling Elouise on what happened between us. But I can't imagine what she could be saying to make Rebecca laugh that much.

Another voice sounds next to me, and I realize that more people have joined our little "conversation". This one I recognize as the gym teacher. "Oh yeah, my neighbors put that model up in their house," he says to the first guy.

Model? I have no clue what the fuck they're talking about.

"Hey Adam," First Guy calls out, "you're in security, right?"

Adam.

My teeth grind just at the mention of his name.

"Uh, yeah." Adam's tone sounds a little worried.

I glance over my shoulder, and see he's moved up so he's just a few paces behind me.

Fucker should be worried.

Not a single part of me believes he was crawling into Elouise's tent on accident last night. But I can't prove it. And as much as he deserves to have his face caved in, his 10-year-old son is on this camping trip, and I can't do that in front of his kid.

I do feel slightly consoled by the sight of his face. Sadly, his nose wasn't broken when he face-planted into the ground last night. But it's swollen, bruised and painful looking.

Over breakfast, I heard someone ask him what happened. His eyes darted to mine before he lied and said he tripped in the dark. One more sign he's a piece of shit. If he really had been lost, he would've admitted the truth.

I might not be able to deliver the justice I want, but Adam's put himself on my radar and I'm not letting that bastard anywhere near Elouise.

"You work for Mazzanti, right?" Gym Teacher asks.

"I used to, I'm at Nero's now." Adam replies.

Feeling my hackles rise at his nearness, I go back to tuning out the conversation.

I just need to get through today without killing someone, so I don't find myself arrested before tonight. Because tonight, I'm staying in Elouise's tent again. And tonight, we're doing more than cuddling.

Chapter 23

Elouise

I'M SO ON EDGE, I'm about to crawl out of my skin.

I was so turned-on during dinner that I was tempted to push everything off the picnic table and lay myself out as a meal for Beckett.

I didn't. Obviously. But that man knows exactly what he does to me, and he tortured me with his closeness all evening.

First, he made stew. And I don't mean he dumped cans of stew into a pot and heated it on a camp stove. No. First, he built a fire. With his bare hands. Then he suspended a large pot - that looked more like a medieval cauldron – filled with water over that fire. And then he used a big, intimidating butcher knife to chop vegetables and beef and herbs and *ohmygod* it was like living in a highlander romance.

By the time he was done prepping, he was down to just a single layer. A thin, long-sleeved shirt that clung to every one of his bulging muscles. Muscles that I slept against last night.

But his torment didn't end there.

After letting everything simmer together, he personally dished out dinner for the whole camp. A sexy lumberjack of a man, lit by firelight, feeding a swarm of children... I don't have dreams of having a hoard of kids but watching his display had my ovaries high fiving each other.

Finally, when I had my own bowl, I thought I'd be free of him. Except I wasn't.

I don't know if he managed to put an invisible "seat taken" sign on the spot next to me, but it stayed open until the man himself sat down next to me. Only it wasn't really a Beckett sized space, so I spent the whole of dinner with his thigh pressed against mine. His arm pressed against my shoulder. His knuckles brushing against the back of my hand.

I didn't want to make it obvious that my blood was smoldering, so I toughed it out. I pretended I was unaffected. I acted like my body wasn't begging for him to pull me onto his lap.

But the second people started to get up, ready for bed, I bolted.

Only, that didn't solve my problem. Because now I'm here, in my tent, wearing my sleep pants and my see-through tank top, huddled inside the extra-large sleeping bag, waiting.

Waiting for Beckett.

I wasn't sure this morning, but now I'm almost positive he'll be coming back tonight.

The looks. The touches. They told me exactly what he was thinking. And he was thinking about me.

I snuggle lower under the covers.

Beckett Stoleman was thinking about me.

Like *that*. And it's our last night, so if he really is interested, he needs to act.

I still can't get over this whole bizarre situation.

It's not that I have terrible self-esteem. I don't. I know I have a lot to offer. Sure, I might not be everyone's dream girl, but I know that I am for some guys. Some guys like curves and brains and a dirty mouth. I just wasn't sure if Beckett was one of those guys.

Honestly, when I try to picture who I think he'd end up with, I flash back to that cursed Christmas Party fifteen years ago. To the perky, skinny, blonde that came in and stole his attention away from me.

I blink away the memory. I don't need to be thinking of that night. Making myself feel insecure will not help my current state of mind.

Whatever I've thought in the past, Beckett is here now. And he's interested in me.

Footsteps approach my tent and I hold my breath.

This is it.

The footsteps walk past.

This isn't it.

I exhale.

Chill, Lou.

Closing my eyes, I work to calm my racing pulse.

Maddie is always telling me about finding my happy place. She's convinced that if I can visualize that peace, then I can experience it in real life.

I probably should have listened closer when she explained the process.

Breathing in, I let the scent of the woodsy air fill my senses.

Calm. I can be calm.

Focusing on my breathing, I don't hear the footsteps that stop outside my tent.

Calm.

The sound of the entrance unzipping has my eyes flying open.

"Beckett?" I whisper his name, suddenly worried it might be Adam again.

"It's me, Smoky," his quiet response settles me, while simultaneously spiking my pulse.

It's strange to just welcome him into my tent, considering I've been avoiding him all day. But having him here gives me an odd mix of comfort and excitement. And my poor heart hardly knows how to handle it.

I left the lantern on, so peeking over the top of the blankets that are still clutched in my hands, I watch as Beckett ducks inside.

He's silent as he closes the flap behind him.

He's silent as he watches me, while moving further into the tent.

He's silent as he pulls his shirt off.

The moisture leaves my mouth and heads straight to my core.

This man... *Christ.* He's built just like my Highlander fantasies. Tall, wide, muscles and thickness and... he's undoing his jeans.

Seriously, what is going on?! Is he just going to strip all the way down? Are we doing this? It? Now?!

Beckett's eyes are on me as he shoves his jeans off his hips. And I have to bite my lip to keep from begging him to go quicker.

There's no way to confuse what's in front of me. Straining against his black boxer briefs is a hard cock. A big, fat, hard cock.

The outline I saw last night did not do him justice.

A small moan escapes my lips before I can clamp them back shut.

I knew he'd be coming back tonight. I mean, I have his blankets. And I was expecting that something might happen between us. But I wasn't expecting this. For him to just strip down and for my body to react like it was doused in a lust potion.

My chest is nearly heaving and I'm glad I'm lying flat on my back because if I'd been standing, I'd have fallen over.

He's just so... manly.

"Elouise?" Beckett's voice fills the tent, skittering across my nerves.

My eyes take their time roaming up to meet his. "Yes?" I breathe the question.

Beckett lowers onto his knees, leaning forward until he's bracing his weight on his hands. "Are you gonna be quiet for me? Or do I need to leave?"

Holy. Shit.

"I'll be quiet," I whisper.

He uses one hand to flip the blankets back.

I release my hold on them, and they fold over at my waist, leaving my top half exposed to the cool air.

I don't need to look down to know that my nipples are screaming for attention. The thin material of my tank top feeling like chainmail.

When he doesn't move, my back arches. "I promise."

His eyes follow the movement, locking on my chest.

"Elouise," the way he says my name sounds like a growl.

I can't believe this is happening. No preamble. No dancing around the topic. Just Beckett getting naked and telling me to be quiet.

Another tremor moves through my body and in a matter of moments I'm going to be embarrassingly wet.

"Beckett," I say his name like a plea.

His eyes stay locked on my chest as he exhales. Then he reaches back and turns off the lantern. Darkness settling between us.

"No one else sees you," Beckett whispers. "Not even a silhouette."

My eyes haven't had time to adjust to the sudden change, so I can't see him, but I can hear him as he moves closer.

The thin mattress beneath me shifts as he climbs onto it.

"And no one hears you," his words brush against my skin. He's so close now.

The blanket over my bottom half gets pushed away, and one of Beckett's thighs presses in between mine.

I open my legs for him. The heat of him seeping into my every pore.

"Not a single sound." His lips brush against my cheek, and I squeeze my eyes shut. "Not a single moan." His breath feathers over my neck. "Not even the smallest groan." His open mouth presses just below my ear. "Not a peep, Elouise."

Then, as if he can see in the dark, fingers suddenly grip one of my nipples.

The sound that leaves my mouth is everything he just warned me against.

He clicks his tongue and releases my nipple, "Bad girl."

Afraid he's going to pull away, I reach my hands out to stop him.

Skin. Hot-to-the-touch skin meets my palms. Because Beckett isn't wearing a shirt.

I have to catch myself before I moan again, because he feels so good. So perfect.

"You want another chance to be quiet, Babe?" I nod my head, not wanting to speak out loud and trusting he'll see the movement. "Good." His teeth scrape against the curve of my shoulder. "Behave this time, or I'll have to find another way to keep your mouth occupied."

More heat surges through me.

I don't know if I've ever been this turned on. This achy.

My legs close around his thigh, seeking friction, but his leg is positioned too low and I can't get the pressure where I need it.

I'm torn between wanting to savor every second and screaming at him to hurry up.

A finger traces along my bottom lip. "Such a pretty girl."

The finger trails a line down my chin. My neck. Between my breasts. Pulling down the front of my tank top. Beckett keeps his finger tugging down on the fabric, moving it from one side, then the other, until both of my breasts are free. The top band of my shirt snug underneath them.

Shivers run over every inch of my body. The cold air. His hot touch. I'm so on edge I'm afraid I might come without any contact at all.

Something ghosts over the tip of my nipple, and I strain into it.

"Patience."

I open my lips to curse at him, but his mouth presses down against mine. At the same time, a large hand envelops my breast.

My senses are instantly overloaded. Our first kiss. The heat of his palm pressing against my nipple. His fingers gripping the soft flesh. The feel of his mouth moving against mine.

Lips. Tongue.

His mouth slants one way and I move the other, deepening the kiss.

A kiss I dreamt about so many times growing up. But even my dreams didn't come close.

My hands reach up and grip his hair. His chocolatey locks are soft, contrasting the feeling of his scratchy beard rubbing against the sensitive skin next to my mouth.

This isn't the Beckett I was infatuated with as a girl. This is Man Beckett, and he's so much better.

When his tongue swipes into my mouth again, I let my lips close around it. Sucking it into my mouth.

I can feel the rumble of approval rolling around in his chest.

Pulling back from our kiss, Beckett lowers his head and sucks one of my nipples into his mouth. Nipping at it with his teeth. Flicking it with his tongue.

I can feel *everything*. And I'm about to burst.

He switches breasts, pulling my other nipple into his mouth. But when he uses his fingers to pinch my other peak, I can't stop the moan that leaves me.

He stops. Lifting off me completely.

"No! Beckett, wait!" I'm panting, but I can't let him stop now. I might die.

He removes his thigh from between mine, but he doesn't go far.

Kneeling next to me, Becket rolls me onto my side, facing away from him.

Before I can ask him what he's doing, he lays down behind me and hooks an arm around my waist, pulling me back until I'm flush against his front. He's the big to my little spoon.

With a few adjustments, he gets one arm under my head like a pillow, and the other splays across my stomach.

My tank top is still bunched up under my breasts, so all that's left separating us are his boxer briefs and my thin sleep pants.

I arch into him and his grip on my middle tightens. "Keep that ass still, Smoky, or I'm going to fuck it."

I can't help it, his words are setting me on fire. And we're leaving in the morning. And I don't even know if I'll see him again after this. And I don't even know if he's talking about doggy style or actually fucking me in the ass, but I find I don't care. I'm so far gone, he could talk me into trying just about anything right now.

Ignoring his warning, I grind back against him.

This time he's the one to groan. "Do you know what you're doing?" he shifts his hips, and I feel the full length of him pressing against me. "Do you understand where this is going?"

"I understand," my back arches. "I'm not some little virgin anymore, Beckett."

The arm under my head bends and I'm hauled higher up against his chest. His hand grips the front of my neck. Not hard. But enough to show who's in control.

"Who took it?" he bites out.

"What..." I try to turn my head back to look at him, but his grip tightens, keeping me in place.

"Who took this sweet little cherry from me?" The hand around my waist is suddenly between the legs, cupping my pussy over the material of my pants.

His hips flex and he thrusts his cock against my ass.

My thoughts are sizzling, but they keep sparking on the same word. "Yours?"

"Mine." In a flash his hand is inside my pants, finding me bare.

He groans into my hair, his fingers gliding against my slit, my wetness instantly coating his hand.

One finger presses into me, just an inch, and I hold my breath.

"You were always too young for me. Too innocent." He pulls his finger out, then pushes back in. "Too fucking young. But not anymore." He adds a second finger in this time. "Now give me a name."

I lift my top leg and hook it back over his hip, opening myself for his use.

"Name?" I'm entirely lost to the climax that's building rapidly inside me.

"A name, Babe. Now." His fingers dip in and out. In and out.

"T-Tim. It was Tim." I stutter, squirming against his touch.

Teeth scrape against my earlobe, "That's the last time you ever say that name." The hand on my throat slowly slides up my neck. "Now remember, you promised to stay quiet for me."

His hand clamps over my mouth as three fingers spear deep into my pussy.

I cry out, the sound muffled into one palm as I grind against the other. The broad expanse of his hand presses against my clit, firm and insistent.

"That's right, Lou," his words are husky against my ear, "work yourself on my hand. Fuck my fingers."

I can't stop moaning. Can't stop grinding. Can't stop clenching around his fingers. His long, thick fingers. The stretch in my pussy. The heat of his body. The hand over my mouth. The press of his hard cock against my ass. The cold air against my nipples.

Beckett rolls his wrist, sliding his fingers even deeper, palm pressing harder against my clit.

"Now, Babe. Come for me now before I shove this dick down your throat."

I implode. Coming so hard bright spots of light dot my vision.

"That's it." He doesn't stop thrusting his hips against me. "That's my girl. You liked that, didn't you." My whole body shudders.

I nod as I roll my hips against his hand one last time, my words dying against his palm.

His chest is rising and falling against my back, his dick still hard against my ass. I press back against him.

His fingers slowly slide out of my pussy, "You want to suck my cock, Babe? You want to swallow me down?"

I nod again, knowing I won't be fully sated until he joins me over the cliff.

"Fuck." His movements become frantic as he untangles himself from me. "Come here." Wet fingers grip my shoulder and roll me onto my back. My eyes have adjusted to the dark so I know what's coming when he lowers his head and licks across my nipples.

My hands claw at his sides, but his dick is out of reach.

Beckett lifts his head to look me in the eye, "Fuck, Smoky, you sure?"

"I want it," my voice still shaky from my release but I can hear the certainty.

I try to push up onto my elbows, but he flattens his hand at the bottom of my neck and pushes me back down.

"Stay."

He shuffles around, removing his boxer briefs, then he's crawling over me. Straddling my chest. "Open up, Babe."

The tip of his dick presses against my lips and I open, eagerly taking him in.

"Fuck!" he whispers.

My fingers grip the outside of his thighs.

Keeping my lips closed around his dick, I run my tongue up and down the underside of his head, flicking against that sensitive spot.

"Fucking hell." His hips start to move.

I hum, taking him deeper.

Beckett lets out another soft curse, then he leans forward placing his hands on the ground above my head.

On all fours, he pumps his hips, burying himself deeper down my throat.

"Shit," another thrust, "Fuck, Babe. I'm so close."

Out and in.

I tip my head back as much as I can, his hips working above me as he fucks my mouth.

His words are labored, "I'm so fucking close."

I use my tongue to run along the length of him. High on the satisfaction I feel at being the one to please him.

"I'm gonna come." He whispers, warning me.

But I don't pull away. I suck harder.

"Get ready, Babe," a hand grips the hair at the top of my head, holding me still, as he pumps into me one last time, exploding.

Overwhelmed with lust, I swallow around his length, taking everything he gives me.

Chapter 24

Beckett

Bright lights dance on the edge of my vision as I pump my hips forward for the final time.

"Goddamn." The word is more of a prayer than a curse, because this woman is a fucking gift.

Blinking away the haze, I look down at the sight below me.

Elouise, mouth wide around my cock, tears trailing down her cheeks, and a wicked gleam in her eyes.

My limbs are on the verge of trembling and as much as I want to stay just like this, I don't want to collapse and actually choke her with my dick.

Carefully, I move off her. Elouise's lips making a small popping sound when my cock pulls free.

Once I'm clear, I drop onto my back beside her.

There's something about trying to be quiet that adds an extra layer of intensity, and my heart is still beating wildly in my chest. But as my blood settles, and the ringing in my ears stops, I wonder if we didn't fail miserably at being quiet.

We lay in the silence for another moment, I figure since I

don't hear shouts from outraged parents, we must've succeeded.

"Wow... that was... wow," Elouise sounds dazed and I can't stop the grin that pulls across my face.

I roll my head to the side so I can look at her, "You can say that again."

Holding my gaze, she mouths *wow* one more time.

I grin harder, and mimic her, mouthing the word back.

She starts to smile but it's interrupted by a full body shiver.

Realizing that we're both sprawled out, exposed to the frigid air, I sit up and quickly rearrange the blankets until we're buried under a pile of fabric.

Elouise sadly takes the time to tuck her fabulous tits back into her tank top, so I snag my boxer briefs and shimmy them up my legs. I don't mind sleeping naked, but if there's a sudden emergency outside the tent that I need to run to, I'd rather be in my underwear than nothing at all.

Laying back down, I pat my chest, "Come here."

With zero hesitation, Elouise shifts closer until she's snuggled into my side. Her arm around my waist, her leg hiked up over mine - the perfect fit.

I want to say something. But I can't think of anything better than *wow*, so I just press a kiss to her forehead.

Elouise lets out a satisfied sound and rubs her cheek against my chest. "Goodnight, Beckett Stoleman."

I smile into the dark, "Sweet dreams, Smoky Darling."

Just like last night, she drops straight into sleep.

My fingers trail up and down her arm, the feel of her soft skin soothing my mind.

As my eyes get heavy, I hug her to me even tighter.

She might think this was a one-time thing, but I'm not done. I'm not even close to being done with Elouise Hall.

Chapter 25

Elouise

With our order taken, the waitress grabs our menus and walks away.

"Well..." Maddie twirls one of her long black curls around a finger.

"Well, what?" I reply, fighting hard against the urge to grin.

She rolls her eyes, "You've been avoiding me ever since you got back from that little camping trip." She lets the curl spring free so she can point her finger at me. "A trip, I might add, that you were dreading. And, you said you'd text me every night. Which you didn't do." I open my mouth, but she wags her finger to stop me. "What you did do was leave me a frantic voicemail about seeing your old crush Beckett. Which, I still don't understand how that's possible. And then proceeded to ignore my calls, leaving me with freaking nothing."

I wait a beat to make sure she's done, "Want me to talk now?"

Maddie crosses her arms, "Not yet." Narrowing her eyes, she gives me her best attempt at a glare, but on her pretty heart-shaped face it's the furthest thing from intimidating. Giving up she huffs, "Ugh, fine. I'm done. Now spill."

The waitress comes back, setting down our drinks. A hard cider for Maddie, and water for me since classes start back up tomorrow.

I take a sip of my water, giving myself another moment to gather my thoughts.

The restaurant, Darling Bites, is noisy, but it's a staple in this small town, and has been here for as long as I can remember. During the day it's the perfect place to grab breakfast and lunch, but once the evening hits, the lights dim, the voices ramp up, and the bar opens.

I let go of my glass and twist my napkin between my fingers, "I didn't call you those other nights because I wasn't alone in the tent."

"Yeah- but didn't you say that Rebecca lady was cool? I can't imagine she'd care about you making a phone call," her brows furrow as she takes a sip of her drink.

"Right. Well..." how do I say this, "it wasn't Rebecca in my tent. It was Beckett."

Maddie tips her head forward, letting her mouthful of booze spill back into the glass.

"Classy," I laugh.

She ignores me. "I'm sorry, what?! Are you telling me that you slept with *your* Beckett, and you didn't even tell me!?"

The way she says *your Beckett* sends a warm possessiveness flowing through my body, but I shove it away. He's not mine.

"Well, we didn't... you know."

She shakes her head. "No, I don't know."

I look around, making sure no one can hear us. But we've snagged a high-top table in the back corner of the bar area, and everyone else is deep in their own conversations.

Leaning closer, I whisper, "We didn't have sex."

Maddie blinks, "Okay... but you did *something*."

I almost ask her how she knows, but she's my best friend. Has been since she cheated off my math homework in the first grade. If anyone could tell something's different with me, it'd be her.

My chin dips down, "We did something."

Memories of Beckett - behind me, touching me, above me - flicker though my mind.

"My oh my," Maddie fans a hand in front of her face, "I can feel the lust from here."

I roll my eyes, but I don't try to correct her. Because she's right. Just thinking about him is making me all sorts of hot and bothered.

"Okay-" she takes a sip, not spitting it out this time, "details. I want all the details."

Considering we share everything with each other, this shouldn't be difficult to do. But I still reach across the table, grab her glass and take a large drink of cider.

Maddie listens quietly as I go through the events day-by-day. But she throws a fit over Creepy Dad trying to crawl into my tent, losing it as any best friend should. Then I explain Beckett coming to my rescue and Maddie flips straight to swooning.

By the time I finish my story – ending on how I woke up alone in the tent on the last morning – Maddie's ordered a second drink and we've nearly finished our burgers.

"I'm so jealous," Maddie grumbles.

A laugh rolls out of me, "You should be."

I feel so much lighter, like some sort of burden has been lifted off my mind just from telling Maddie about Beckett. I knew he'd been consuming my thoughts, but I hadn't realized how much it'd been weighing me down.

Maddie sags against the back of her chair, "Seriously

though, I haven't had sex in..." she drums her fingers on her chin, "I don't even know how long it's been."

"Technically, I didn't have sex either."

She scoffs, "No, you just had a hot-as-hell fingerbang and a face fuck session with the man you've been pining over for 23 years."

I grin, "I mean, if you're gonna word it like that."

"You're the worst."

I grab the bottle of ketchup and squeeze more onto my plate. "I won't deny that it was a good time." I pop a fry into my mouth. "But you could be getting some too, if you took the time to start dating."

"Not everyone has a childhood crush to just walk back into their life and sweep them off their feet," she gestures around the room. "How am I supposed to meet anyone new while living in this dinky town and working all the damn time?"

When I lift an eyebrow, she waves me off, knowing what I'll say.

We've had the online dating discussion too many times to count. Granted I've never used a dating app either, but I'm also not the one who's complained for *years* about wanting a boyfriend.

"So-" Maddie starts, changing the topic, "did you make plans to see each other again?"

"No," I sigh and it's my turn to sag in my seat. "I don't know if he had something pressing to get to, but he was gone from the campsite when I woke up. Like all the way gone. He didn't even stick around to get his sleeping bags."

"I mean, that could be good..." Maddie drums her fingers against the table. "You said it was high end stuff, so he'll prob-ably want it back."

"Maybe," I shrug a shoulder, "but we didn't exchange numbers or anything so I'm not sure how he'd accomplish that."

Maddie purses her lips and hums.

Shaking off the thought, I sit up straighter, "I just wish I knew what he was thinking."

Maddie laughs, "Right. As if men have any fucking clue what they're thinking themselves."

"Fair."

A devilish look comes over Maddie's features, "Okay so now that I know the good stuff, I need you to remind me what he looks like. I remember when he came into the coffee shop that one time, but that was forever ago and I just remember him being hot. And I remember you making a fool of yourself."

"Har har," I fake laugh then heave out a breath, "I dunno. He's just hot. I'm not good at describing people." I let my gaze track over the people in the restaurant, like I might suddenly find Beckett's doppelganger. "He looks like..."

My eyes keep jumping around, no one close enough in appearance to even point out.

Until movement near the door catches my attention.

My stomach clenches and a wave of nausea rolls through me.

"He looks like that," I whisper, staring at Beckett as he walks past the bar and towards the main dining area. Not alone.

Cueing into the change in my tone, Maddie leans into the table and lowers her voice, "Wait, is he here?"

I nod, watching as the waitress brings Beckett, an attractive woman, and a kid to a table. They're just at the edge of my sight line, but when the waitress stops to set the trio of menus on the table, Beckett drapes his arm over the woman's shoulders.

I only got a glance of her as she passed, but she looked to be about Beckett's age. And she's pretty. Her light brown hair and features reflected back in the small boy standing just behind them. He looks to be about 8 years old and something about him feels vaguely familiar, but I can't focus on him right now. I'm too zeroed in on the woman leaning against Beckett's chest. At the smile on his face as he looks down at hers.

When the waitress moves, allowing them to sit, I quickly face back towards Maddie.

Her eyes are wide as she stares back at me, "It might not be what it looks like."

I choke out an unamused laugh, "I don't think I'm lucky enough for that cliché to be true."

"Are you going to confront him?" her face pales as she asks the question. Maddie hates confrontation more than she hates spiders.

The shake of my head has her visibly relaxing, but I still feel on the verge of throwing up.

The sense of betrayal is so thick over my skin that it feels physical. How could he have hidden this from me? And to be here, in this busy restaurant, in the town I live in... Does he really think no one will find out?

"I want to leave," I whisper.

Maddie reaches out, placing her hand flat on the table, "Go. I'll take care of the bill."

"Are you sure?" I ask, feeling bad about sticking her with my meal, but knowing that I can't stay here a moment longer.

"I'm sure."

I glance around, "You don't think he'll see me, do you?"

Her mouth twists, "I can walk past their table and make a scene. Draw the attention away from the door."

I almost smile, "How would you do that?"

"I could accidently dump a pitcher of beer over his ugly head."

"I love your face," I tell her, meaning it more than I ever have. "But I think I'll just pull my hood up and slip out."

123

"I love your face, too," the look Maddie gives me is so full of sympathy that I almost break.

Not giving myself time to start a mental breakdown, I slide off the chair and pull my jacket on, yanking the hood up over my head. It might look a little weird, but it's not so out of place that I'll draw attention.

I pull my keys out of my purse and clutch them tightly as I walk between the tables, aiming for the door, letting the cool metal hold my attention.

It's not until I'm stepping outside that my discipline slips.

As the door swings shut behind me, I glance across the restaurant, and lock eyes with Beckett.

Chapter 26

Beckett

F*uck*.

Chapter 27

Elouise

GRUMBLING, I give the cabinet door an extra hard tug.

I shouldn't be mad at the cupboard, it's not like this is new behavior. This same door has been getting stuck since I was tall enough to reach it.

Snagging my Darling Elementary travel mug off the shelf, I set it in the designated cup spot and hit brew on my coffee maker. I don't always bring coffee with me to class, usually the two cups I have while getting ready for the day are enough. But this morning I need all the caffeine I can get.

After catching Beckett's gaze last night, I literally ran to my car. I don't really know why. I guess some part of me was worried he might get up from his cozy table and chase me down.

He did not.

I even watched my rearview mirror the whole five-minute drive home, but no one followed me.

It took me hours of pacing, and worrying, and feeling sick to my stomach, to realize that Beckett wouldn't just magically show up. Because he doesn't know where I live. Or, well, he doesn't know that I live here again.

After college, I moved back to the Twin Cities and worked at a couple of schools. But four years ago, I saw an opening in Darling Lake and I applied.

I wasn't sure if I'd want to move back to the little town I grew up in, but walking back into my old school for the interview I felt the connection I'd always been looking for. So, I took the job. And when, two years later, my parents decided to sell their house to live the RV lifestyle I decided to buy it from them.

I know everything there is to know about this house. It's close to work. And now it's mine.

Glancing around the kitchen, I see all the projects that I've wanted to do since moving in but that doesn't make me love it any less.

The three-bedroom, two-bathroom house was built in the mid-80's and still has all of the original finishes. Orangey oak cabinets, doors, and trim throughout. Scuffed wood floors. Boring off-white laminate countertops. And windows that need replacing but still let in tons of natural light.

It took a little adjusting to get used to sleeping in the master bedroom, but no way was I going to leave it empty. I'd dreamed of having an en suite bathroom my whole life and now it's finally mine.

My coffee machine chimes, letting me know it's done.

Hefting my bag over my shoulder I head for the door, thinking – not for the first time – that I should get a pet. Someone to say goodbye to when I leave for work.

Ten minutes. I have ten minutes until I get to school, and then it's game time. If I walk into my classroom still in a funk over Beckett, my kids will pick up on it immediately.

I grip my wheel tighter as I back out of my driveway.

Beckett's already consumed too much of my time. I won't let him ruin today too.

The image of him with his arm around that woman flashes in my mind, and I squash it as I start down my street.

There are two options for what I saw last night.

First, it wasn't what it looked like. That there's some sort of reasonable explanation. I don't know what the fuck that explanation could be, but I suppose the world of probabilities says there's a chance.

The second, and more likely scenario, is that he's a cheating piece of shit and I was complicit in his adultery.

It's the last part that makes me want to gag.

"I'm fine." I say it out loud, but my words are shaky, so I say it again. "I'm fine."

Pulling up to a stop sign, I grab my phone and select the Fuck It Playlist on my phone.

GAYLE plays loudly through the speakers and I sing along with her lyrics, nearly screaming them into the interior of my car. But my mind still won't let go of the memories.

Beckett wrapped around me.

Beckett whispering into my ear. Licking up my neck.

Beck over me. Thrusting into my mouth.

I reach forward and turn the volume up.

Time for this man to leave my thoughts once and for all.

Chapter 28

Elouise

WHEN THE FINAL bell of the day rings, I sag in relief.

To say today was taxing, would be a gross understatement. The combination of my crappy mood, my lack of sleep, and the kids' overall inattention after a week off from classes was just about as much as I could handle.

But we're not done yet.

"Alright, kiddos, grab your projects and line up at the door."

Picking up an array of science projects, the kids do as asked. When everyone is ready, I lead them down the hallway towards the cafeteria – which doubles as our gym.

Thankfully, there's already a handful of parent volunteers and other teachers standing by to help the kids get set up at the right tables.

I don't know whose bright idea it was to have a Science Fair the first day back after spring break, but surprisingly all of my students had something prepared. Some obviously better than others, but hey, I'm not judging.

With the kids in good hands, I head back towards my classroom.

Thirty minutes.

I have thirty minutes to sit and find my chill before the fair starts.

Entering my now quiet room, I close the door behind me and walk the few paces to my desk. It's not an overly comfortable chair, but I still drop into it as though it's an ergonomic throne.

I should really use this time to get ahead on tomorrow's lesson. Maybe write a few things on the board. But I won't. I just want some peace and stillness before I have to wander through the cafeteria, listening to overelaborate explanations of potato batteries.

Crossing my arms on top of my desk, I lower my cheek against my wrist and close my eyes.

Breathing in, I will my mind to clear. But instead of blackness, chocolate hair and golden eyes greet me.

I squeeze my eyes tighter.

Go away!

Meditation Beckett floats closer.

Stop it, you asshole!

Inhaling, I focus back on the darkness. Forcing his handsome face out of my mind.

Just as his visage starts to fade, the sound of my classroom door clicking open breaks the last of my focus.

Popping my eyes open, I lift my head and find Mr. Olson stepping into my room.

I resist the urge to clench my teeth at this uninvited interruption and sit up.

"Hi, Mr. Olson," I try for a smile.

He uses one hand to push the door shut behind him, the other holding a bottle of water.

His smile is genuine, "You really don't have to call me that when students aren't around. Richard is fine."

This is not the first time he's brought this up, and I wish he'd take the hint and leave it alone. He's never been anything but friendly towards me, but I just don't feel comfortable having that level of familiarity between us.

I let my smile relax into something more real. "Sure." *I don't mean it.* "So..." he's the one that just walked into my room, but the silence is awkward, and I feel the need to fill it. "How was your first day back?"

His reply is just as stiff as I expected. He's happy to be back... Blah blah, so on and so forth.

I mean, I love my students too, but the poor guy must have zero social life if he's this eager to get back to work.

I nod along, but want to hiss when he asks me about my day.

Talking with Mr. Olson is not how I want to spend – I glance at the clock – my eighteen minutes of freedom, but I know that's not gonna happen. So, I sigh and tell him about all the spilled glitter that happened during our Art Hour.

Chapter 29

Beckett

WITH ALL THE commotion of the Science Fair, no one stops me when I walk into Darling Elementary.

I'm early. The fair doesn't start for another fifteen minutes or so, but I have something I need to take care of first.

There's no map on the wall telling me which teacher is where, and it's been decades since I've stepped foot inside these walls, but I know that the fourth grade classes are in the opposite corner of the building from the front entrance.

The building itself is just a large rectangle. The large cafeteria is just inside the main doors to the left, across the hall from the principal's office. Straight ahead is one of the two perpendicular hallways making up the rest of the school. With classrooms on the outside, the center of the building is filled with the art rooms, the music room, and custodial storage. With a couple perpendicular hallways connecting the two sides.

Walking past the noisy fair set-up, I cut across to the hallway I need.

My steps echo against the cinder block walls, and I feel an odd tightening in the center of my chest.

I don't know what drew my eye to the hooded figure slinking out of the restaurant last night, but when my eyes landed on Elouise's I knew I was in trouble. I knew what it looked like.

Every part of my being wanted to get up and run after her. Chase her down to explain.

But I didn't.

I didn't want to make a scene.

I didn't want to risk running through the crowd only to lose her.

And, evilly, a part of me didn't want to correct her. A part of me was relishing the look on her face.

Not the pain. No, I feel terrible about that. But the jealousy... Hell, the jealousy in her eyes was beautiful. Reassuring me that I wasn't alone in this new and sudden obsession I felt between us.

Approaching the first of the two fourth grade classrooms, I see the door is open and the room is empty. A small plate next to the door tells me this room belongs to Mr. Olson.

So, my girl has the room at the end of hall, one down from Mr. Fucking Whistle.

As I get closer, I can see that her door is closed, and I start to worry that maybe I missed her. I figured she'd have stayed to walk through the Science Fair but maybe she didn't, and she's already gone.

Then I hear laughter. Her laughter.

It's distinct. Sweet, light, and perfect.

But she's not alone. And the other voice filtering through the door belongs to a man.

Keeping my steps light, I peer through the small window and see the back of a man standing just inside the door. I can't see his face, but I recognize his stupid blond haircut. As if it's not enough that he works in the room next to

Elouise, he has to be here. After hours, chatting her up. Laughing.

My hands tighten into fists.

Feeling the slightly unreasonable need to be violent, I take in a breath and slowly blow it out.

There's nothing wrong with two friends talking.

Mr. Olson's voice is muffled against the door, so I lean closer to hear it.

"You really are the best!" he says, shaking his head, but I can hear the annoying-as-fuck smile that's pasted on his face.

Tilting my head, I catch a glimpse of Elouise at her desk. And she's smiling.

Okay, enough of this shit.

Mr. Olson raises a water bottle to his mouth, and I take the opening.

In a single movement, smooth enough to make it seem like I hadn't looked through the glass, I turn the handle and shove the door open. Hard.

The edge of the door collides with Mr. Olson's shoulder, jolting him forward, and causing his hand to clench around the bottle, sending a torrent of water out the spout, down his throat, up his nose, and all over his face.

I pause beside him, clapping a hand down roughly on his back, "Whoops."

Chapter 30

Elouise

ONE MOMENT, I'm talking and laughing with Mr. Olson. The next, I'm staring, open-mouthed, as Mr. Olson seemingly attempts to drown himself with his water bottle.

And then Beckett is there.

It takes a moment for my brain to catch up to my eyes.

Beckett.

Here.

In my classroom.

Looking at me like... like he owns me.

I plant my hands on my desk, like I'm going to stand up, but my legs don't cooperate. I'm too stunned.

Beckett keeps his eyes on me as he addresses Mr. Olson, "I heard one of the parents up front asking for you."

Instead of replying, Mr. Olson just continues to cough. His face is red, and it looks like he's trying to glare at Beckett, but it's hard to tell. No doubt the unexpectedly inhaled water making it hard to speak.

Not sure what to say, I lift a hand in a small wave as Mr. Olson backs out of my room.

The moment he clears the doorway, Beckett uses his foot to swing the door closed. And just like that, we're alone.

But that doesn't matter.

It doesn't matter that it's just the two of us.

It doesn't matter that the last time we were alone he made me come all over his fingers.

It doesn't matter that just the sight of him reminds me of the taste of him.

It doesn't matter because he's a lying, cheating, douchebag.

He's not mine.

With that reminder, I force down the fluttering in my belly.

"What are you doing here, Beckett?" I keep my voice level, trying to hide the hurt that I still feel.

He steps further into the room, looking around, taking it in.

I don't like it.

I feel like he's already seen so much more of me than I've seen of him, and this is just one more layer he gets to peel away. Another reminder that I don't know anything about Beckett The Man.

Even though I don't want to, I can't stop myself from taking him in.

Worn black work boots. Faded and perfectly fitted dark jeans. And a grey cotton shirt, covered with a heavy black leather jacket.

He should look like an everyday guy, but he looks like he just walked off a calendar photoshoot. *Asshole.*

Stopping just a foot in front of my desk, his gaze finally rests back on me.

"Hi, Lou."

His tone is warm, and kind, and it makes me want to slap him in the balls.

"Why are you here?" I snap it this time.

The corner of his mouth twitches and my anger flares.

I push up and stride around the desk to face him. He's still so much taller than me, but at least this way he's not lording over me.

"I saw you," I shove my finger into his chest. "And I know you saw me, seeing you."

Beckett doesn't back away. He leans in, increasing the pressure on my fingertip. "And what did you see?"

This prick.

"I saw you! With her!" my voice cracks and I snap my mouth shut.

I start to drop my hand away, but Beckett traps it with his own, flattening my palm to his chest.

He lowers the volume of his voice, "And that makes you mad?"

His calm demeanor is making this whole thing worse. He's acting like it's no big deal, like none of this matters. And me... I can't pretend it doesn't matter. I've tried. But I can't.

Heat builds behind my eyes and I blink.

Not wanting, or needing, to explain myself, I ask him again, "What are you doing here?"

I hate that the fight has left my tone, leaving nothing but disappointment and sadness in its wake.

"I'm here for the Science Fair," his large hand tightens around mine. "My nephew is a third grader here, and he's very excited to show me his mealworms."

Nephew?

Beckett nods at my unspoken question, "The woman you saw me with, that's my cousin, Natasha. And that was her son, Clint. I call him my nephew, because I don't actually know what you're supposed to call your cousin's kid."

"She's your cousin?" I repeat, needing to hear it again.

He nods, his free hand reaching out, palming the back of my neck. "Cousin. Family."

She was his cousin.

Could it really be that easy?

"You're single?" I ask.

Beckett nods, "I'm single."

Am I this lucky? Was last night honestly one of those *it isn't what it looks like* moments?

"No girlfriend?"

The edge of his mouth pulls into a smirk, "Nope."

I want to believe him. I want to believe him so badly.

"Wife?"

He shakes his head, "No wife."

"Dating anyone?" I whisper.

It feels like he's telling me the truth, but I can't leave any questions unasked. I won't be able to deal with this sort of heartache again.

"I'm not dating anyone." He leans in closer, his fingers flexing around my neck. "How about you, Smoky Girl? Any more guys I need to chase off?"

"There's no one." Once the words are out, I feel even more foolish. I'm not trying to sound so desperate, we only had one actual night together. I shouldn't be this broken up over thinking he'd cheated on someone with me. Yeah, that'd be bad. Terrible even. But it should've just made me angry, not heart broken.

Then his words register, "Wait, what do you mean chase off *more guys?*"

"Babe, what happened last night was a misunderstanding. But you," he pulls me closer, "I've already had to deal with two assholes. How many more are out there trying to take what's mine?"

I'm not usually left speechless, but this whole conversation puts me on my back foot.

"Two?" Once I think about, I assume he's referring to the

night Adam tried to crawl into my tent, but... I glance at the now closed door. "You can't mean-?"

I swear his jaw flexes. "Mr. Standing In Your Classroom Trying To Flirt With You. Yeah, I'm talking about him."

His tone is so serious, it almost makes me laugh. Almost.

"Mr. Olson was not flirting with me." I tell him, not sure I believe it.

"Gotta convince yourself of that before you're able to convince me," He tips his head down, mere inches left separating us. "Now, are you gonna let me kiss you, or do you want to question me some more?"

I use my free hand to press a finger against his chin, keeping his face where it is, "One more question."

He lifts his brows, encouraging me to continue.

"You knew that I saw you last night, so you had to know what I assumed." Even knowing the truth, an unpleasant feeling roils through my stomach. "Why didn't you stop me? Correct me?"

His smirk is not what I was expecting, "Promise not to hit me?"

I scowl, "No."

He lets out a breath of laughter, before his face turns serious, "I liked seeing your jealousy."

My brows furrow together.

For an instant he lets go of my hand, snagging my other one, and before I can react, he has both my hands pressed to his body.

We're still standing, him palming my neck while keeping my hands trapped between our chests, and it feels more intimate than anything else we've done before.

"Thoughts of you have plagued my mind since the moment I stepped out of that damned tent." He bends towards me, "I wasn't just going to walk away. That wasn't going to fucking happen. Sooner or later, I was going to end up right here, chasing you right to your classroom. The one place I knew where to find you. Only I wasn't sure you wanted to be found." His breath fans over my lips. "But then I saw you last night, and I knew exactly what you would've assumed. And you looked hurt and angry and beautifully jealous. And even though I hate that I put those emotions on your face, I relished in their meaning." He angles his head, putting his lips next to my ear. "It meant you wanted me too."

Shivers trace down my spine as his words roll over my skin.

I really should hit him. I wish I wanted to hit him.

"You're a dick," I whisper, with no real anger.

"I certainly am. But I'm not a liar. And I'm not a cheat."

The last of my tension seeps from my bones. I believe him. And as mad it makes me, I understand him.

"Okay," I tell him quietly.

"Okay?" he questions.

My head tips in the smallest nod, "Okay, you can kiss me now."

Like magnets that have finally been released, we gravitate into each other.

His lips press against mine, warm and firm. A caress.

It's slow. Slower than it was before between us. Like we're taking our time to taste each other. And he tastes... decadent.

I lean in, needing the warmth of his body against mine. Suddenly freezing without him.

Beckett tilts his head further. The brush of his stubble against the sensitive skin at the side of my mouth is the perfect contrast as his smooth tongue searches for entry.

I let him in.

Buzz.

The hand on the back of my neck, slides up into my loose hair and I moan.

Buzz.

My hands are still trapped between us, Beckett's grip never loosening.

Buzz.

Buzz.

Buzz.

Breaking the kiss, Beckett leans his forehead against mine, "Fucking hell."

Releasing my hands, but not my neck he reaches into his pocket to pull out his vibrating phone.

"The fair has started," Beckett's exhale is full of sexual frustration. "Clint's making sure I haven't forgotten."

"Oh," and then I remember where we are, "Oh!"

A door slams somewhere down the hallway, solidifying the fact we're standing in my classroom, making out, on our way to doing so much more.

I clear my throat, "We should go."

"Yeah," Beckett closes his eyes, "give me a moment."

Now that my hands are free, I glance down at the front of his pants. Or more specifically the prominent bulge at the front of his pants.

I bite my lip, "Take your time, Champ."

He cracks an eye open, "Champ?"

"Trying on a nickname." I laugh, "No good?"

"No good."

Taking a moment, I run my hands over my hair and straighten my clothes.

I wasn't expecting to see Beckett here today, but I feel decently cute in my dark wash skinny jeans and pale blue thick-knit sweater. Teaching a roomful of rowdy fourth graders means that function takes precedence over style. But I managed to make it through the day without spilling coffee, food or paint on myself, so that's a win.

Seeing that Beckett looks ready to go, I snag my bag off the desk and start for the door.

"Not so fast."

I halt, "What?"

"I need your number."

When I don't immediately reply, Beckett shows me the screen of his phone with a new contact open. "Number, Babe."

My pulse ticks up.

I want to give him my number. I want him to call me. But...

"Is this a good idea?" my fingers twine together in an effort to keep them from tugging at my sweater.

Beckett narrows his eyes, "Yeah, Smoky. This," he uses a finger to point from my chest to his, "is a good idea."

The pulse between my legs is saying *yes*, this is a good idea. But my brain is still in play, and I'm trying to listen to her.

"What do you mean by *this*?" it's my turn to gesture. "I'm not asking for a commitment, or anything like that. I just..." I huff out a breath, "I don't even know where you're living. Are you just back for a visit? Are you leaving again soon?" My hands slap down against my sides. "It's fine if that's what this is, but I want to make sure we have the same expectations."

Beckett takes a step closer, "If I said I was just back for the week, you'd be okay with spending a few nights together?"

My tongue swipes against my lower lip. "I wouldn't say no," I admit.

And it's true.

I'm not opposed to a booty call, friends with benefits, fuck buddy – whatever you'd call it. But I know how I work, and if that's what this is, I need to know ahead of time, Or else my heart will get too invested.

Said heart gives a discreet cough and eye roll. Reminding me I'm more than a little invested already.

Beckett holds my gaze, "And if I told you I was back for good?"

A flutter ripples behind my ribcage, "Are you?"

He nods. "I don't know exactly where I'm gonna live, here or closer to downtown, but I'm in Minnesota to stay."

The look in his eyes is so serious.

"Really?" The hope of my younger self leaks into my words.

"Really. I'm staying in Darling Lake, at my cousin's place for now. I get to spend time with Clint and use him as an excuse to not share a roof with my parents." He blinks like the thought alone creeps him out. "Do you live in town?"

I smile, "I bought my parent's house."

Surprise covers Beckett's face, and the feeling of catching him off guard pulls my mouth all the way into a grin.

He grins back, "So, you gonna give me your number now?"

I take the phone from his hand and tap in my number, noticing he's labeled the contact as Smoky Hall.

Beckett takes his phone back, typing out a text to my number before hitting send.

"There," he tucks the phone into his pocket then holds his elbow out to his side, "shall we?"

Looping my arm through his, I shake my head, "A first date at the 3rd through 5th grade Science Fair. How are you ever going to top this?"

He pulls the door open, holding it for us to walk through. "I'm sure I'll think of something."

Chapter 31

Beckett

ELOUISE SMILES at me from across the cafeteria and – for the hundredth time – I remind myself that we're in public, surrounded by children and I can't do a goddamn thing about my desire to claim her completely.

Our talk in the classroom went better than I'd hoped. But I should've known better. Elouise is a smart, reasonable person and everything I told her was the truth.

I regret causing her pain, but I don't regret putting our feelings out in the open. I like her. She likes me. And I'm getting too old to dick around anymore. I don't know that I want forever. I'm not entirely sure I believe that's a real thing anymore. But whatever this ends up being, I'm not gonna let her slip through my fingers before it even starts.

"Uncle Beckett!" Clint's unnecessarily loud shout is accompanied with a tug on my shirt.

"Christ, kid, I'm right here," I tap the side of my head with my palm, like I'm trying to knock my hearing back in place.

"You're not supposed to say that," he lifts his eyebrows and looks so much like his mother I almost shudder.

Same light brown hair, same light brown eyes, same judgmental stance. It's uncanny.

"Yeah, yeah, you can tell on me later."

"Can we go?" he yanks on my shirt again and I bat his hand away.

"Um," I look around at all the lunch tables still covered with posterboards, and experiments. All the kids standing next to their displays. "I don't think so."

"Why not. I'm bored," His sigh is soul deep.

Usually I'd agree with him, but watching Elouise walk through the aisles as she listens to the kids describe their projects has been immensely entertaining.

Before we entered the room, she disentangled her arm from mine. I felt the loss of her warmth immediately, but I didn't say anything. This is her place of work, so I understand wanting to stay professional. Even if professional in this case includes lackluster Styrofoam volcanos and petri dishes showing the amount of bacteria on the drinking fountain spout.

But Elouise didn't ditch me. She walked with me right to Clint's table, introducing herself as Miss Hall, one of the 4th grade teachers.

Clint was instantly enamored with her. Can't really blame him since I feel the same way, but it did irk me a little that he spent the first five minutes telling her about his dumb meal worms without sparing me a single glance. I'm his uncle. I'm the one he should want to impress.

When she gracefully excused herself to move to the next table, Clint turned to me and told me he wanted her as his teacher next year. I nodded, understanding. I'd want her as a teacher too, and not just because she's hot. She's patient, the exact sort of thing I needed when I was Clint's age, really the sort of thing every kid needs.

The small human at my side drops down into the plastic

seat attached to the table, melting into the surface with a dramatic groan.

"What time is this supposed to go til?" I ask him.

"I dunno. Forever," he moans.

I let him see my eye roll, "Keep an eye on your worms. I'll go find out when we can leave."

Clint's limp body perks up, "Kay!"

Picking my way through the clusters of parents, I aim myself towards Elouise. She's not here as an official chaperone, but she'll know what time this is supposed to wrap up.

When I turn to head down the next aisle of tables, my eyes are drawn to a man stepping out of the cafeteria and into the hallway. His dark buzzed hair, triggering a memory.

Son of a bitch.

Changing my trajectory, I stride towards the doorway.

This dickhead is getting a piece of my mind.

Stepping into the hallway, I look both ways but I don't see him.

Fuck.

I was only seconds behind him. He couldn't have gotten far.

I step further into the hallway, looking out the front doors and seeing nothing, I turn back and notice the door to the boys' bathroom swinging closed.

Gotcha.

A few strides later, I'm pushing into the bathroom.

It's small. Just two stalls, both doors open, two urinals and two sinks.

Adam has his back to me, hunched over the shorter-than-usual urinal, relieving himself.

There's no lock on the door, but that's okay. I only need a minute.

He hasn't heard me enter, so I take a few quiet steps closer and wait for him to finish. I don't want to startle a man while he's still peeing and end up with piss on my shoes.

Finally done, he straightens back to his full height, which is still well below mine, and zips himself up.

I'm hardly surprised when the prick doesn't press the lever to flush.

Adam turns around and lets out what can only be described as a shriek when he spots me. But the memory of him crawling into Elouise's tent prevents me from feeling any humor.

His unwashed hands fly up to his chest, "Holy shit, man, you startled me! Didn't hear you come in."

Keeping my eyes on him, I take one step closer, so he has to tip his head back a little to hold eye contact.

"Your kid out there?" I ask, staring into his eyes.

My question clearly isn't what he was expecting, and he takes a step back, "Y-yeah." He takes another step back. "Why would you ask something like that?"

With one step, I close the distance between us again, "Because no kid should see someone beat the shit out of their dad."

Adam's eyes widen and he holds his hands up in a placating gesture, "Dude, chill."

"Chill?" I let my aggression seep into my tone, "you should be fucking thanking me. Because this is your one warning."

His voice goes up an octave, "What'd I do?"

At my expression, he takes another step back, bumping the back of his knees against the bowl of the urinal, throwing him off balance. His arms flail but he has nowhere to go. His knees bend as he tips back, pressing his ass against the vertical wall of the dirty urinal.

Moving forward for the last time, I don't stop until the toes of my shoes are pressed against his. Pinning him in place.

"Stay away from Elouise Hall. Don't talk to her. Don't

fucking look at her. Don't so much as think about her." I squeeze my fists tighter, fighting the urge to punch him. "You didn't accidently crawl into her tent that night. And if you make me think too hard about what your intentions might've been, I'm going to rip your spine out through your mouth. So don't push me." His breathing has picked up, and his eyes are wide. "If I hear you're harassing her, if I hear you so much as breathe on her, I will end you. And I *will* hear about it, because she's mine. You hear me? Elouise is mine."

His nod is frantic.

I lean in a little closer. "And if you try that shit with any other woman, I'll find out and sink you to the bottom of Darling Lake. Because I'm back. And just like Elouise, this town is mine."

Adam's mouth flops open and closed, but no sound comes out.

"Glad we understand each other," I show my teeth and dart my hand out. He flinches away from me, but I don't hit him. I depress the lever to flush the urinal, causing the water to stream down across his back.

Satisfied, I head for the door. "And wash your fucking hands."

Chapter 32

Elouise

When I catch myself checking my hair in the rearview mirror for the third time, I squeeze my eyes shut and turn off the car.

"Just get out." I tell myself. "It's fine."

Shoving my phone into my purse, I climb out and cross the street.

It's Friday night in downtown Darling Lake and the block is predictably quiet.

Beckett sent me a text Monday night after parting ways at the Science Fair, asking me out on a date. I said yes. Of course, I said yes. And even though we've... *done stuff*, I'm still nervous.

The fact he's had his hand in my pants, and his mouth on my tits, doesn't make me feel more confident about tonight. Honestly, there's a part of me that hardly believes that night in the tent even happened. Like maybe I made it all up.

Which is dumb. But that's brains for you. They're dumb.

My reflection looks back at me as I approach the glass store-front, my carefully straightened hair flying all over in the cool breeze.

Since we decided to meet at BeanBag for coffee, I went for casual. Casual, but it still took me two hours and dozens of combinations to find something I felt comfortable in.

I ended up in a pair of distressed jeans that hug my ass in a way that keeps the jiggling to a minimum, a low cut – and kind of snug – black tank top, and a thick multicolored cardigan. It's low key enough that I'd wear it out with friends, and the tank is more revealing than something I'd wear to work. All in all, I feel pretty. And when the tiny voice in the back of my head reminds me how smoking hot Beckett is, I shove that voice into a box and wedge it into the shadowed corner of my mind. Because he seems to want me just as much as I want him.

Pushing the door open, I'm greeted with the soft tinkling of a rain stick filled with coffee beans and the scents of coffee and cinnamon bread.

The shop is expectedly quiet. There's a college aged girl sitting at one of the tables, laptop open, headphones on. And there's an elderly gentleman sitting near the crackling fireplace, with an honest-to-god newspaper in his lap.

Before I start towards a table, I spot a familiar head of black curls.

"Maddie!" I hiss out her name.

From her spot near the register, her head whips in my direction. "Hey," she lifts her hand in a little wave.

At least she has the grace to look guilty, hunching her shoulders and cringing.

I hurry to the counter, looking over my shoulder to make sure Beckett's not about to walk in.

"What are you doing here?" I ask, keeping my voice low so the employee stacking cups further down the counter doesn't overhear – not that she's paying any attention to us.

Maddie leans over the counter towards me, staying just as

quiet, "I needed to come in to do some paperwork. I'm not spying on you!"

I roll my eyes, "Bullshit. I know as well as you do that your *paperwork* can be done from your laptop at home."

After having worked here since we were 15, Maddie became the proud owner of this location a few years ago after BeanBag decided to go the franchise route. Which is a whole other story, but the point is that I know how she runs this business. And I know she wouldn't be here unless she wanted to be.

"Okay, fine!" Maddie huffs, "I want to see Beckett. So, shoot me!"

"You did see him! At the restaurant!" I remind her.

She shakes her head, "That doesn't count. I only got a glimpse at him. He was too far away, and I was too much of a chicken to try and walk past his table when I left. Plus," she holds up a finger, "I was planning to be in my car before you got here. I was just gonna watch him walk in."

I snort, "Creeper."

We stare at each other for a moment, then both break out in grins.

Maddie glances at her watch, "Which, I might add, you'd never even know about if you weren't so freaking early."

Catching myself a moment before I scrub my palms over my face and mess up my makeup, I drop my hands to my sides. "I've been dying of nerves all freaking day and didn't want to be late."

Maddie snorts, "So you left a half hour early for a three-minute drive?"

"Basically."

Her smile turns soft, "Don't be nervous. This might feel like a first date, but you two already know each other. Think of it more like catching up."

I bite my lip. "I know. You're right."

"And, I mean, he's already petted your kitty. So..."

We stand in silence, blinking at each other before we both fall into laughter.

I can feel the tension leave my body with each shake of my shoulders. Even though I picked this time because I knew Maddie wouldn't be here to stare at us, talking to her is exactly what I needed to relax.

"What's so funny?"

The deep voice startles a yelp out of me.

Beckett's large hand presses softly against my lower back and I can feel the warmth even through my thick sweater.

My eyes catch the stunned look on Maddie's face before I look up at Beckett, and I completely understand the wide-eyed stare my best friend is giving him.

In a black t-shirt, black zip up hoodie, and the same worn jeans I saw him in on Monday, Beckett looks as hot as he always does.

I don't even understand how someone can look so good, all the time, but I can't tear my eyes away.

I clasp my hands together to stop myself from reaching up to stroke the stubble covering his handsome face. I know what his hands feel like, but I'm dying to experience that beard between my thighs.

He clears his throat, "Evening, Smoky."

"Hi, Beckett," my voice comes out breathy, and if Maddie wasn't so mesmerized by Beckett, she'd probably make fun of me.

The smile he gives me sends a tendril of warmth all throughout my body as his hand slides across my back, until he's palming my hip and pulling me into his side.

Good god, why are we even here? I should've just invited him straight to my bedroom.

Beckett's chest expands, "You look nice."

Usually *nice* wouldn't be a word I'd preen over, but the way he says it...

Welp, that's it. One minute in and my panties are already toast.

"Thanks," I lean a little harder into his side. "You don't look so bad yourself."

The smirk on his face is so cocky, I'm tempted to pinch him.

"Umm, you guys want some coffee?" Maddie's timid voice reminds me we aren't alone.

"Oh, uh, Beckett, this is-"

"Maddie, right?" he cuts me off, holding out his hand.

Maddie's cheeks flame a brighter red than I've seen in years. Her mouth opens, but instead of responding she snaps it closed again and shakes his hand with a quick nod.

Beckett's easy smile tells me this isn't the first time a woman's been rendered speechless by his looks.

"Nice to see you again," I don't know if he's referring to the restaurant last weekend, or if he remembers her from all those years ago, but Maddie doesn't seem to care, she just keeps staring.

I look to Beckett, "I know what I'd like, if you're ready to order."

He dips his chin, "You first."

Straightening myself to face Maddie, I ask her for a caramel latte and Beckett requests a black coffee.

Maddie's biting her lip so hard when she takes his credit card, I'm worried she'll start bleeding any second.

When she hands it back, she musters the courage to speak again. "Go ahead and sit down, I'll bring these over when they're ready."

Maddie's wide-eyed gaze is on me, but I catch Beckett slipping a twenty into the tip jar on the counter. It's a nice gesture, and it's not lost on me that he did it when he thought no one would see him. Never mind the fact that Maddie will send all the money home with the other employee.

Leading the way, I weave between a smattering of tables towards the private back corner. The round table is scarred, small and my favorite seat in the house.

I'm reaching for one of the chairs when Beckett's hand tightens in the fabric of my cardigan across my back.

Forced to stop, I stand still while Beckett reaches past me and pulls the chair out from the table, "Allow me."

Taking the offered seat, I can't stop the smile spreading across my face, "Why thank you."

Seating himself across from me, Beckett rests his elbows on the table, "I might be a prick some of the time, but I know how to behave on a date."

"I'll be sure to tell your mom she raised you right."

Beckett laughs, "Hell," he shakes his head, "she'll have a field day when she hears about this."

My brows raise, "You gonna tell her?"

He rolls his eyes, "If I don't, I'm sure my cousin will."

The thought of Beckett's female family giving him a hard time fills me with delight.

"Do they still live around here? Your parents?" I ask.

He nods, "Yep. I know the day is coming that they'll eventually have to move out of that house and into a senior housing type place, but they're still both active as ever."

I smile. I don't know his parents well, but because of our brothers' friendship, I've met them plenty of times.

Maddie's approach halts our conversation, and we exchange a chorus of thank you's as she sets down our drinks.

After I promise we don't need anything else, Maddie backs away from our table, putting herself behind Beckett so only I can see her. With her eyes wide, she fans her face and pretends to pant.

I do my best to ignore her, wrapping my hands around the warm latte in front of me.

"What about your parents?" Beckett taps the side of his coffee with his fingertips. "You said you bought your old house?"

Maddie stands behind him and feigns a faint, then finally spins and walks away.

"I did," I purse my lips to keep from laughing at my friend. "I think it's been... two years already." I shake my head. "That seems crazy."

"Did they just want to downsize, or what made them move?"

"Oh, they downsized alright." I roll my eyes, "They bought an RV and have been terrorizing the entire countryside with their antics ever since."

"They're having fun I take it?" Beckett asks with a crooked grin.

"That they are," I nod. "They head to the southern states during the winter, then travel back north in the summer. Keeps them out of my hair for half the year at least."

"There is that," Beckett agrees.

There's a moment of silence while we both sip our beverages.

"So how about James? What's he up to?"

My mouth pulls up in a half smile, thinking about my brother. "He's exactly the same."

Beckett laughs, "No surprise there."

"He's got a pretty nice apartment in downtown Saint Paul that's walking distance from the bank he manages. And because James never stops complaining about it, I know Tony still lives in Seattle, and that they never get to see each other."

Beckett smirks, "I hear those same complaints from my mother. You'd think Tony moved to another planet for how she acts."

"Mothers will be like that," I slowly spin my coffee cup between my hands. Beckett must sense I'm about to ask a question so he stays quiet, waiting for me to continue. "You said you're staying with your cousin and helping out with Clint..." there's no good way to ask this, and it's not like it really matters, but I'm curious. "Are you, um, are you working anywhere?"

When Beckett doesn't answer right away, I drag my eyes up from the tabletop and find him grinning.

"What?" I ask, exasperated at his look.

"Smoky, are you asking if I have a job?"

The grin on his face makes me think that he must, but he still hasn't answered the question.

I sit back in my chair, "It's a fair question."

"It is," the fool is still grinning.

I cross my arms, "I just want to know if I should feel guilty about letting you pay for my coffee."

My comment must catch him off guard because he lets out a bark of laughter.

"Because I can, you know, pay for my own stuff. Teachers might get paid shit, but I don't need you to buy me things."

His tone softens, "I know, Elouise."

Elouise.

The syllables feel like satin on my skin.

My arms uncross and I lean forward, resting my hands on the tabletop.

Matching my movement, Beckett reaches across, placing his large palms over the backs of my hands. "I kinda love the fact that you don't need me." His thumb rubs across the sensitive skin of my wrist. "It means you're here with me because you *want* to be."

I raise one of my shoulders in a half shrug, "I'm caught up on my shows. And you aren't terrible to look at."

He narrows his eyes, "Cute." His fingers encircle my wrists, holding my hands in place. "And to answer your question, yes, I'm gainfully employed. I actually moved back to Minnesota because of work. I was ready to be done with Chicago and the timing felt right."

We kinda talked about this, back in my classroom, but I clearly needed this added reassurance that he's back to stay. I don't consider myself a fragile flower, but I can feel myself slipping under his spell already and I'm happy he won't be disappearing.

"Is your work near here?"

He makes a noncommittal sound, "My main office is in Minneapolis, so not too far. We do property management, so unless I'm needed at a job site, I can usually work from wherever. The glory of laptops, virtual meetings and all that."

I sigh. "Must be nice."

He chuckles, "It is. Unfortunately for you, being a teacher is kind of an in-person career."

"True. I can't even imagine trying to teach a bunch of 9 and 10-year-olds online. But I do get summers off, so there's that."

Beckett's eyes hold mine, "Sleeping in. Breakfast in bed. Afternoons lounging in the sun. I can picture it now."

Darkness has settled outside, but I swear I can feel the warmth of the sun on my skin as he speaks. Because in this image he's painting, it sounds like he's there with me. Like he's already planning on it. Even though summer is months away.

Needing to touch him, like he's touching me, I rotate my hands until they're palm up.

His hold on me tightens, "I don't want to rush you."

"You're not," I cut him off before he tries to make excuses for this pull between us.

"Good. Because every night when I shut my eyes, I see you." He leans in closer. "I see you, underneath me, with my cock buried in your throat." That heat builds between my legs, flashing out into the rest of my body. "I see you writhing and moaning and swallowing me down." *I'm panting. I think I'm panting.* "And I need to see that again. Only this time," he tugs on my hands, bending me over the table towards him, "I'm going to do it with my cock sunk deep inside your pussy."

Releasing one of my hands, Beckett cups the side of my face, holding me still as he closes the distance between us.

It's only for an instant, but when his lips press against mine every nerve ending I have alights with pleasure.

"Tell me you want that too," his words ghost over my mouth.

"I want that, too," I whisper back.

"That's my girl. Now invite me over."

Not realizing my eyes had closed, I open them, finding Beckett's golden gaze staring back at me, "Will you come home with me, Beckett Stoleman?"

"I thought you'd never ask."

Chapter 33

Elouise

Waiting next to my car in the dark garage, I watch as Beckett climbs out of his truck, his long strides closing the distance between us up the driveway.

The drive here was the longest three minutes of my life. Just enough time for me to freak out, get myself under control, and freak out again.

His footsteps sound like the beat of a drum reverberating through the quiet neighborhood.

Breathe, Elouise. Just breathe.

Beckett doesn't break stride when he reaches me, he just hooks an arm around my waist and propels me through the door that leads into the house. I hear the sound of him blindly slapping at the garage door button, and the matching rumble of the door lowering. And a second after the house door clicks shut behind us, I hear the soft clunk of him turning the deadbolt.

We take a moment to kick off our shoes, then Beckett is back to guiding me forward. Through the living room, past the kitchen, and up the stairs.

I don't know if he's been up here before or if he's just good at guessing, because we pass my old room, a bathroom, James's old room, and then we're there. At the open door leading into the master suite. My room.

Framed photos from family vacations line my pale blue walls. My queen-sized bed, nightstands, and dresser are made of chunky wood painted a silvery grey. And white curtains match my white bedding. Bedding that's unmade. The blankets still tossed back from when I got up for work this morning, and that somehow makes this moment feel even more intimate. Because this is it, the real me, and Beckett's here anyways.

Beckett's chest expands against my shoulder as he inhales. "It's perfect. Exactly how I imagined," his voice is a low rumble that I feel *everywhere*.

Before I can respond, Beckett is striding across the room to the door that leads into the master bath. Reaching inside the doorway, he flips on the light, causing illumination to streak across the room. Across the bed.

From the other side of the room, Beckett faces me, "I need to see all of you this time."

My throat works, but I can't think of anything intelligible to say. Instead, I take off my cardigan.

One piece of clothing, that's all I've removed. But he's looking at me like I just stripped naked.

Fuck it.

The distance between us gives me the confidence I need to strip. So, keeping my eyes on his, I grip the bottom of my tank top and pull the material up over my head.

He doesn't move closer, but he drops his hoodie to the floor at the same time.

Thank you, past self, for wearing cute underwear today.

With trembling fingers, I undo my pants and slowly drag them down my legs.

Beckett's chest is heaving, and as I stand upright, he reaches back with one hand and tugs off his t-shirt up over his head.

While his shirt is covering his face, I unclasp my bra and let it fall away from my body.

A choked sound leaves Beckett when his vision clears, and he sees that I'm left in nothing but my thong.

While he works to undo his belt and jeans, I hook my fingers in the top of my panties and discard them into a pile with the rest of my clothes.

"Goddamn," Beckett wets his lips and takes one step, moving to round the foot of the bed towards me.

But I step to the side, putting the bed back between us.

He stops, and a wicked gleam fills his eyes. "Babe," he says it like a reprimand while he palms the erection straining the front of his boxer briefs.

I tip my head towards his hand, "Take them off."

The look in his eyes is predatory, but he doesn't hesitate. And before I can blink, he's completely naked.

Jesus.

My eyes won't look away. Can't look away. I had him in my mouth, down my throat, but I didn't get to see him. Not like this. And dear god, he's perfect.

Beckett uses one hand to squeeze the base of his cock, "This what you want, Smoky?" His other hand grips his length, stroking up and down.

I can't do anything other than nod.

"On the bed." It's Beckett's turn to command.

And it's my turn to obey.

Not thinking of anything beyond pleasure, I climb onto the bed, reclining back against the pillows.

Beckett steps up to the foot of the bed, the glow from the bathroom casting him in light and shadows.

S. J. Tilly

I'm waiting for him to tell me what to do next. But he doesn't. Instead, Beckett releases his hold on himself and darts his hands forward, gripping me by my ankles.

In one swift motion, he pulls me all the way down the bed until my ass is right on the edge.

A shocked gasp escapes me, turning into a moan when he lifts my feet into the air, his grip loosening so he can slide his hands down to my knees, then the inside of my thighs.

Spreading me wide, Beckett moans, "Fuck, Babe."

With nothing else to hold onto, I reach up to grab my own tits. Squeezing them, pinching my nipples.

Beckett's eyes dart back and forth from between my legs to my chest, and he lets out an even louder groan.

"Beckett," his name is a plea. I need more. I've never been more turned on in my life and I need more.

Instead of responding, he drops to his knees and closes his mouth over my pussy.

My back arches off the bed, the sudden sensation causing me to release a strangled cry.

"Oh my god. Beckett. Oh my god."

His tongue laps at me. Against me. Into me.

And when his lips close around my clit, my eyes snap shut.

"Beckett!"

Lost. I'm completely lost in the feeling of him.

His warm breath, soft lips, talented tongue. His fingers pressing into the sensitive skin of my inner thighs.

I'm close. So close.

Then he stops, and a whine crawls out of my throat.

When I pry my eyes open, I see Beckett standing again. "Do you have condoms?"

I blink at him a few times.

Oh, yes, condoms. Because we're smart adults.

"Drawer," I pant while stretching an arm out, pointing to my nightstand.

I almost stop him, wanting to tell him I'm on birth control and that I can't wait another second before he's inside of me, but I don't. That decision is best left for when we're both thinking straight, and when I can form complete sentences.

Beckett slides the drawer open, and his soft curse reminds me that there's a small pile of vibrators sitting there waiting to greet him.

"Oh, um..."

"Another time," Beckett cuts me off, then digs around until he finds the unopened box of condoms.

Turning to me, he holds it up, making a show of breaking the seal, "You've been a good girl. And that makes me very happy."

His eyes are pure lust and I feel his words prickle over my skin. Praise from Beckett is the aphrodisiac I didn't know I needed in my life.

I watch as he steps back between my spread thighs, slowly rolling the condom down his length.

Holding the base, he presses his tip to my clit and my back arches, my head pressing back against the mattress, my eyes automatically closing.

"I told you before, Smoky. Eyes open."

His palms run up and down the outside of my thighs, finally curling around the top, gripping me. "Can you do that for me?" He pulls me closer to him, sliding my ass further off the edge of the bed. "Can you watch what happens next?"

"Yes." I nod my head, my hands tangling in the blankets at my sides. "Yes."

I feel his cock bump against my entrance.

"Eyes on me."

My mouth opens to promise him that I will, but he slams

forward, burying the full length of his cock inside me. And instead of giving him a promise, I give him a cry of pure pleasure.

So good.

So big.

So much.

There's no waiting, no pausing. Beckett pulls back, almost all the way out, then thrusts forward again. His moans mixing with my own.

Over and over.

His hand grips me. Pulling me closer. Keeping me grounded.

Each time our hips meet, I can feel the vibration roll through my body. My breasts jiggling with each hit.

Just as my eyes start to close, a pinch on my nipple has them flying back open.

"If you want to come, you'll keep those pretty eyes open."

Chapter 34

Beckett

FUCK.

She's too much.

She's perfect.

Watching her tits bounce with every thrust brings me closer and closer to climax. But I'm not ready to be done yet. This was the perfect position to see her, all of her. But it's still not enough. I need to feel her surrounding me.

"Goddamnit, Babe. You feel so good," I grit out the words.

Seating myself as deep as I'll go, I press forward, pushing her back further on the bed. And when the edge of the mattress stops me, I put one knee, then the next up on the edge of the bed.

Never withdrawing from her wet heat, I hook an arm under her waist. "Hold on to me."

Knowing exactly what I want, Elouise wraps her arms and legs around me and I crawl us both up the bed.

She clenches her muscles around me, and my cock twitches inside her. She's the best thing I've ever felt.

Reaching the center of the bed, I lower my hips first,

pressing her ass into the mattress and pushing my cock as deep as it'll go. My eyes want to roll back, but I won't let myself miss a single expression that crosses her face. Because she loves this. She loves this as much as I do.

Elouise adjusts her legs until her heels are digging into the backs of my thighs. Urging me to stay inside her.

My arms buckle and I drop my weight onto my elbows, our chests pressing together.

With my lips pressed against her ear, I pull my hips back until just an inch is left inside her. "You want more?"

She nods.

I press another inch back in. "You *need* more?"

"Yes." Her voice is strangled. "Yes, Beckett. Please."

Catching her lobe between my teeth, I sink into her and we both groan.

Our bodies move together in a way that shouldn't be possible.

Rocking. Moving. Like we've done this a hundred times before.

Elouise grips my hair in one hand, the other clawing at my back, holding me close. "Oh... fuck... Beckett..."

Her nipples are pebbled against my chest. Her body heaving beneath mine.

The more frantic she gets, the more she pulls me under with her.

"Do you need to come?" I growl between clenched teeth.

"Yes! Please, yes!"

I can feel her roll her hips against me. Her clit rubbing against the base of my cock.

I grind into her. Matching her motion. Pressing harder.

Her breathing is erratic. Her movements jerky. And the intensity of it has me right there on the edge.

"Go over, Elouise." I press my lips to her warm skin,

pressing my hips down, grinding right where she needs me. "Come for me."

As if she was waiting for my permission her body tenses, imploding around me, and I follow.

I feel like I'm in a daze. I don't even remember rolling off Elouise. Let alone cleaning up and getting back into bed. But now that I'm here, laying on my back, with my satisfied woman draped half over me, there's no way I'm leaving.

"I'm gonna stay over." I tell Elouise, toying with the ends of her hair.

She hums a response, rubbing her cheek against my chest and I take it as an agreement.

Smiling into the darkness, I feel a sense of peace fill the room.

I didn't think I was unhappy before. Or unfulfilled. But now... Well, now I'm starting to wonder if I knew anything at all.

Chapter 35

Elouise

LIGHT FILTERING through a gap in the curtains flickers across my closed eyes.

Morning.

Habit has me trying to roll out of bed, but the arm tucked around my waist tightens, keeping me secured to the warm body behind me.

Fingers rub against the soft cotton covering my body, "When'd you put this on?"

Beckett's voice is rough from sleep, making me smile. He sounds adorable like this.

Relaxing back, I answer him, "When I got up to use the bathroom."

"Hmm," I feel him nuzzle the back of my head, "I prefer you naked."

My mouth pulls into a grin, "Is that right?"

A low sound leaves Beckett before he slips his hand up my shirt, cupping my breast, while pressing his erection against my ass.

I automatically arch into the pressure, moaning in response.

"God damn, Smoky. I don't know what I like better." His hand slips down until his fingers dip under the band of the thin sleep pants I pulled on. "The way you feel." One finger slips between my folds, brushing against my clit. "Or the sounds you make."

Right on cue I groan at his touch.

His teeth drag down the side of my neck, "Yeah, just like that."

My hand reaches back, searching for skin, wanting to feel him like he's feeling me.

He pushes my hand away and moves his hips back enough to grab the top of my pants and pull them down below my ass. "I need to have you."

It's like each word he speaks arrows straight to my core. "I'm ready."

His fingers glide over my slit, testing the truthfulness of my statement and he lets out his own groan. The rumble deep against my back.

But then the rumbling continues...

My eyes flutter back open.

The sound is coming from outside and... And it's getting louder as it gets closer.

And closer.

Oh no.

Alarm bells start sounding off in the back of my brain.

Oh hell no.

My body tenses.

Beckett's hand drops away from my pussy as he pushes up onto one arm. "What is it?"

The rumbling stops, and a sick feeling of *oh-please-no* fills my gut.

Frantically, I squirm myself out of bed, tugging my pants back up as I rush to the window.

"Oh no, oh no, oh no..."

Sure enough, when I pull the edge of the curtain aside, I see exactly what I'd feared.

My parent's RV. Parked in my driveway.

"Babe?" I can hear Beckett climbing out of bed behind me.

But I can't answer him. I'm too busy freaking out.

"Lou, what's wrong?"

Quickly turning, I lodge my hands against his chest to keep him away from the window.

The slap of my hands against flesh reminds me that he's naked. Unbidden, my eyes drop to his cock and a pulse throbs through my body.

He's entirely naked and still hard.

No time! I mentally shout at my libido.

I shake my head and force my eyes back up to his. "You have to go."

"Go?" the sound of a slamming door filters into the house and his eyes narrow. "Elouise, who's out there?" his tone has shifted from concern to anger, and I realize he must think I'm hiding him from another man.

Only it's worse. So much worse than that.

"My parents are here!" I hiss, giving him a shove. "Put your clothes on!"

"Your parents?" Beckett's eyebrows shoot up.

"Yes!"

I stand frozen for half a heartbeat, watching Beckett scoop his pants off the floor, before darting into my closet, ripping off my pajamas as I go.

In record time, I've switched to leggings, a sports bra, and an old college hoodie. I don't look like I'm ready for the day, but hopefully I don't look like I just rolled out of bed with Beckett.

Beckett!

Rushing back out of the closet, I find him pulling his shirt on.

A glance at the clock tells me it's not even 8:00, but years of being a teacher means my parents know that I don't sleep in.

And then the knocking starts.

Shit! Shit!

"Out!" I almost shout it at Beckett, then lower my voice. "You have to get out!"

Another round of knocking.

I groan, and briefly pretend I'm in a world where I'm still fast asleep, wrapped warmly in Beckett's arms.

Clearly done with knocking, the doorbell chimes throughout the house.

Thankfully, my parents insisted on me changing the locks when I bought the house. Their reasoning was that it would stop them from coming in unannounced. But that obviously didn't translate to them not showing up unannounced.

Beckett steps in front of me and grips my upper arms, holding me still, "Elouise, you need to relax. I've met your parents before."

A small strangled sound leaves my throat, "Not like this!" I wave my hand around the room.

Oh god, I'm panicking.

The doorbell sounds again.

"Maybe you can hide?"

Beckett grins. "Nah, I think I'll just go let them in."

Before I register his ridiculous words, he's striding out of my room.

"What!?" I chase after him, "Beckett, you can't do that!"

"Why not?" he doesn't slow down, tossing the question over his shoulder as he descends the stairs.

I hurry to catch up, "Because you don't get how they are! They'll get the wrong idea!"

He stops at the bottom of the stairs and spins to face me; my momentum sends me crashing into his chest. Thankfully, he's rooted in place and doesn't so much as budge with the impact.

The seriousness in his eyes makes me feel like I'm about to get scolded, "Babe, they'll get the right idea."

Then he leans down, presses his lips to my forehead, and heads back towards the door.

Tingles from his stupid kiss zip over my skin distracting me.

But he doesn't get it. He thinks they'll get the idea that we're dating, which I think we are. But in reality, my mother will jump straight to oh-my-god-they're-getting-married idea.

Snapping out of my daze, I run the last few yards between myself and Beckett, "Wait!" but before I reach him, he unlocks the front door and swings it open.

Chapter 36

Beckett

"Elouise, what took..." Mrs. Hall's voice trails off as her eyes widen, catching sight of me.

It's been at least a decade since I've seen Lou's parents, but I recognize them immediately. A little greyer, but they look almost exactly the same.

"Morning, Mrs. Hall," I hold my hand out and she fumbles a bit to take it, head tilting like she's trying to place me. Tipping my head down, I give her my most charming smile, "It's me. Beckett Stoleman."

Her mouth pops open and the look of surprise reminds me so much of Elouise that my smile grows.

I know I should probably feel severely uncomfortable right now, but I don't.

Mrs. Hall clasps her free hand around the back of mine, not letting go, "Beckett Stoleman! I can't believe it! You're so grown up!" I almost snort. At 38 I'd hope so. Lou's mom gives me a once over and shakes her head. "Sweet baby Jesus, you sure did grow up!"

"Mom!" Smoky's gasp has my laugh breaking free.

Mr. Hall pats his wife on the shoulder, "Let the poor boy go, Hun."

Instead of letting me go, Mrs. Hall pulls me in for a hug. Only she's even shorter than Elouise so I have to bend down to hug her back.

Lou is grumbling something from where she's still stuck behind me, since I'm blocking the doorway.

Mr. Hall just rolls his eyes at his wife's behavior, "It's best to just roll with it, son."

He seems awfully calm for finding me in his daughter's house so early in the morning. I'm not sure if he hasn't put it together yet, or if he's just handling this in a very mature way.

"Okay, Mom," Elouise grips my shoulder pulling me back a step and dislodging the hug, "might as well come inside before this becomes any more of a spectacle."

"Has she always been such a prude?" I ask Mrs. Hall, as we all move into the house.

She sighs, "She really has."

I think Elouise says something along the lines of *I'm going to kill you* but her words are smothered by her mother's hug. Mr. Hall shakes my hand before stepping into the house with the rest of us, closing the door behind him.

It takes a minute for all of the greetings to finish, but when they do, I watch Elouise as she twists her fingers together, clearly trying to figure out how to play this.

Humor brews inside me, as I watch her cheeks get even pinker, "I guess I'll make some coffee."

Trailing behind the Hall family, I follow them into the kitchen where Elouise busies herself measuring water and coffee grounds.

Mr. Hall asks me how my parents are doing, and I keep an ear on Lou and her mom as they discuss how her students are getting along. And this all feels just as right as Elouise felt in my arms this morning.

The timing might not be what we planned, but I don't regret this turn of events.

I can feel Elouise's hesitancy in pursuing this relationship. I don't know if it's our brief history, our brothers' friendship, or the small town that has her so leery. So, it might've been shitty of me to force the issue by opening the front door, but I didn't want Elouise to push me out a back door – or hide me in a closet – because I wanted her to face this thing between us. And there's no hiding from this now. One way or another, Elouise and I are in this together until we figure out what *this* is.

By the time the coffee is poured, Mr. Hall has donned an apron and is elbow deep in flour making a batch of homemade pancakes.

"Come sit," Mrs. Hall gestures to me to come closer, pulling out two of the chairs around the dining table.

We sit at the same time, then she turns her chair so it's facing me.

Elouise pinches the bridge of her nose, looking like she wants to trade her coffee for a cocktail, "Mom."

"What?" her mom looks back at her with mock innocence.

"We haven't even had breakfast yet."

I choke a little on my coffee. I know what Lou meant, but it's the perfect reminder of what we did last night to build up our appetite.

Realizing how it sounded, Elouise drags a hand down her face. "I just mean it's too early for the third degree."

Truthfully, I'm glad Elouise interrupted. I can only imagine the sort of questions my own mother would ask in this situation, and I'm guessing Mrs. Hall would be just as direct.

And it's not that I'm trying to keep secrets from Lou, but

there are some topics – like our romantic histories – that are best discussed when it's just the two of us. And we haven't had enough alone time to share everything that still needs to be said.

Lou and her mom are still debating the merits of morning interrogations when I hear the front door click open.

Damnit, I'm better than this. I chastise myself when I realize I didn't check to make sure that the door got relocked after the Halls came in.

I silently push back from the table, closing my hands into fists as I move to intercept the intruder.

"Where are you going?" Elouise breaks off her conversation with her mom to call after me.

I can hear heavy footsteps before I even exit the kitchen. Whoever just entered the house isn't even trying to be quiet.

This older style house has a small threshold between the kitchen and living room, and that's where I find him.

At the sight of me, the man a few years younger than myself halts.

When I keep approaching, he takes a step back, shock covering his features. And it's that expression that makes it all click.

I stop, a few feet left between us and release the tension in my hands.

"James," I don't say his name too kindly, still feeling worked up over hearing someone walk into my girl's house unannounced.

His eyebrows lift until they meld into his shaggy brown hair, the same shade as Elouise's. "Beckett?" His brows shift back down, furrowing, "What the fuck are you doing here?"

That attitude brings me back 20 years. James had a tendency to be a little shit when he felt like he had something to prove.

A smirk pulls across my mouth, "I'll give you one guess."

I shouldn't goad him. I really shouldn't. Not when his parents are no doubt seconds from appearing. But I can't help it. And when I see it click for him, my smirk turns into a grin.

"You son-of-a-bitch."

Chapter 37

Elouise

"BECKETT, WHAT ARE-" my eyes move past Beckett's broad shoulders and lock on my brother. I don't hide my groan of annoyance, "You've got to be kidding me."

"Hey, sis," James' tone is just as disgruntled as I feel, but I don't know what he has to complain about. I'm the one who's morning is being interrupted by my entire freaking family.

"Hey, brother," I say with fake cheeriness, "Why are you here?"

"Why is this asshole in your house?" he nods towards Beckett.

"Asshole?" Beckett mimics the word, and I don't have to look at him to know he's smirking, "You used to like me just fine."

James sneers, "That was before you were fucking my sister."

I tense.

I mean, he's not wrong, but the way he says it makes it sound so degrading. Like Beckett is taking advantage of me, rather than this being a mutual decision between adults.

Beckett must not like James's words any more than I do because he takes a step towards James. "We can be adults about this, or we can go outside and *talk*." He bites off the verb and I get the distinct impression he doesn't actually mean talking. "Either way, you don't say shit like that to Elouise."

Tension simmers between them and James looks like he wants to take a swing at Beckett.

"Guys," I lay my hand on Beckett's forearm, my fingertips pressing into his bare skin. "Play nice."

Mom calls out from the kitchen asking where we went, and I send a pointed look at James. But he's just glaring down to where I'm touching Beckett's arm. And when I look up at Beckett, I see he's glaring right back at James.

I tighten my grip, "Please."

Beckett's shoulders lose some of their tension and he turns his head until he's looking down at me, "Alright, Smoky."

"Thank you," my smile is genuine, because even if this whole situation is immensely fucked up, I like that he's standing up for me.

I see him bending down, I know what he's going to do, and I don't make any effort to stop him as he presses his mouth gently to mine.

"Aww, come on!" James complains at our show of affection.

I feel Beckett's lips curl into a smile against my own, and I hold up a middle finger towards my brother.

Beckett breaks the kiss and hooks an arm around my shoulders.

Before he can turn us around, I smile at my brother, "That'll teach you to barge into my house."

Laughing, Beckett guides us back into the kitchen.

My dad looks up from his current batch of pancakes and addresses Beckett, "Everything okay out there, son?"

"Son?" James almost shouts as he enters behind us, "He's not your son, I am."

The sound of surprise that Mom makes at James's entrance is all the confirmation I need to know they didn't plan this. She's terrible at pretending.

"What are you doing here?" Mom shrieks, pulling James in for a hug.

"Hey Mom," he hugs her back and even though I'm annoyed at all of them for just showing up, it's nice to see everyone together. "You told me you were coming into town, figured I'd surprise you." His eyes raise over the top of Mom's head and narrow on me, "I think we all got a surprise today."

Rolling my eyes, I pull out a chair and sit at the table next to Beckett.

I finished setting the table before I went to check on Beckett in the hallway, so now we're just waiting on Dad to wrap up.

"Sit, sit," Mom waves James towards the table as she grabs another setting for him.

James stomps the few steps to the table and stops directly across from Beckett. With his eyes locked on my guest, James noisily drags the chair away from the table.

The two of them glare at each other until my dad sets down the large stack of pancakes telling us to dig in.

With carbs and coffee being passed around the table, it's easy to pretend this isn't a total clusterfuck as people settle into conversation.

James keeps asking Beckett questions about his time in Chicago, but Beckett mostly ignores him or answers with his own questions. I don't know why my brother is being such a dick. He's always been a bit protective, but I honestly didn't think he'd be this bothered by me being with Beckett.

Forcing the final pancakes onto *the boys,* Mom leans back in her chair with a huge smile on her face, "This is so nice, just like the old days."

James snorts, "Not exactly like the old days. Back then what these two are doing would be illegal."

Dad laughs but Mom cuts James a look that has him shutting up. Then she turns to Beckett, "We're only planning to stay for a few days, but maybe we could do a lunch with your parents? It's been so long since I've seen either one of them."

Beckett dips his chin down, "I think they'd like that a lot."

Mom beams and I slowly slide my hand over to rest on Beckett's thigh. He's really getting more than he bargained for this morning.

"Perfect! We were going to stay in the driveway here," she glances at Dad, "but maybe we should find somewhere else to stay."

As much as I want them to do just that, I shake my head, "No, don't do that. You can stay here."

They've done it before, and I know that – for the most part – they'll stick to their own space.

"You sure?" Dad asks and I nod.

Beckett settles his hand on mine, threading our fingers together.

Nothing like jumping straight into the deep end.

Beckett uses his free hand to pull out his phone and I watch as he texts his mom asking about doing a get together. Based on the number of exclamation points, I think it's safe to say that Mrs. Stoleman is just as excited about this as my mom is.

He waits for a break in conversation, "My mom said that next Sunday afternoon would work, and that they'd love to host, if you can stick around that long."

Mom doesn't even check in with Dad before agreeing, and

that's how I know her claim of only staying a few days was total bullshit to begin with. "Just let us know what to bring."

Beckett tips his head, "Will do, Mrs. Hall."

"Oh please," she waves a hand in dismissal, "call me Mom."

I choke on my coffee, but the sound is drowned out by James' curse.

Chapter 38

Elouise

"Night, Mom."

I let her give me one last hug before I shut and lock the front door. Dad's already waiting for her in the RV, having gotten it hooked up to water and electricity earlier in the day.

It was a little weird the first time they stayed in my driveway, but they insist they're fine out there and I've given up caring what the neighbors think.

Flicking off lights as I go, I snag my half-finished glass of wine and head upstairs.

Mom and I polished off most of a bottle of wine while watching Second Bite, our favorite baking competition, but I'm not about to let the last sips go to waste.

Beckett left shortly after breakfast, and I was able to slip away long enough to take a shower and compose myself. Then the day was spent catching up with my parents and avoiding questions about my relationship status.

Alone in my bedroom, I make sure the curtains are fully closed before stripping down and pulling on the same pajamas I frantically changed out of this morning. Since I only wore these pajamas for a few hours last night, I'm not gonna feel bad about putting them back on. Plus, the knowledge that I was wearing them when I woke up with Beckett wrapped around me, makes me feel close to him.

Wow, Lou, you sound like a lovesick tween again.

Draining the last of my wine, I drop onto the bed face-down. I need to slow my emotions down before my heart falls completely in love with Beckett all over again.

My parents camping out in my driveway should do a good job of that for the next week at least.

A soft buzzing sound emanates from my nightstand, and I lift my head enough to reach for my phone.

I'm expecting it to be Maddie, since I texted with her about the RV debacle earlier today, but my heartrate ticks up a notch when I see the caller is someone else.

Rolling onto my back, I hit accept, "Hello."

My voice comes out a little breathy and I wonder if maybe the wine has affected me more than I realized.

"Hey, Babe," Beckett's tone is just as husky. "How was the rest of your day?"

I smile at the ceiling, "Uneventful. Thankfully."

He chuckles, "Glad to hear that."

My breath heaves out, "I'm so sorry about this morning. That was..." I drop a hand against my forehead, "I don't even know how to finish that sentence!"

"Don't apologize, it wasn't all that bad."

I snort because it was. It was that bad. We've barely had one date and my mom already told him to call her Mom.

"Smoky," his voice trails through the phone and wraps around my body, "don't dwell on it another moment."

"Okay," I agree, knowing I'd say yes to just about anything when he sounds like that.

"You alone?"

It's an innocent question, but it sends a flush up my neck, "Yes."

He lets out a hum of approval, "Good."

I feel myself squirm against the bedspread, "Why is that good?"

"Because I can't stop thinking about what was about to happen before we got interrupted this morning. And if I'm stuck thinking about it, you should be too." *As if I could forget.* "And I can't wait until next weekend to hear those sweet sounds you make."

Heat. Blazing heat fills my body.

"I can sneak you in some night after my parents go to sleep."

"If I could, I would, but I gotta leave for a few days."

My eyes, which had slipped close at the sound of his voice, snap open. "Leave? Where are you going?"

Chapter 39

Beckett

Squeezing my eyes shut, I wish I could take the worry out of Elouise's tone, "I have to run back down to Chicago to take care of a few things, but it's just for a few days. A week at most."

Her sigh floats through the phone and straight into my chest, "That sucks."

I crack a smile at her willingness to be honest, "It does suck." I glance back to the door of my borrowed bedroom, making sure the handle is locked. "Which is why I need your attention now."

"What do you mean?"

I palm my already hard cock through the thin material of my shorts. "I'm gonna have some late nights, and you'll be getting up early for class, so this might be the last chance I get to hear you moan for a while." Her indrawn breath only makes me harder. "You understand me, Babe?"

"Y-yes, what do you want me to do?"

I bite down on the groan that tries to leave my chest, "Put me on speaker."

Just because I'm trying to be quiet, doesn't mean she has to be.

There's a soft shuffling as she sets down the phone, "Okay, I did it."

"That's my girl." I squeeze my dick harder. "Now I want you to use both your hands to play with those glorious tits." I give her a second to do as I say, "Pull your top out of the way so you can feel that soft skin against your palms. I want you to squeeze them. Feel their weight." Her breathing is picking up, so I know she's doing what I'm asking. "Rub your nipples with the pads of your thumbs." She moans and I'm insanely jealous of her hands. "Does it feel good, Lou? Do your tits feel nice?"

"Yes."

Her one-word answer is a whisper, but it's as effective as if she yelled it.

I let go of my cock long enough to shove down my shorts, before wrapping my fingers back around my length.

"I want you to lick the tips of your pointer fingers and thumbs. On both hands." I slowly stroke myself up and down. "Did you do it?"

She lets out a muffled sound that I take as confirmation.

"Use those fingers to lightly pinch your nipples. Roll them around." My breathing picks up to match hers. "Are your nipples hard? Are they ready to be sucked on?"

"Yes, Beckett."

"Pinch them harder." I increase my own grip. "Harder still." She moans and I work to make my voice commanding. "Do as I say and pinch them harder."

Elouise follows my directions and her small cry of pleasure echoes around in my skull.

"That's right, Smoky. Don't be shy. Let me hear it. Let me hear how I'm making you feel."

187

"Fuck, Beckett," she's panting and if I'm not careful I'm going to come before she does.

"How do you feel?" I need to know more. I need details. "Don't stop touching those pretty pink nipples. Keep pinching them and tell me how you feel."

"It's... I'm..." she groans, "Oh, Beckett, I'm so wet."

"*Shit.*" I stop stroking myself and squeeze the base of the cock. "How wet, Babe? Slide one of those hands down inside your panties and tell me how wet you are."

There's a pause as she holds her breath, then it's back, choppier than before.

"Tell me." I remind her. "Use your words."

"I can't... God, I'm almost there."

"Are you dripping for me? Is your pussy ready for my cock?" I'm gritting out the words between clenched teeth.

"Yes. Yes, I'm soaking wet. Can I come?" Her question is the submission I didn't know I needed, and my balls tighten in anticipation of release. "Please, Beckett, let me come!"

Over the sound of her heavy breathing, I can hear the sounds of her fingers frantically working the slick spot between her legs.

"Rub that clit for me, Babe. Rub that clit and come for me." I can't control myself any longer, my hand matching her pace on the head of my cock. "Come for me now."

There's a hitch, then her moan fills every inch of my awareness.

With a thrust of my hips, I explode, coming all over my stomach and hand and cock.

"Fuck, Smoky," my heartbeat won't slow down, "I'm really gonna miss you."

Chapter 40

Beckett

PULLING MY TRUCK TO A STOP, I climb out and stare at the familiar brick façade, surprised at my lack of emotion.

This beautiful brownstone was my home for the last three years, and though it served me well, just a few weeks away from it has the place feeling foreign. And that's how I know I'm doing the right thing. My accountant threw a fit when she heard I was going to sell. But even though my business is literally property management, I specialize in large commercial buildings not individual homes. Plus, with a price tag of a few million, a one-time sale is worth it.

Walking up to the front door, the lock clicks smoothly as I turn my key, and I step into the foyer bracing myself for the week of bullshit ahead.

I cleared out the majority of my stuff before I left, leaving only enough furniture and personal belongings to stage the home properly. But the call I got from my realtor yesterday means that I need to get the rest of this shit out of here, and fast. Because the new owners want to sign by the end of the week.

And even minimal staging ads up when it's a 7,000 square foot home.

Of course I could just pay someone to do this for me, but I prefer to handle things myself. My cousin would call it being cheap, but I like to think of it as being responsible with my money.

Elouise will still be at school, so I resist the urge to pull out my phone to call her and instead start my walk through of the house.

Last night, after we both came down from our little phone-sex high, Elouise quickly hung up. Clearly embarrassed about what we'd done. I was tempted to stop over this morning before I left town but I knew if I went to her house, I'd end up fucking her. And not that I didn't want to do that, but I had a six hour drive ahead of me and she had to get ready to teach the nation's youth.

Being a responsible adult sucks.

Making my way into the kitchen, I find a small pile of mail on the breakfast table. I changed my address to my cousin's place in Minnesota, but there's always a few lingering items.

Flipping through, I see a letter from my lawyer. Considering the paperwork has all been signed, and my bill has been paid, I decide to ignore the envelope. That's a topic I'll deal with on another day.

Chapter 41

Elouise

THE PHONE only rings once before Maddie picks up my call.

"Aren't you supposed to be at that barbeque thing right now?" She asks, with eyebrows that I'm sure are raised.

I groan, "We're about to leave."

"Okay..." she lets the word hang.

We've talked about this stupid Stoleman-Hall family get together about a dozen times since the RV incident last weekend, so it's fair that she's wondering what the problem is now.

"I can't figure out what to wear," I admit.

Maddie makes a humming sound, "Yeah, I get that. Are you currently dressed?"

"Yes."

"Give me the rundown."

Maddie dates even less than I do, but like any woman, she understands the struggle of finding the perfect outfit.

I stare at my reflection in the full-length mirror on the back of my closet door. "I'm wearing that black wrap dress you like, but I feel like it's too fancy."

"Oooo yes, keep that on. It makes your tits look great!"

"Maddie! Our parents are going to be there! I'm not going for sexy."

I can almost hear her rolling her eyes. "Whatever, don't be a prude."

I snort, "Pot. Kettle."

She ignores my dig, "It's kinda cold so you could wear that light blue jean jacket you have and your yellow flats. Then you'll look like a perfect Spring Virgin."

A laugh bursts out of me, shaking loose the feeling of dread that's been sitting on my shoulders all morning. "Thank you, I needed that."

"You're welcome! Now go get in the car with your parents and brother and drive over to your boyfriend's parent's house." She starts laughing so I grumble a goodbye and hang up the phone.

Resigned to my fate, I take Maddie's advice, finish dressing, and hurry out of the house.

Everyone is already waiting in my brother's flashy SUV. I tried so hard to get him to stay home for this. He's been driving back and forth from his place to visit with Mom and Dad, so I thought I could convince him to take a day off. But that didn't work. And no matter what he says about wanting to see Mr. and Mrs. Stoleman, I know he just wants another chance to grill Beckett.

"You look wonderful," Mom clasps her hands together as I get into the backseat next to her.

"Thanks, Mom," I sigh.

Thankfully Dad and James are already in the middle of a conversation, one they continue as we drive over to the Stoleman's.

It's not far, as the crow flies, but Darling Lake the town was built along the shoreline of Darling Lake the lake, so there's no quick routes around the sprawling body of water.

But on the plus side, the sun is shining and it's a pretty drive.

In any normal situation I wouldn't be meeting a guy's family after one date. But this isn't a normal situation. And if I'm being honest with myself, my feelings towards Beckett aren't normal either.

I'll acknowledge that I was mildly obsessed with the boy growing up, and I was shocked by the man when he walked into my campsite a couple weeks ago. But this knotted feeling in my chest isn't simple infatuation. It's more than a childhood crush. I know what that feels like. It's fun and present but hollow. Because I was pining over the idea of him. But this new feeling... it's so much more consuming than I know what to do with. Because these are real feelings for the real Beckett.

Which is probably why today feels like such a big deal. Like I'm getting a second-chance introduction to his family, where they can see me as something other than James's little sister.

My mom's hand lands on my knee, and she gives me a squeeze, but thankfully she doesn't try to fill my head with platitudes.

When we pull up to the white one-story home it's exactly how I remember. White painted siding, dark blue shutters, and a neat iron fence surrounding the yard.

James parks in front of the house, and I make sure I'm the first one on the sidewalk leading to their front door. I may feel over-whelmed, but I'll be damned if I let my brother knock on the door.

My pulse is embarrassingly high when I tap my knuckles against the wood surface. It's been nearly a week since I've seen Beckett, and the stress of missing him is starting to show in my nerves. He hadn't planned on being in Chicago this whole time, but he said things kept popping up that he had to take care of. I'd say I understand, but I still don't really know what he was doing down there. Something for work, I think.

We talked a few times, texted most days, but it was all brief. Too quick. And I need more. I need more Beckett.

My eyes nearly close, thinking of all the things I want to do to the man, when the door in front of me swings open.

The scent memory of this home hits me like a wave, and I'm suddenly thrown back 15 years. The sensation is so extreme I have to fight the desire to turn and run.

I'd been expecting Beckett to answer the door, but it's not him.

"Hello, Dear!" Mrs. Stoleman pulls me in for a quick hug before holding me at arm's length, beaming at me, "It's so nice to have the families together again! This is going to be so much fun!"

"Hi, Mrs. Stoleman," it's impossible to not smile back. "Thanks so much for having us."

She brushes off my thanks and I step aside, letting her run through a similar greeting for the rest of my family before corralling us inside.

Mrs. Stoleman tells us that her husband is out back by the grill, then she and my mom start chattering away. I don't know how I was expecting Mrs. Stoleman to act, but I'm a little surprised she hasn't made any comments about me dating Beckett. I guess she's taking it all just as calmly as my parents did.

We're halfway to the living room when my mom pats her old friend on the back, "It's so nice of you to have us over."

Mrs. Stoleman smiles at her, "Of course! When we heard you were in town, we knew we had to do it."

Mom nods then decides to ditch subtly, "I mean, it was a bit of a surprise, but I'm glad you're just as excited about Beckett and Elouise dating as we are."

Mrs. Stoleman stumbles as we step into the large living room, "Um, what?"

The look on her face is a mix of shock and horror. Like she just heard the most horrible news.

Wait... did she not know about me and Beckett?

What does she think this is all about? Why wouldn't Beckett tell her? Does he think it'll be funny to tell her together, in person?

Mrs. Stoleman has stopped walking, "But..."

In a confused daze I walk past the pair of mothers, into the open living room.

Movement across the room catches my attention, and I turn toward it, prepared to ask Beckett what the hell he was thinking, except it's not him. It's someone else.

The figure rises from the couch, unfolding her long limbs, straightening her already perfect clothes.

We stare at each other for a long moment, the buzzing in my ears distracting me from the memory that's trying to break through my psyche. Because she looks... familiar.

Her blonde hair is curled into smooth waves, and the smile on her face is gentle, but there's a hardness in her eyes that I recognize.

But from where?

"Who are you?" My mom's tone is borderline rude, but I have the same question.

The woman looks at Beckett's mom, but she's still rooted in place near the hallway.

Straightening her already rigid shoulders, the blonde steps closer, holding out a hand for me.

Taking it out of reflex, we're palm to palm when she introduces herself.

"Hi, I'm Kira. Beckett's wife."

Wife?

Her grip releases, and my hand slowly lowers back to my side.

Wife.

I take a trembling step back.

Wife!

Beckett's married?

My mom curses and my dad murmurs something before rushing out the patio doors to the backyard.

Mrs. Stoleman finally finds her voice, "I don't understand what's going on!"

The woman... Beckett's *wife*... doesn't look so cocky anymore. But she's still here. In Beckett's parents' house. A welcome guest. And then it hits me. Like a brick to the face, the pieces slam together.

Sitting in this very house. Wearing my red velvet dress. Having Beckett talk to 15-year-old me like he actually sees me. And then she comes in. Kira. The lap-sitting, attention stealing bitch.

"Where is he?!" my brother's angry voice slices through the air.

Mrs. Stoleman sputters before replying, "He's getting cake."

Cake? He's missing this disaster because he's getting cake?

A laugh starts to build in my chest, but as it rises, it morphs into something much sadder and I clamp my lips together to hold it in.

Wife.

The hurt doesn't take over in a single moment. It's not just suddenly there. But there's something about it that just feels inevitable. Like I'm standing at one end of a long illuminated hallway, watching as the lights click off, one at a time, until the darkness is right in front of me.

Mom says something to me, but I can't listen. I need to get out of here before that last light clicks off. Before the shadows swallow me whole.

"Elouise, honey," Mom reaches out for me.

I take a step back. "I need to go," I whisper.

"But-" she starts to argue.

But I shake my head, "It's a misunderstanding."

It's not. It's so not. Whatever this is, it's malice. It's awful. And I can't be here for one more second.

"Please stay." I plead, knowing that's the only way I'll be able to quickly leave.

"Yes, this must be a misunderstanding," Mrs. Stoleman repeats, grasping for straws.

A mixture of anger and empathy fills my mom's features, but she nods, letting me pass.

It's not that I think anyone will have a nice lunch after this, it's just that I need to leave *right fucking now*. Because if I wait, Beckett might come back, and I can't face him right now.

Not now.

Not ever.

Keeping my head down I hurry down the hall.

Footsteps follow me, and I know it's my brother before he even speaks.

"Lou..." his soft tone kills me.

Keeping my eyes on his chest, I'm able to cling to my composure for another heartbeat. "I'm okay."

"You want a ride outta here?" When I shake my head, he holds out his precious keys, "Wanna take the car?"

I shake my head again, shoving my feet into my shoes. I'll walk. I don't know where, but I know I need the space, the air, to keep me upright.

When he doesn't move, I chance a glance up at him.

His jaw works before he shoves the keys back in his pocket, "He's a fucking prick."

I bite down hard on my lip and nod.

James only hesitates a moment before he holds the door open, letting me step through. And as soon as I hear the door close behind me, I run.

Chapter 42

Beckett

CLIMBING the steps to the front door, I balance the cake box in one hand.

Of course, Mom ordered an elaborate cake for today's little gathering. It just would've been nice for her to mention it sooner, not thirty minutes before Elouise and her family were supposed to show, especially considering the bakery is 20 minutes away.

I feel bad I wasn't here when Elouise arrived – since I'm trying to make a good impression on her family – but it's more than that. I miss her. I want to see her. Touch her. Smell her. It's been too damn long since I've had her near me, and I'll be rectifying that now. To hell if it makes our families uncomfortable, I'm gonna be touching some part of Elouise from now until the moment I bury myself in her pussy later tonight.

Digging my key out of my pocket, I remind my body that we need to keep it together for a few more hours. I can't walk in with a boner.

When I pull the front door open, I expect to be greeted by sounds of laughing and talking. But I don't hear... anything.

James's vehicle is parked out front, so I know they're here. But the place is quiet as a graveyard.

Kicking the door shut, I stride down the hall towards the kitchen and living room.

As I get closer, I hear hushed voices.

Stepping out into the great room, I see my mom standing in the corner talking quietly to Mrs. Hall. They haven't seen me yet, so I watch them for a moment, and it looks like my mom is consoling Mrs. Hall. But... that doesn't make sense. Why would she be doing that?

And it dawns on me. I told Mom that Elouise and I had reconnected, but I hadn't exactly spelled out that we were dating. I'd assumed that my cousin would gladly fill in those details. Then I left for a week and it completely slipped my mind to prepare my parents. Not that it should be a big fucking deal. My family loves the Halls. They shouldn't be acting this weird.

Looking through the closed patio doors, I see our dads standing next to the grill, but it doesn't even look like they're talking.

Seriously, what the hell is going on?

"What-" I start to ask, but before I can finish asking, my attention is drawn across the room.

I turn towards the movement, expecting to see Elouise. Only it's not her. The face staring back at me is familiar, but it's not the woman I want. And it takes my brain a long second to register who I'm looking at.

"What the fuck?" My words are a whisper of disbelief.

"Yeah, what the fuck!?" James' angry shout hits me the same time that his palms connect with my chest, shoving me backwards.

Too stunned to even notice his approach, I stumble back,

releasing my grip on the cake. The box thumps to the ground as I catch my balance.

"You lying, cheating, piece of shit!" James comes at me again, but I'm ready this time so I deflect his hands.

He reaches out yet again and I shove him away, "Knock it off!" I snap at him, "What-" I spin around to face Kira. "What the hell are you doing here!?"

She has the sense to look sheepish, "I came to see you." She glances away, "I didn't know you were seeing someone already."

James scoffs, "You have your wife over here apologizing after catching you with some other woman."

"Ex!" I toss my hands up, "My *Ex*-wife. We're divorced!" I glare at Kira, "And *already*? Really? We've been separated for over a year. I think I'm well within my rights to start dating again."

Murmurs sound around us, and I hear the back door open. Perfect, the dads are listening too.

"Divorced?" Elouise's mom repeats the word.

And my mom huffs, throwing up her hands, "No one tells me anything!"

My fingers pinch the top of my nose, "Mom, I told you we were getting a divorce."

"I didn't know it was done!" She rings her hands in her apron and I instantly feel like a jackass. "When Kira said she was here to see you, I assumed that you'd reconciled. And that I'd misunderstood why you were bringing Elouise over."

The turmoil in my mind freezes, my fractured thoughts suspended as my brain catches on one word.

Elouise.

Taking two more steps into the room, I whip my head around. I was so stunned to see Kira, I didn't even realize that Elouise was missing.

Understanding crawls up the back of my neck and I turn towards Kira. "Did you seriously walk in here, introducing yourself as my wife?"

When she glances away, I have my answer.

Cheeks I once thought I loved turn an ugly shade of red. But I don't feel any pity for Kira. It's not shame tinting her flesh, it's embarrassment at getting caught.

"Fuck!" I bark. "What are you even doing here?" I hold up a hand before she answers and a derisive laugh escapes me, "You know what. I bet I can fucking guess. But I don't want to hear it. If you have anything to say to me, send it through the lawyers."

My mom gasps, probably at my tone, but I don't have time for this.

Turning on my heel, I stride back towards the front door.

What a fucking disaster.

Heavy footsteps follow me down the hall and I know it's James.

"It's only been a couple minutes," he says.

I rip open the front door, "Did she drive?"

"No, she wanted to walk." He heaves out a breath as I try to decide which way she'd leave. "Shit man, I'm sorry. I should've asked questions."

This isn't his fault, but I don't look at him because I'm so pissed I might punch him, "Apologize by getting my greedy ex out of my parent's house."

As soon as I got over my shock at seeing her, I figured out what Kira is doing here. She must've heard that I sold my company in Chicago and now she wants some of that money.

Too fucking bad.

Not waiting for a response from James, I run to the sidewalk. Trusting my instincts, I turn deeper into the neighborhood. If she's on foot, I'll be too.

She could be trying to walk home, or to the lakeshore. Or she could just be wandering the streets, angry and hurt, because I'm the dumbass who didn't tell her I was divorced - that I'd been married. And I'm such a dumbass I didn't even tell my parents that the divorce had been finalized, simply because I didn't want to talk about it.

Fucking hell, she must think I'm a cheating asshole. Again.

An invisible rope cinches around my heart and I break into a sprint.

Chapter 43

Elouise

"STUPID." I chastise myself out loud. "*Stupid. Stupid. Stupid.*"

I can't believe I fell for it. The bullshit Nice Guy act. The way he made me feel special. Made me feel like... like he wanted more from me. All of me.

But a wife?! *A fucking wife!* What am I supposed to do with that?

And I can't even try to pretend that she's just some delusional woman, like she's lying, since Beckett's own mother let her into their house. Let her sit there as we walked in. Let her shake my hand, introducing herself as Beckett's wife, as though she wasn't plucking my heart straight out of my chest with her words.

My knuckles drag across my chin, wiping at the tears dripping down my cheeks.

I'm so disappointed in myself. How did I not see it? A 38-year-old man living with his cousin and nephew. A man who doesn't even seem to have a job. Who hasn't really told me anything about his life.

Seriously, what do I even know about him. Like actually know about him.

Is he really even back? Or was this just some sort of extended visit home and he decided to have a fling?

My brain fights back at that last thought, because why would he invite me to his parent's house if this was supposed to be some sort of secret sex-cation for him? And why would he not have taken the opportunity to hide when my parents showed up that one day in their freaking RV?

But I can't think about those moments right now. There's no point in trying to reason this one out. This isn't going to be a "it's not what it looks like" incident like it was when I saw him with his cousin at the restaurant. This one is pretty cut and dry. The evidence crystal clear in front of me.

With angry movements, I swipe through my phone and select Maddie's name.

She answers on the second ring, "Calling me from the bathroom already?"

Her laughing tone catches me off guard and I end up replying with a strangled sound.

"Oh my god!" Maddie's playfulness switches instantly to concern. "What happened?"

I take a moment to pull in a breath and calm myself, but the lack of response just sends Maddie into more of a panic.

"Elouise! What's wrong? Oh my god, talk to me!"

"I'm fine," my voice is quieter than I'd like, but it's steady. "I just need you to pick me up."

"Okay," I can already hear the sound of her grabbing her keys and running out of her house. "Where are you?"

Knowing this neighborhood well, I give her the name of a small park a few blocks over.

"Be there in four!" Maddie confirms before hanging up.

My fingers flex around the phone and I make my next right, moving further away from thoughts of Beckett and closer to my escape.

Chapter 44

Beckett

Breathing heavily, I dart across yet another street.

I can't find her.

If she gets away from me today... *Fuck.* I don't know what it'll take to get her to listen.

My boots thunder against the sidewalk, but I don't slow down. *I can't.*

If I can just find her, I can clear this up. I know I fucked up. I totally get it. But I can make this right. I can make her understand.

She has to understand.

My eyes scan the street ahead of me, but there's still no sign of her.

Reaching the next intersection, I stop.

It's been too long. She's been gone too long.

Sucking in a breath, I turn to the right. And spot her.

There's a city park between us – a small field, with a basketball court, a copse of trees, and a playground taking up the entire block. The slides block my view as she walks, back to me, on the far side of the park, but it's her. I know it's her.

I want to shout for her, but now that I have her in my sights, I need to calm down. I can't be a stressed-out mess when I reach her. If I am, I won't say everything the way it needs to be said.

Walking calmly, I cross the street to the park and watch Elouise, her hips swaying in a pretty black dress. She looks... Goddamnit, she looks amazing. She dressed up for today. And instead of me being there to greet her, she was on her own to be blindsided by my secrets.

She lifts a hand to wipe at her face and another dagger of self-loathing slides between my ribs.

She's crying. Elouise is fucking crying!

I'm such an asshole.

Cursing myself in my head, I quicken my strides.

But just as quickly, a motion in my peripheral snags my attention, and my steps slow.

There's a man.

My steps slow even further.

He's standing near the trees, turned towards Elouise. His hood is pulled up over his head, blocking my view of his face.

Is he...?

I stop, torn between reaching Elouise or figuring out why this guy has every one of my instincts on edge.

The man steps away from the trees and heads straight for Elouise.

Oh, hell no.

Changing my trajectory, I start to run towards a spot between them. I don't know what the hell he's planning, but I'm putting an end to it.

He's not running, and he hasn't seen me, but he's so much closer to her than I am. And I can't risk him reaching her first.

Pushing myself to go faster, I shout out Elouise's name.

Her shoulders stiffen, but she doesn't stop walking and she doesn't turn around. But the man does.

His head whips in my direction, but his features are a blur, large sunglasses blocking most of his face from view anyway. But whatever glimpse he got of me must've been enough. Turning back the way he came; the man breaks into a run.

Do I go after Elouise, or do I go after the man?

Torn, my fists clench and I take one more stride forward.

Elouise. It's always gonna be Elouise.

Once more, I change direction towards my girl. But a moment later a small white car slows down as it pulls up to the curb next to Elouise. I have one heartbeat to worry that it's someone else trying to take her, but then Elouise darts towards the vehicle, climbing in willingly.

"Elouise!" I call again.

But her only response is the slamming of the car door. Then she's gone.

I spin in the direction the man went, but he's already out of sight.

"Fuck!"

Chapter 45

Maddie

For the fourth time in the past ten minutes, my gaze travels to the bakery display case – eyes lingering on the delicious looking cinnamon roll.

"No, Maddie. You don't need it," I say it out loud this time, like that might make a difference.

Except it doesn't.

I only get these beauties in on Fridays and this batch looks extra gooey. And it's the last one. And it's already mid-afternoon so the breakfast crowd already got theirs. And there's no one here to witness. And *oh my god I don't care, I'm eating it!*

Decision made, I wipe my hands down my apron and slide open the glass door letting the scent of sugary wonder waft out.

My mouth is already salivating, and by the time I rip off the first piece of flakey, buttery, goodness I'm afraid to look down, sure I'm drooling on myself.

"Fuck me," I moan, as the first taste hits my tongue.

I love Elouise. She's my very best friend in the world. But sharing my one-bedroom apartment with her for the past several days – as she hides from Beckett – has been exhausting. And not even in a bad way. I've loved seeing her so much. It's just that we've spent every night polishing off a new bottle of wine, watching every Drew Barrymore movie we can get our hands on, and I'm more than a little sleep deprived.

Elouise isn't tall but considering I'm barely over five feet I insisted on being the one to sleep on the couch. She fought me the best she could, but she's the one dealing with heartbreak, and I'm the one who's too much of a light sleeper to share a mattress with another body.

Ripping off another chunk of my roll, I swipe it through the frosting pooling on the small plate before shoving it into my mouth.

Forcing the stress of calories out of my mind, I focus back on Elouise and her situation.

We've talked it over – Beckett's supposed *wife* – and the more I think about it, the more it doesn't add up. There's definitely something fishy going on, but I think there's a lot more to this story.

Elouise's mom told her to go talk to Beckett before making any decisions, hinting that she knows more details about the situation. Elouise agreed that she would, but then her parents took their RV and left town the next morning and Elouise still hasn't taken any of Beckett's calls.

I need to convince her to talk to him. But I'm not sure how to do that.

Swallowing, I lick my fingers and reach for the pastry. I know I should savor this piece slowly, but instead I rip out the center coil, the very best part of a cinnamon roll, and shove it into my mouth.

It's too big to eat at once, but there's no going back now. So, I let my eyes fall closed as I chew.

Holy Crisco this is amazing.

The cinnamon sugar is beginning to become one with my soul when I hear the tinkling sound of the door opening.

Feeling like I've been caught with my hand in the cookie jar, my eyes snap open. And then I freeze. Because it's *him*. It's Beckett. And he's striding towards me, a mission clear in his features.

My hands fly up to cover my mouth, sure my cheeks are puffed out like a chipmunk's.

Oh my god, this isn't happening.

I start to chew as fast as I can, way too aware of my face heating.

When he stops across the counter from me, I hold up one finger, then turn away, giving him my back.

Dying of mortification, I try to not actually die from choking as I frantically chew and swallow what's in my mouth.

Wiping my lips off with the back of my hand, I turn back around and think that maybe dying would have been the better choice.

No wonder Elouise is running from him. He's so stupidly attractive I don't even want to look him in the eyes. But I force myself to, finding that his serious expression has softened with amusement.

"You alright?" he asks, and my blush reaches a whole new level.

I nod. Then nod again, "I'm good. Um, what can I get you?"

I glance over my shoulder, towards the menu board, but I already know that's not what he's here for.

"I need to talk to her," he states, confirming my assumption.

When I force myself to look at him again, I notice there's no longer a trace of humor.

I nervously bite down on my lip. I hate confrontation. All of it. Any of it. And this is already stressing me out.

This isn't for me. It's for Elouise.

Mustering all of my courage, I roll my shoulders back and face Beckett straight on, "She doesn't want to see you."

My heartbeat is skittering all over the place, but Beckett doesn't act angry. He doesn't yell or throw things or call me names, he just nods.

"She's mad," I add, feeling bolstered, Then I shut up. I've read about negotiation tactics before and wonder if he's trying to use the silence to get me to talk.

But Beckett nods again, "I'd be mad too."

Ooookay. He's being agreeable. I don't really know what to do with this.

At a loss, I just nod back in return. All too aware that most of this conversation has been us moving our heads up and down.

"Maddie," he sighs, "please. I need to talk to her."

I'm back to biting my lip.

"She's staying with you, right?" he asks. "Can you at least tell me that? That she's okay?"

My nod is slower this time. I don't know how much Elouise would want me to say.

Well, I know she'd *tell* me that she doesn't want anything to do with him. But that'd be her stubborn head speaking. I think her heart might have other ideas.

Beckett bends over, resting his elbows on the counter, his head dropping in defeat, "I'm not married."

"I knew it!" the words come out at a near shout, startling us both. "I mean," I continue at a lower volume, "I was pretty sure. I pulled a – never mind. It doesn't matter. But you're not married? Like not at all?"

Bolstered by my excitement, Beckett straightens back to his full height, "Not at all."

I tilt my head, while I watch him. "Then why'd that chick introduce herself as your wife?"

He heaves out a breath, "She's my ex-wife."

My brows raise, "Um, I feel like Elouise would've mentioned it if you were married before."

Beckett runs a hand through his hair, "I didn't tell her."

Still stressing over the whole encounter, I channel my inner P!nk and cross my arms over my chest. "Probably should've mentioned that. Don't ya think?"

"Yes," the way the word crawls from his clenched teeth tells me he's probably had this conversation a time or twenty with himself. "And I'd like to explain myself to Elouise, but she won't answer her phone and she hasn't been home. And I really don't want to barge into her classroom-"

"Again," I butt in.

"Again," he repeats. "But I'm running out of options. And patience. And I hate that she's spent this whole week thinking I'm a cheating bastard."

I let my arms drop to my sides, "If I tell you where she'll be tonight, you have to find a way to make her listen. Because if I do this, and you mess it up, it's going to be *me* that she takes it out on."

"Please," he pleads. "I promise I won't fuck it up."

I'm torn, but staring into his intimidating eyes, I find I believe him.

Chapter 46

Beckett

Filing into Darling High School, I'm a little thankful for the crowd of bodies around me slowing my progress.

We're in the Performing Arts part of the building, and even though I didn't spend much time on this side of the school when I was a student here, I'm still hit with a wave of nostalgia. Only instead of calming me, that nostalgia just mixes with my nerves causing a sludge of unease.

I was confident in my persuasion skills right up until I parked my truck a few minutes ago.

Cornering Elouise as she sells tickets for tonight's play – a musical version of Clueless – is not ideal, but it's all I got.

My steps slow, and I let a pair of grandparents pass me, biding my time.

I've had so much time to plan what I was going to say to her, but now I can't remember a single goddamn word.

The crowd shifts and for the first time in a week, I see her. And she looks fucking beautiful.

Something loosens around my ribcage, and I feel like I can finally breathe again.

No more waiting.

This is it.

I'm gonna get her back.

Reclaiming my place in line, I shuffle ahead until there's only two couples ahead of me.

Elouise is sitting behind a small card table, with a stack of folded programs in front of her and a small tablet with a card reader in her hand.

Half her body is covered, but it doesn't matter, because even sitting there in a hard metal chair, she's glowing. Fucking glowing in a white sweater that looks as soft as I know her skin to be.

The dramatic lighting of the auditorium lobby shines off her wavy chestnut hair. And even with her head tipped down, I can tell she's smiling. The curve of her cheeks, the light laughter in the air. And when she brushes her hair over her shoulders, I swear I can smell the citrusy floral of her shampoo from here. A scent that's been haunting my dreams.

She lifts her head and hands the credit card back to the man in front of her, then the next couple steps up.

The closer I get, the more settled I feel.

This is right. Everything about *us* is right. And it's time for her to understand that.

Completing the payment, the couple ahead of me picks up a pair of programs then move on, heading for the auditorium.

She's tapping something into her screen, still looking down, when I hold my credit card out. "One ticket, please."

I watch as she stills, her pointer finger still pressed against the screen.

After an eternity of seconds, she lifts her head, her eyes meeting mine, and the universe clicks in place.

"Hi, Smoky," I keep my gaze on hers, and see the flicker of anger at my use of her nickname.

Good. Anger I can deal with. It's *hurt* that'll kill me.

Her jaw clenches as she reaches out to take my card, making sure our fingers don't accidently touch.

Elouise looks down as she selects the number of tickets, then swipes the card. The screen swirls as it thinks, then signals the transaction complete.

But she doesn't hand me my card back. Instead, she keeps it in her palm, on her lap, and looks past me to the next person in line.

"How many tickets?" she asks the family behind me.

She's craning her neck to see them, so I step to the side of the table and allow them to approach.

The dad of the group smiles at Elouise, "Four, please."

She smiles back, but instead of taking his offered card, she swipes mine.

He looks back-and-forth between me and Elouise, but she doesn't offer an explanation other than, "You're all set. Enjoy!"

The dad does another double take, then pushes his family along.

Making no move to look at me, Elouise greets the elderly couple that steps up next. The woman tries to hand over money, but Elouise waves them off, "Your tickets are free tonight." Then she swipes my card again.

When the process repeats for a third time with a single attendee, I can no longer hide my smile. And this time, when they walk away, I'm the one who calls out, "Enjoy the show!"

The next family moves to the front of the line, and I count a total of eight people.

Having seen the same thing, Elouise sighs and holds my card up for me to take back. At $12 a pop, this family will cost nearly $100 and she's trying to give my card back. I nearly grin. She's pissed, obviously, but she's not so pissed that she'll try to spend all my money. It's cute.

But instead of taking the card back, I cross my arms.

With a roll of her eyes, she turns back to greet them.

As she types in the ticket quantity, I move closer and lower myself until I'm kneeling on the rough industrial carpet next to her. My joints protest the movement, but I want to be eye-to-eye when I say this, even if she chooses not to look at me.

"I'm not married." I keep my voice low, the drone of milling bodies in the large lobby preventing anyone but her from hearing me. "The woman you met was my ex-wife." She doesn't acknowledge that I'm talking, but I watch her grip on the tablet tighten. "I'm sorry I didn't tell you about her. I wasn't trying to keep it a secret, I just..." I shuffle closer on my knees until my chest is nearly against her shoulder. "I'm not proud of my failed marriage, and I didn't want to spend the little time we've had together talking about it." The image of Elouise brushing away tears after fleeing my parent's house slams into my brain and my chest is back to aching. "I'm sorry. I'm so fucking sorry you found out the way you did. I didn't mean to hurt you. I never want to hurt you."

A new family steps up to the table but I don't move my eyes away from Elouise's face. "The divorce was finalized a few days before I moved back, but we've been separated for a long time. I haven't lived with Kira for over a year."

Elouise still isn't responding to me, and I'm not sure how to take that.

I place a hand on her thigh, the denim warm under my palm. "I brought a photo of my signed divorce papers if you want to see them," I offer, feeling like a total dumbass.

When Elouise slides my card through the reader again, she's a little more forceful than she's been on the previous occasions.

I grimace, "I'd really rather not call my ex, but I will if you need to hear it from her."

Elouise tells the family to go ahead, then turns her head just enough to see me, "Why did your mom think you were still together?"

"Because I'm a shitty son," I admit, knowing it's true. "I told her when we separated that we were going to get a divorce. But like I said that was a year ago, and for once in her life, my mom didn't pry, and I didn't bring it up again. I figured she didn't ask because she knew I wouldn't want to talk about it. But when Kira showed up on their doorstep, with the worst fucking timing ever, my mom assumed we'd reconciled. And that you and I were just friends." I tell her, urging her to believe me.

She watches me for a long moment, "Maybe that's all we should be."

"No!" my fingers dig into the softness of her thigh, and I take a breath to calm my tone. "No. That's not what we are. We're more than that."

"It was one time," she's trying so hard to appear unaffected by the conversation, but I can feel her thigh trembling under my grip.

"Babe, that was just the first time."

The rise and fall of her chest quickens, and I know she's reliving the same memories I am.

I press in even closer, "I swear to you, that I'm telling you the truth. I'm an idiot. An asshole. A total piece of shit for letting it happen the way it did. But I promise that I'm not lying. I'm not married. Her and I are over. And if I wasn't such a crap son, I would've told my mom everything. About Kira. About us." She's not saying anything, and I don't know how to take it. "I'm so fucking sorry, Babe. I wasn't trying to keep secrets from you, or keep you a secret from anyone else."

"Uh," a stranger clears their throat, "two tickets, please?"

The stream of people pouring into the lobby has slowed but the line is still long enough that these interruptions won't stop.

"Charge me for the rest of the tickets," I tell her, flexing my fingers.

Elouise and the stranger both turn to look at me, but I nod to the tablet.

"Um, what?" she perplexes.

"Charge me for the tickets."

She glances at the line of people, "How many?"

I tap the screen, "All of them. Whatever's left to fill the auditorium."

"I don't think we're gonna sell out."

"Lou."

"Okay." Her eyes are wide, but she taps at the screen, "It's-" she tilts the screen in my direction, "It's a lot, Beckett."

"Will you sit with me?"

My hand hasn't left her thigh, and I feel her shift as she thinks, "You can't talk during the play."

"But you'll let me sit next to you?" I ask again.

Her nod is slow, but it's still a nod.

I take my card from her hand and pass it through the reader myself, "Then it's worth it."

Chapter 47

Elouise

I'VE LOST my damn mind. Or maybe it's Beckett who lost his mind, spending $2,000 on tickets to a play that I'm sure he doesn't actually want to sit through. But as I let him guide me towards the back of the auditorium, I think over everything he said.

I want to believe him. He sounds genuine. And as much as I don't like admitting it, his story is believable, even if it makes him sound like an idiot. Because honestly, I could see my brother doing the same thing. Only our mom would never have just *let it go.*

Or would she?

Before my parents left town, Mom did make me promise to talk to Beckett. And the more I think about *that* the more I wonder if she didn't get this whole backstory the day of The Incident. Which just makes me want to kick myself. If Beckett is really telling the truth, did I spend the whole week hiding at Maddie's suffering through a broken heart for no reason at all.

No, not no reason. No matter the truth, I was still put into

the horribly humiliating situation of having "his wife" introduce herself to me in front of my entire family.

When we reach an empty row, Beckett gestures for me to
go ahead, and I shuffle through until we're almost to the other
side. I want easy access to an aisle out of here if I decide to run.

We haven't spoken since he bought the tickets. He just
stood by silently while I created a small sign letting people
know that the rest of the seats tonight were free.

I took my sweet time, so by the time we settle into our seats
there's only a few moments before the play begins.

Beckett turns in his seat, but right on time, the lights dim
and the play starts, silencing him.

As the lights lift for intermission, I realize that I haven't paid
attention to a single line delivered by the young actors. My
thoughts were already a mess and then five minutes in Beckett
draped an arm over my shoulders. My first reaction was to
tense against him, but he didn't pull away. He waited for me to
relax, then he started to lightly skim his fingers through the
ends of my hair, sending tingles up and down my spine and
thoroughly squashing any bit of concentration I had left.

My mind just can't settle on an answer. I want Beckett. I
want to be with him, see what this pull between us could turn
into. But I don't want to be that woman who believes every lie
her man tells her. We've barely even dated, and this is already
the second time I've suspected he was in another relationship.
Sure, the first time was me jumping to the wrong conclusion
when I saw him with his cousin and nephew, but this whole

wife thing is a different ball game. And it's not about him being married before. I don't care about that. Lots of marriages fail, at least this shows that he's willing to try. But...

I shift to face Beckett, causing his posture to instantly straighten, "I'd like to see it."

The look on his face is stuck somewhere between puzzlement and humor as he glances down to his lap.

I use the back of my hand to smack into his chest, "Not that, you idiot. The divorce papers."

"Ah," his humor slips away.

Beckett removes his arm from my shoulders to dig out his phone and tap through his emails to find the right one.

With his selection made, he sets the phone in my hand.

I've never seen a divorce decree before, but when I zoom in the names and dates are easy enough to read. But I read through twice just to be sure.

Handing the phone back, I ask the question I need answered most, "Do you still love her?"

A guilty look crosses his face even as he shakes his head, "No, I don't." When I narrow my eyes, he sighs, "The relationship we had was never... healthy."

I just give him a look, silently suggesting he continue.

He drags a hand down his face. "We were *that* couple. The on-again-off-again will-they-won't-they pair. We eventually did, when we shouldn't have, and the marriage lasted less than two years."

"Why'd you marry her?" I can't help myself from asking.

He shrugs. The stupid man shrugs. "It seemed like the right thing to do. We were mid-30's, too old to keep doing the back-and-forth. She wanted to live together, I said we should be married first, she said okay, and then I found myself married."

I snort out a laugh, "That all sounds awfully passive of you."

The side of his mouth tips up, "There's a reason I strive to be in control now."

His hand over my mouth.

His dirty words in my ear.

"Are you gonna be quiet for me?"

No. Nope. Not going there. Not right now.

"So, you're not in love with her anymore." I state, and he shakes his head. "And you don't want to get back together."

"Fuck no."

"Then why was she at your parent's house? Does she still want you?"

He's shaking his head before I even finish my question. "Kira doesn't love me anymore than I love her. But she does love money."

"Money?" I repeat, like the idea of Beckett having a lot of money is ridiculous.

He huffs out a bitter laugh, "The irony is, her dad insisted we sign a prenup."

My eyebrows raise, "She's rich?"

"Not her, her dad. He was worth, I dunno, millions, and I was just starting my business. Guess he worried I'd use her to funnel all his money into my own business. Who knows? But the result was an iron clad agreement where we'd keep our finances separate for the first ten years." Beckett's smile gradually grows to a grin. "Best decision we ever made, though Kira would argue otherwise."

I tilt my head, thinking back through all our interactions. The times he said "my company", how he laughed when I asked if he had a job, spending a small fortune on these damn play tickets.

"I take it your company did well?" I ask.

He lifts a shoulder, "After selling off the Chicago branch,

I'm worth more than Kira's father. And that doesn't seem to be sitting well with her."

Millions.

I feel my mouth pop open. He'd said that other guy was worth millions.

It doesn't matter.

I repeat to myself. Twice.

It doesn't matter that he's actually loaded. Like, stupid loaded. Because I don't need his money. I don't want his money. I just want to be with someone I can trust. And that means no more secrets. For either of us.

"I recognized her," I blurt out.

It's Beckett's turn to look confused, "Kira?"

I nod, "Yeah." I'm already regretting bringing this up. I don't know why it seems so much worse now, knowing what she became for him. Even if he doesn't love her anymore, or ever, if I'm supposed to believe that. "From your parent's house actually." I nearly laugh, realizing it's the truth. "She was at that Christmas party."

I see when he remembers the moment I'm talking about. The moment that meant so much to me at the time. The moment his future wife ruined.

"Aw, hell." He grips one of my hands in both of his. "I'm so fucking sorry, Smoky. For all of it."

The sincerity in his voice weaves its way between my ribs and ties itself around my heart.

He means every word, and it's suddenly hard to swallow.

One hand lets go, moving to cup the back of my head.

Beckett pulls me in closer, pressing his lips to my forehead, his words whispering over my skin, "I'm sorry."

I don't have an answer for him, not yet. And when the lights dim, letting us know intermission is almost over, I'm thankful for the reprieve.

Applause fills the auditorium as all the actors step onto the stage for a bow, and I lift my head from its place on Beckett's shoulder.

The second half of the play was even more stressful than the first, because I believe him. His explanation. His apology. All of it.

And now I need to decide what to do next. Should I just accept his apology and move forward. Or should I just end this here? I don't want to stop seeing Beckett, but that's kinda the whole point. If I felt this bad after only a couple weeks, how much worse would it feel if I were with him longer?

As the clapping dies down, I lead us out of the row of seats. Following the crowd out.

I know Beckett's right behind me because his palm presses into my lower back, infusing heat straight into my blood. And I can't think with him this close. And I certainly can't be trusted to make a good decision if I walk into that dark parking lot with him at my side.

I need distance from his overwhelming presence, so I have room to think.

"I have to pee!" I immediately cringe at my exclamation, but it works and Beckett pauses. "Stay here."

Not waiting for his confirmation, I step away, slicing a path through the crowd toward the restrooms.

Then, without looking back, I let the flow of people guide my steps until I'm walking out the main doors in a sea of bodies.

Chapter 48

Beckett

WATCHING ELOUISE WALK AWAY, I stuff my hands into my pockets trying to conserve her heat that I still feel on my palm.

Tonight seemed to go well. Obviously, I haven't fixed everything. That can't be done with one apology. But I think she believes me, which is only step one. Because I need her to forgive me. For several things, but mostly for being an idiot.

I let a deep inhale fill my lungs.

Being able to put my hands on her tonight brought a calm over me that I haven't felt all week.

My eyes follow her movements as Elouise weaves between bodies streaming for the exit. She steps behind a tall body and disappears from my view.

A second passes, then another, and when I don't see her reappear, I take a step to the side. Finally, I catch sight of her soft brown hair. Except she's changed direction.

Wait...

Is she...?

Her pace picks up, and I watch, stupefied, as she walks out the front doors.

Goddamnit.

I shake my head, as the urge to shout her name wars with the urge to laugh. I swear this minx is a surprise every damn day.

It takes me too long to push my way through the crowd, so by the time I make it outside, I've lost her.

Fuck.

If I was a smart man, and I'm clearly not, I would've found her car right when I got here and parked next to it.

Not ready to give up, I weave my way through the rows of cars. But the lot goes in both directions, and the scattered lights don't do enough to illuminate and identify all the people milling about.

I wander for a few minutes but seeing no sign of her I accept defeat.

Letting out an audible sigh, I turn back and head toward my truck. Cutting across the dark parking lot, I let my mind replay the events of the evening and I find myself feeling proud of Elouise. My girl might have given me the slip just now, but she also listened. I came here thinking there was a good chance she'd throw something at me and tell me to go fuck myself. But that's not her. She's smart and kind and more mature than I'll ever be.

Then I think about the look on her face when she swiped my card that first time for someone else's tickets and a grin forms on my lips.

Clever little brat.

If I'd still been a broke college kid, that would've had the desired effect. But instead of coming off devious, she just came off as cute.

I'm still grinning when I step out into the last lane between me and my truck, and the sound of an engine revving is the only warning I have.

My brain registers the noise and my body reacts on instinct, jumping backwards, landing me on my back between two vehicles.

The adrenaline rush is instant, and I have a split second to feel like I overacted before the crunch of metal on metal reverberates through the air.

I'm already scrambling back on my hands and heels when the car to my left starts to slide towards me. The menacing sound of the revving of the engine gets louder.

"What the fuck?!" I yell even as I keep moving, the car on my side still getting closer.

Shouts are sounding from somewhere nearby, but the noise in front of me has my full attention.

The engine gives one last loud rev and the front corner of the car to my left slams into the car on my right.

"Shit!"

I've made it to the rear bumpers, the V created between the cars just wide enough for my shoulders.

There's a loud scraping sound, followed by squealing tires as the car that caused the wreck speeds away. But with the front of the cars pressed together in front of me, I don't catch even a glimpse of the vehicle.

Thudding footsteps alert me to the approaching witnesses, and as they get closer, I notice the bouncing beams of light coming off of multiple phone flashlights. This makes me realize just how dark it is in this part of the lot. Pushing up to my feet, I look around and see that three of the closest parking lot lights aren't working.

Someone calls out to me, asking if I'm okay. I raise a hand, letting them know I'm fine as I step forward and look at the damage on the cars that nearly crushed me.

If I hadn't heard the revving, or if I'd moved any slower...

The darkness feels heavier when I realize the car that

almost hit me never turned their lights on. I definitely would've noticed the beams before stepping out from between the cars.

Seriously, what the fuck?

Chapter 49

Elouise

His breath is hot along my skin while his lips graze my neck, sending tingles up and down my spine.

"Beckett," I groan out his name, not caring about our surroundings.

A large hand clamps over my mouth, as his body shifts until he's above me, pressing me into the floor.

"Hush, Smoky," teeth nip at the curve of my breast. "You don't want to get caught, do you?"

My head shakes even as I try to ask him for more, but his palm is still silencing my words.

I writhe, not caring about the dirty carpet beneath me. And when his teeth scrape over my nipple I reach out and grip the base of the chair next to me.

Then his mouth moves lower... and lower... my heart rate increasing as he inches closer to where I want him. Where I need him.

Strong hands pry my naked thighs apart and I groan.

Shushing fills my ears... getting louder... until it's all I can hear.

Opening my eyes, I look up and find an entire auditorium full of people looming over me, with judgmental looks in their eyes and fingers in front of their lips.

"*I told you to be quiet,*" *Beckett says, before lowering his face between my legs.*

I want to tell him to stop. We shouldn't do this. Not here. But then his tongue laps against me, and then all I can hear are the wet noises between my thighs. The strokes of his tongue sounding like the strikes of a hammer.

Hammer?

My eyes pop open.

For a second, I almost expect to find a bunch of disapproving adults staring down at me, but it only takes me a few blinks to come back to reality and I recognize my bedroom ceiling.

I let out a deep sigh.

This obsession with Beckett is affecting my dreams.

But after a few more blinks I realize that the hammering sound didn't end with my dream.

"What the...?"

Throwing back the covers, I glance at the clock, shocked to see I slept past 9:00.

I'm settling my feet on the floor when the hammering stops. My palms scrub over my eyes. And I have just enough time to think that I'm totally losing it when the unmistakable sound of an electric saw filters in through my window.

"Seriously?"

With an un-ladylike grunt, I stand and shuffle to my window. Pulling the curtains open, I see that Beckett's truck is parked in my driveway. I can still hear the sounds of a power tool, but I can't see him.

Half awake, I trudge down the hall, down the stairs and

across the living room, stopping only to unlock the deadbolt before yanking open the front door.

I had a suspicion of what I might find, but that didn't prepare me for the site in front of me. Because it's not just Beckett. It's Beckett in a tool belt. With little bits of sawdust stuck in his hair and a sweat-dampened white shirt clinging to his broad back.

Facing away from me, Beckett leans over a bench, moving his saw across a board, and just like that, my ovaries pop out of my body and roll across the porch, in an effort to get closer to the testosterone on display.

The way he's bending highlights the fact that his jeans are molded to his ass. And, fuck me, even his usual black leather work boots look hot.

"Jesus Christ," I mutter. "I had no chance."

Beckett straightens but before he can turn around, I snap the door shut. If I'm going to deal with him, looking like that, I need to change.

And brush my teeth.

Ten minutes later, I'm opening the front door again. Only this time I step out onto the porch, closing the door behind me.

Beckett's standing at the bottom of the short set of steps, still looking hot as hell.

He smiles, "Morning."

I lift a brow and hand him a mug filled with black coffee,

taking my own over to the wicker bench in the corner of the porch.

In leggings, a sports bra and hoodie, I'm far from put together, but everything is held in place. And after throwing my hair into an extra-messy bun, I feel like myself.

Settling onto the seat, Beckett holds his ground as we take matching sips of coffee, our eyes locked over the edges of our mugs.

"So," I make a point of looking around, "what's going on out here?"

Beckett mimes my action, slowly looking at the tools and lumber scattered around my porch and yard. "Just replacing some of your floorboards."

I can see the ones he's already done, their color slightly lighter than the others.

"Oh?" I infuse the *why* into my tone.

He shrugs, "I spent a lot of time here this week," he taps his foot against the steps, "and noticed a few bad boards."

"You spent a lot of time here?"

Beckett nods, "Yeah. Waiting for you."

Oh.

Really?

"You did?"

"Of course, I did."

His simple answer hits me square in the chest. "When?"

He looks exasperated at my question. "Every day, Elouise. I came here every single day since the disaster at my parent's house because I needed to see you. Explain to you what happened. And as I paced back and forth across this damn porch, I couldn't help but notice that a few things needed to be fixed. And so here I am, fixing it." Beckett sets his coffee on the railing and climbs the steps, crossing over the newly replaced flooring until he's right in front of me.

He smacks a hand against his chest. "Me. *I'm* fixing it. Because the thought of some other man over here, working to make your house a safer place, makes my blood fucking boil." He leans down, hands braced on either side of my shoulders, caging me in. "I don't think you get it, not yet, but you're mine, Smoky Darling. You're mine to touch and spoil and keep safe. And while you're letting that sink in, I'm gonna do what needs to be done. Because the only thing worse than thinking about some strange man fixing your rotten floorboards, is the thought of you being unsafe. I won't fucking have it, Elouise. So don't ask me to. The last time I saw you injured it nearly killed me."

My pulse is skittering. His intensity is such a contrast to the calm Beckett from last night, pleading with me to believe him. This Beckett... *fuck,* this Beckett is hot.

"When did you see me injured?" is the only question I can think to ask.

"Do you remember that kick ball game?"

My heart skips a beat.

He can't... he can't possibly...

"When that little prick from down the street knocked you over?"

I nod. Because I know exactly what day he's talking about. It's a memory that's formed my existence. The moment that started everything. One I've relived countless times in the years after. Because it's the moment I fell in love with Beckett.

But I was sure – I *knew* – it meant nothing to him. Just a random fleeting moment in his life.

But... My lungs fight to inflate. But I was wrong. Because if what he's saying is true... *Oh my god...* that means that same moment meant something to him too.

Beckett's hands move to my shoulders, dragging his palms down my arms as he lowers himself into a crouch.

Beckett's gaze holds mine, his tone softening, "Seeing you

235

sprawled on the blacktop that day... it broke something inside of me. Or maybe it fixed it." His fingers squeeze mine. "I was always *aware* of you after that. Every time I saw you, or heard your name, or thought of you, a feeling of protectiveness would overcome me. It wasn't like it is now. It wasn't filled with this *need*. You were just a kid back then." His chest expands. "But you aren't a kid now."

The air between us fills with a tension I can feel. Past and present colliding and forming something new.

How is this possible?

"You..." I trail off. Not sure what to say after that.

The corner of his mouth twitches but he doesn't attempt to fill the silence. He just lets me take in the meaning of his words.

We're still staring at each other when my phone starts to ring, and I make no move to answer it.

When it continues to ring, Beckett reaches into my sweatshirt pocket and pulls out my phone. "Answer it." He punctuates his statement by flipping my hand over and setting it in my palm.

"Beckett-"

"Better yet," he cuts me off then taps the screen, "Maddie?"

There's a pause on the other end of the line before my friend's voice sounds over speakerphone. "Um, yes?"

"Are you at home or at BeanBag?"

"I'm at the shop. Is everything okay? Where's Elouise?" She sounds curious but not too alarmed.

"Everything's fine. Elouise is gonna come hang out for a bit."

"Beck-"

He cuts me off again, while he hangs up on Maddie. "Go. I need to wrap up here, and if you stay, you'll just distract me."

Rather than arguing, I let him help me up.

He's right. Not that I care about the front porch. It's more that if I stay, I'll end up tearing his clothes off in about, oh, five minutes. And what I really need is time to process the emotional bomb he just dropped on my childhood.

Beckett presses his lips to my forehead then turns back towards his tools.

Chapter 50

Elouise

AFTER GRABBING my purse off the counter, I went out through the garage, leaving without saying anything else to Beckett.

The drive to BeanBag passes in a blur. My mind still focused on what he admitted crouched before me on the porch.

I'm glad I put on halfway decent clothes before facing Beckett because I didn't even think to check over my appearance before leaving.

Finding a parking spot, I climb out of my car and head into Maddie's shop. The familiar scents of coffee and pastries greeting me when I pull open the door.

After having Beckett answer my phone, I'm sure she knows I need the full Best Friend Treatment, which means privacy. But Maddie's busy ringing up a customer, so I make my way behind the counter and help myself to our Freak Out Spot.

It's a square of extra thick squishy mat that's been here for years and has been strategically placed behind the tallest section of counter. Lowering myself to the ground, I settle my butt into place and tip my head back against the cupboard.

238

Smoky Darling

Maddie and I discovered the privacy of this spot back when we both worked here in high school, Maddie has just made it a little more comfortable. It's mostly used for panic attacks, and while I might not be quite there, I'm close. So, I close my eyes and listen to Maddie's movements as she makes a pair of lattes, trying to compose my thoughts.

A few minutes pass and my heart rate is finally slowing back to normal when I hear the door open then close as the customers leave.

"So..." Maddie trails off, her footsteps stopping at my side.

"So..."

"I take it the volunteering last night went well?"

Maddie's question has my eyes slowly opening. I watch her for just a second and see the guilt written across her features.

"You're the one who told him where to find me?" I shake my head, realizing how stupid I'd been to not even think about *how* he found me.

Maddie drops to sit on the floor facing me. "I'm so sorry! He just came in here looking for you and you know how I am with confrontation!" Her eyes widen, "Not that he was confrontational or anything like that! I just mean-shit Lou... Beckett is super-hot!"

A loud laugh bursts out of me, "Oh, trust me, I get it."

"I really am sorry," she says, quieter this time.

"It's okay." I blow out a breath, "Honestly, I'm glad you did it."

"Yeah?" Maddie perks up, clearly relieved, "Want to tell me what he was doing still at your house this morning, answering your phone?"

"It wasn't like that."

Her brows raise, "You just had a hot guy sharing your bed all night, but it somehow wasn't *like that*?"

I roll my eyes, "I mean he didn't sleep over."

Maddie scrunches up her features, "So what, he came over for breakfast?"

With I sigh, I tell Maddie everything that happened. About him showing up at the High School. About the tickets and sitting through the play together. About me bailing on him and then me waking up to him fixing my porch.

"That's..." Maddie shakes her head, "wow."

"That's just the start of it." I sit up straighter, "Do you remember that kickball game when we were like seven? The one where Beckett threw the ball at that kid who knocked me over?"

"Remember?" she snorts, "You talked about that game for weeks afterwards. It was the day you *fell in love with Beckett.*"

I swallow, "He brought that game up today."

The memory of his words hits me square in the chest and I barely notice Maddie's gasp.

I know he didn't have the same sort of crush on me as I had on him. I get it was different. But if my younger self had known...

But that doesn't matter now. Because life may have sent us traveling down separate paths, but we managed to find each other right back where we started.

My throat tightens and the tears I've been fighting since driving away from my house finally win.

"Ohmygod, don't cry!" Maddie scoots closer, already sniffling.

"Why are you crying?" I start to laugh but it just comes out as more tears.

"I don't know! Because you are!" Maddie snags a stack of napkins off a shelf, handing me half, before rubbing her own tears from her face. "Why are you crying?"

"It's just... This feels like heartbreak and hope all wrapped together. And..." I squeeze my eyes shut, "and because I think I still love him."

Maddie shrieks.

Chapter 51

Elouise

MADDIE'S REACTION startles me so much I jerk back, thumping my head against the cupboard.

Her hands fly over her mouth, "Oh my god, I'm sorry! Are you okay? I'm so sorry?"

I rub my fingers over the throbbing spot on the back of my head, "I think you just scared five years off my life."

"I'm sorry." Maddie keeps her mouth covered, but I can tell she's smiling. "But, I mean, come on!" she's back to shouting. "You can't just tell me you're in love and expect me not to react!"

She has a point. Maddie's the biggest hopeless romantic out of everyone I know. Crying her way through every single romance movie ever created.

Just as she starts to ask a question, a throat clears from the other side of the counter, scaring us both. Her recent outburst must've covered up the sound of someone entering the coffee shop.

Collecting herself, Maddie brushes off her pants as she

hurries to stand, greeting the customers as though they didn't catch her sitting on the floor.

Her easy tone and cadence are soothing to listen to, so I close my eyes and let the familiarity of the space calm my soul.

I know what I want to do. Hell, I know what I'm going to do. I'm going to see where this goes. I'm going to date Beckett Stoleman.

I just want to take at least a few minutes to think it over. Make sure I'm not being some blinded-by-love fool. Because as completely unlikely and ridiculous as it might seem, I am in love with him. And it's not the same infatuation I had with him when I was growing up. That was... hero-worship, hormones, and innocence. It felt like love, but what teenaged Elouise felt doesn't hold a candle to the feelings I have for Beckett now. This love is built on his kindness and willingness to help. His protective nature. Honesty. And the way he fucks me, like he's trying to leave his mark on me for days to come.

The love I feel now is far from innocent, and so much more fun.

Before Maddie can hand off the drinks she's currently making, the rain stick at the front door alerts us to another customer entering.

I feel guilty about not helping, since she's clearly working alone today, but it's been a long time since I've made a real latte and I'm sure I'd just slow her down, so I stay put. Listening as Maddie hands off the drinks and greets the next customer.

I start to think about Beckett showing up here, asking Maddie for my whereabouts, and how awkward that probably was for both of them.

My lips pull into a smile at the thought, and I listen to the newcomer order a black coffee to go.

The male voice sounds somewhat familiar, but I can't focus on it, my mind too distracted by sudden thoughts of Beckett.

S. J. Tilly

Beckett sitting in this very building with me drinking his own black coffee. Beckett following me up to my bedroom. Beckett watching me undress. Beckett burying his face in my pussy.

Heat blooms between my legs.

Maddie shuffles around me, moving back to the counter, handing over the coffee.

I don't even know what was hotter, Beckett eating me out and taking me for the first time. Or Beckett throat fucking me on the forest floor.

The heat turns to molten lava.

Good god, that man is talented.

Maddie asks the customer if there's anything else he needs – in a tone that really means *why are you still here* – but I don't listen to his response, because I'm done thinking.

Taking my phone out, I pull up Beckett's contact and tap out a text. Before I can overthink it, I hit send.

Me: I think we should date.

Those three little dots dance on the screen seconds later.

Then his answer appears.

Beckett: Good. I'll pick you up at 7:00.

Chapter 52

Beckett

I SHIFT my truck into park, planning to go ring the doorbell, but Elouise is already coming out the front door.

For a moment, I'm frozen in place.

She's just so damn pretty.

Her hair is pulled back into a high ponytail, her lips are painted a soft pink, and she's wearing a dress. A fucking dress. The grey material fluttering around her calves. The navy cardigan and little matching shoes making her look every inch the teacher she is. And, god help me, I've never wanted to fuck a teacher more in my life.

Gritting my teeth against the urge to drag her back inside by her hair and do just that, I get out and stride around to the passenger door, opening it a moment before she reaches me.

"Hi," her voice is breathy, and I wonder if she's having the same thoughts I am.

"Hi," I take the small purse from her hands and set it on the dashboard. My truck isn't obnoxiously high, but I still place my hands on her waist under the guise of helping her up.

Thankfully she doesn't swat my hands away, letting me keep them on her as she climbs up, settling into the seat.

"Thanks," Elouise bites her lip as she glances over at me.

I don't know why she's acting so shy all of a sudden, but I kinda like it.

The skirt of her dress is draped over the side of the seat. It's not actually in danger of getting shut in the door, but I want the excuse to touch her again. Gently grabbing the material, I slide my fingers under her thigh, tucking in the hem of her dress. It's a simple movement, but still causes her to draw an inhale. Which draws my attention to her chest and sends a rumble through my own.

Now that she's up close, all I can see is the low cut of her dress. And fucking hell, her tits look amazing. I want to face-plant into them. Feel that warm soft flesh against my cheek.

"It's not really fair," Elouise's words snap my eyes back up to meet hers.

"What's not fair?"

"I gave you this to look at," she dips her chin down, gesturing to her cleavage, "but you're completely covered." She presses a hand against my chest.

This minx.

Keeping a straight face, I hold her gaze, "I'll wear my scoop neck next time."

Elouise snorts out a laugh and whatever uncomfortableness had been sitting between us melts away.

Unable to resist I lean into the hand she has pressed against my chest and lightly kiss her temple.

I want to linger, but if I don't step away now, we'll never make it out of the driveway.

"Watch your hands," I tell her, stepping back.

When she clasps them in her lap I shut the door.

Back in the driver's seat, I grip the gear shift but pause. I don't know why I hadn't done it before, but I take this moment to try and see us objectively. Me with my usual jeans, scuffed leather work boots, and a black cotton shirt. Elouise looking cute-as-fuck in a dress and coordinated accessories. Me in my twelve-year-old truck, living with my cousin, working part-time at my own company. Elouise owning her own home, working full-time as a teacher, changing the future.

Noticing my delay, Elouise turns in her seat to look at me, "What are you thinking about?"

Not wanting any more secrets, I decide to answer honestly, "I'm thinking that you're too good for me."

The way she huffs and rolls her eyes pisses me off. She thinks I'm joking.

I take my hand off the shifter, open my door, climb back out and circle around the front of the truck.

Her eyes dart down to the door lock as I near her.

"Don't you dare." I see her consider doing it anyway, but something on my face stops her.

Yanking the door open, I lean in, crowding her space.

My right hand lands on the center console and I use my left to grip the side of her neck. "I wasn't joking," I tell her, my thumb pressed to the hollow of her throat, "you are too good for me."

Her eyes widen, "But you have-"

My grip tightens, her warm flesh giving under the pressure, "So help me god, if you say something about money right now, I'm gonna spank you so hard you won't be able to sit tomorrow."

A small moan vibrates against my fingers and my dick strains in response.

"Fucking hell, Smoky, you're just proving my point. It's not even your beautiful face, or perfect body." I can feel her throat work through a swallow. "And it's not just the way you respond

247

to me. It's everything you are, from the inside out. You're *good*. You're just... good."

I let my forehead rest against hers. I didn't mean to make this so intense; I just can't seem to control my emotions when it comes to this woman.

Her exhale feathers over my lips, "You're good too, Beckett. I wouldn't be here if you weren't."

My little fire-starter. Of course, she would feel the need to say something nice.

I smirk, "I'm not *that* good."

To prove my point, I give in to desire, drop my head and sink my teeth into the soft swell of her breast.

Chapter 53

Elouise

WITH A SHOCKED CRY, I shove Beckett away. He laughs before stepping back and shutting my door, giving me precious few seconds to get myself under control before he gets back in the truck, again, and finally backs us out of the driveway.

Beckett leaves the radio off as he navigates out of my neighborhood. He'd texted me earlier to tell me he was on nephew duty and that I should eat dinner before our date, but that we'd go out for a nightcap. He didn't tell me where we were going and I'm tempted to ask, but instead I let the silence settle around us comfortably.

The sun has already set but looking out the window I catch glimpses of the moon reflecting off the lake. The final bits of ice on the surface have finally melted, giving way to spring.

He turns onto the one main street that runs through town, but he heads away from where most of the bars are located. My curiosity builds, but the answer comes quickly when Beckett flips on his blinker and steers us into the Dairy Queen parking lot.

As is typical, there are a few cars lined up at the drive-thru so Beckett pulls up behind the last car.

When he turns to see my reaction, I don't even try to hide my grin.

His own lips tug into a smile, "I take it you approve?"

"I approve."

I mean, who needs a cocktail when you can have ice cream.

The line of cars shift forward, and Beckett lowers his window in anticipation of being next. The scent of chocolate drifts in and my mouth begins to water.

"Know what you want?"

I nod, "Chocolate dipped cone, please."

He makes a sound of approval, then surprises me when it's our turn to order and he gets the same thing for himself.

As we once again wait our turn, the sounds of the night filter in through the open window. Neither of us says anything. This feels like a settling period, like we need the quiet to bring us back to some sort of equilibrium.

So much has happened in the last 24 hours. Beckett coming to the high school and our conversation there. My slipping away. Him showing up at my house and laying *everything* out this morning. Admitting things I'd never even dreamed to hope for. And now... this. This simple outing to the local DQ that should feel silly, but actually feels perfect.

Beckett pulls up to the window, hands over cash, and hands me one of the chocolate coated ice cream cones. The perfect swirl on top just begging to be eaten.

It's a strictly drive-thru establishment, so when Beckett pulls away from the window he maneuvers one-handed into an open parking spot in the little lot. Some cars just drive off, but we're not the only vehicle over here doing the park-and-eat.

The car a few spots down from us has a group of teenagers in it and seeing them is when it hits me – why this feels so perfect. This is the exact sort of date I dreamed of going on with Beckett when I was young. I can even remember sitting in this very lot, my family in the car eating our treats, and me pretending it was Beckett I was with instead.

"I need to tell you something," I say the words before I can chicken out.

"Alright."

Hearing him turn in his seat, I look away from the teenagers and face Beckett. "I-" My cheeks fill with air, and I blow the breath out slowly, closing my eyes. "I was in love with you for... so long. That kickball game, the one you brought up this morning, that started my, um, infatuation with you. I remember telling Maddie about it the next day. And probably every *next day* for several weeks." I squeeze my eyes shut even tighter. "And I wasn't just obsessed with you for the summer. It was, oh my god, it was *years*. Like all the way up to that damn Christmas party, when I finally swore off my feelings for you. But even that didn't stop my stupid heart. Because when I saw you at BeanBag that time when I was working there in high school and I spilled hot coffee all over myself, I fell all over again. And so this... it just all feels a little surreal."

I slowly crack my lids open, expecting the worst since Beckett didn't make a sound during my admission. But instead of judgment, I find Beckett staring at me with a big dopey grin on his face.

When he still doesn't say anything, I widen my eyes, "Well?"

His grin stays in place as he shrugs, "What can I say? I'm fucking irresistible."

"Oh my god," I shake my head, "I'm in love with an idiot."

The words are out before I even realize what I'm saying.

But instead of freaking out at my accidental declaration, Beckett's grin turns into a smirk, "Like I said, I'm irresistible."

Fighting the blush that's trying to consume my whole body,

I roll my eyes, "Uh huh."

Keeping his eyes on mine, Beckett opens his mouth and bites off the top half of his ice cream. Teeth sliding through the freezing cold dessert.

My mouth drops open, "Ahh! What are you doing?"

Beckett chews twice then swallows the whole mouthful and I'm positive my face reflects the disgust I feel.

"What?"

"Isn't that cold?" I ask, not sure why I have to explain my reaction.

"I guess," he takes another massive bite and I have to look away.

"I can't watch that," I say with a shiver.

"How are you supposed to eat it?"

"I dunno, like a human," I reply, carefully biting off a piece of the chocolate coating.

Beckett laughs, "And how am I eating it?"

He takes another bite, obliterating the rest of the ice cream piled on his cone.

I eye him, "Like a German Shepard."

Beckett starts to laugh, then freezes as he works to swallow what's in his mouth and not spit it out.

I give him a look that says "see" then continue to work on my own cone.

I can feel Beckett's gaze on me while I catch the dripping ice cream with my tongue. Licking the vanilla goodness carefully, one section at a time.

"I'd have said you need to eat it quickly in order to not make a mess, but clearly you've mastered this skill."

In answer, I smile at him as my lips close over the top point.

By the time I finally finish, Beckett has shifted around in his seat several times and looks ready to stomp back over to my side of the truck.

Chapter 54

Beckett

THIS WOMAN IS TRYING to kill me.

First, it's those tits. Then she admits she's in-love with me. Fucking in-love with me! And as if that wasn't enough, watching her eat that goddamn cone was the final dagger through my heart. I haven't figured out the details yet, and 24 hours ago I would've said I wasn't certain, but I'm certain now, this woman is my future.

"I'm taking us back to your place," I slam the car into drive the second she pops the last bite of ice cream into her sweet mouth.

Elouise doesn't make any comments about my somewhat reckless driving, nor does she comment on my single-mindedness. But it doesn't escape my attention that she's pressing her legs together. And if she keeps squirming around like that, I'm not gonna make it the last two minutes it's gonna take to reach her house.

Gripping the steering wheel in my left hand, I reach over with my right and press my palm down onto the top of her thigh.

S. J. Tilly

Her leg stills, and then I feel the slide of her fingers over mine. She doesn't try to dislodge my grip, she just laces her fingers between mine.

I slow as we approach a 4-way stop sign, but seeing no one else on the road, I drive through.

She tries to stifle her snicker, but I hear it.

"You okay?" her innocent tone is belied by her fingertips tracing over my knuckles.

I wasn't quite sure if she realized how much of a tease she was being, but now I know. She's absolutely fucking with me.

Her driveway appears in front of us, and I pull in – stopping a few feet from her closed garage door.

Feeling the tension growing between us, Elouise scrambles out of her seat, slamming the truck door. But her shorter legs are no match for my own so I'm right behind her by the time she reaches the front door.

I don't give her space. We're past that.

Bracing my hands on the doorframe, I press my front into her back. My hard arousal throbbing against the soft roundness of her ass.

Elouise arches her back, pushing into me, but keeps her head down as she digs through her tiny purse.

"Open the door, Babe." I lean down, inhaling against the top of her head, "I need to be inside you."

She whimpers before letting out a few quiet curses, "I don't have my keys. I forgot to switch them over when I grabbed this bag."

"Fuck," I exhale the word, grinding into her.

She tries the handle, but it doesn't give. I'm not happy about being locked out, but at least she didn't leave her house wide open.

Reluctantly, I step back, "We need to get you a lock with a passcode."

Elouise waves the comment off, "It's okay, follow me."

She turns and hurries down the stairs heading back towards the garage. I expect her to stop at the garage door and open it with a keypad, but she keeps going and I notice there's no keypad for the garage door either. *I'll need to change that.*

Staying behind her, I follow as she turns around the side of the garage. I wait for her to stop and pick up one of those fake rocks with a key hidden in it. And I'm ready to lecture her because those aren't safe. Thieves know how to spot them. But she doesn't do that. She keeps walking, down the side of the garage and then around to the back. It's dark back here, and with the trees blocking out the moonlight I can hardly see where I'm stepping. Whatever her plan is, this is not safe. It's too dark and anyone could be hiding back here.

Elouise finally stops and I see she's standing in front of a backdoor leading into the garage.

I'm still wondering where the key for this door is, when Elouise grips the handle, leans her shoulder into the door, pulls up on the handle, and swings the door open.

She steps into the dark garage, calling "come on" over her shoulder, and a static haze starts to fuzz the edge of my vision.

Following her into the pitch-black garage, I kick the door shut behind me.

Unlocked.

She left this door unlocked.

Apparently having done this before, Elouise walks through the pitch-black garage to the door that leads into the house. And without the accompanying sound of a key in a lock, she opens that door too.

Unlocked.

The entire way into her house was unlocked.

A soft glow fills the doorway, silhouetting Elouise as she

steps up into her house. And the static in my brain is now a full volume buzzing.

I shove the door shut and flip the deadbolt in place.

Elouise has slipped her shoes off and is standing barefoot in front of me. Looking sexy, and cute, and extremely fucking vulnerable. The perfect picking for a predator.

"This is *Not* acceptable!" my volume is low, but I can feel the intensity of my words crackle in the air between us.

She freezes, holding still as I take a step closer, "But I thought you wanted to-"

My jaw flexes as my hand darts out and grips the base of her ponytail. "What I want is for you to be safe." I growl, the full breadth of my emotions coming into focus. Anger at her for being so foolish. Anger at myself for not checking that everything was locked up. And a bitter mix of helplessness and worry because what if...

The haze intensifies.

"What are you talking about?" Elouise pants, eyes wide.

"I'm talking about you living in a house with a door that isn't locked!"

Her mouth forms an O as it clicks together. She reaches up to place her hand on my biceps. The look on her face tells me her next words are meant to placate me. "It's always been like that." But as soon as she says it, she realizes her mistake.

"Always." Keeping my hold of her ponytail, I walk her backwards towards the living room. "It's *always* been like that?" She stumbles but I loop my other arm around her waist to keep her upright. Her feet skid across the floor as I take the final few strides to the couch.

"Beckett-"

I don't wait for whatever excuse she's going to try. Changing my hold, I spin her sideways, so her shoulder is against my chest and her hip is pressed against my cock. I hook a forearm around her stomach and use my other hand to bend her over.

"What are-" her words turn into a squeal when I lift her into the air, bent in half over my arm.

"Feet up," I snap. And her knees bend.

With one step to the side, I drop myself into a sitting position on the arm of the couch, Elouise draped perfectly over my lap. Face inches away from the seat cushion, feet dangling in the air.

"Beckett, what are you doing!?"

"Teaching you a fucking lesson."

Reclaiming my grip on her ponytail, I hold her in place while my other hand pulls up the hem of her dress until a pair of lacy white panties are revealed.

The material stops just above the bottom curve of her ass, covering most of the cheek. *That won't do.* I tug the material until it's bunched in my fist and give it a firm tug. The movement snugs the material between her cheeks, and since I'm pulling from the back, it's tightening along her front, putting pressure on her pussy.

She moans, and I tug it a little harder.

"God, Beckett..." she wiggles in my grip and images of that unlocked door snap back into the forefront of my mind.

"If you know what's good for you, you're gonna shut your mouth and take your punishment like a good girl."

I release my grip on her panties, the material secured between her ass cheeks and out of my way.

"Punishment?"

In answer to her question, I let my hand come down against her bare flesh.

She shrieks, and I rub my hand over the sting, only for a

moment, then I spank her again. The sound of skin on skin going straight to my dick.

Elouise squirms, and I smooth my hand over the pinkening flesh. Seeing my mark on her hits me straight in the chest, and I let my hand slap down against her other cheek.

She cries out, but it's not pain filling her tone. It's desire.

Her head strains against my grip on her hair, but when I adjust my hand so it's not tugging on her scalp so hard, she strains forward until the tug is just as tight as it was before.

"Fuck." I growl, pulling her hair a little harder. "You like that, don't you?"

She groans.

"Answer me, Dirty Girl. Do you like this? Do you like having your hair pulled and your ass slapped?"

Her whole body shudders against my lap, "Yes. Beckett... Oh my god. I'm so wet."

My hand comes down on her bare skin again. And again. "Fuck. You're so fucking perfect."

Unable to take it anymore, I grip her waist and stand.

"I'm taking you now." I warn her, spinning so she's facing the armrest where I was just sitting. "I hope you're on birth control because I'm fucking you bare and you're gonna take it."

She braces her hands against the edge of the couch and bends at the waist. "I am. I'm ready. I want it."

My hands fumble opening my jeans. My fingers finally flipping the button open and releasing the zipper. With a few more quick movements my cock is freed, hard as steel, precum glistening at the tip.

Her dress is still bunched around her waist, and I stroke myself twice before I let go of my dick and use both hands to roughly pull her panties down to her knees. The evidence of her own arousal dampening the material.

The sight is too tempting.

Bending down, I shove my face into her core, licking from her clit to her little pink asshole.

Her hips jolt and I grin. *This is gonna be fun.*

Chapter 55

Elouise

My entire body is on fire. My ass is deliciously sore. My pussy is throbbing with need, clenching around nothing, and Beckett just... holy fuck he just licked over my asshole, and I've never felt anything like that before.

I lean my forehead against the arm rest and look down. My bare feet against the wood floor. My cute and probably destroyed underwear around my knees, stopping my legs from parting any wider. Beckett's steps forward, one scuffed work boot on either side of my spread feet. Trapping me. Surrounding me.

His jeans feel rough against the sensitive skin on the back of my thighs.

"Beckett, please!" I beg when he doesn't move fast enough.

I watch one large hand snake around the front of my thigh, moving towards my core. Then in a blur of motion, his hand slaps up against my spread pussy.

Holy. Fuck.

The first tremors signaling an orgasm ripple through me, and I moan.

I feel his cock press against my entrance, and I arch back, trying to impale myself on him.

He stills and I want to cry.

"Tsk tsk, Baby. You wait and take what I give you."

Another slap hits directly on my clit a second before he shoves his full length inside me. Splitting me. And I shatter.

Beckett slams into me, over and over again, while my pussy clutches at him. My climax is so intense, even my throat clenches and I have to fight to pull in air. The waves of pleasure crash over me, but I can tell there's more. There's a ledge inside me and I feel like I'm teetering on the edge, but I can't make sense of it because *oh my god* I don't think I've ever felt anything like this.

Beckett grunts with each thrust. His hips meeting my ass each time.

He's so deep. So fucking deep.

I have to tell him.

"You're so deep."

I'm not sure I say it loud enough for him to hear, but he answers me with a hard slap to my ass and I clench around him.

"That's right, Baby. I'm so fucking deep." Another rough thrust. "This pussy is mine. This ass is mine."

I moan in response; words are no longer possible.

His hips slow, just the smallest amount, and my eyes open again. I hadn't realized they'd closed but his change of tempo has a warning light flaring to life inside of me.

His palms rub the skin of my hips. Sliding up, then together, gripping my ass in both of his large hands. I feel his fingers dig into my flesh as he rotates his hands, then he's... ohmygod he's pulling my cheeks apart.

His cock is still sliding in and out of me. All the way in, almost all the way out.

There's a sound I can't understand and then a wetness trickles down my crack.

Did he? Did he just spit on my ass?

Something swipes over my asshole, and I jolt, but the fingers gripping me tighten.

"Relax." Beckett himself sounds anything but relaxed, but I try to obey.

My eyes slide shut, and I picture what he's doing to me. Standing behind me. Watching. Spreading me wide.

What has to be his thumb slides over me again. There.

It's too much.

But I need it.

How did I not know that I needed this?

My back arches and Beckett lets out a dark chuckle. "My perfect girl."

Then he presses his thumb into me.

My entire awareness narrows onto his every movement. His hand. His cock. The dual movements in and out of me. The way his cock is rubbing against this place inside of me. This place... *Oh* god... He doesn't stop. Everything inside me is building around this need to... release. His thumb... goddamn why does that, "feels so good" I moan out loud.

He increases his speed, "That's right. Take it all, Baby."

The hand that was still gripping my ass lets go and slides around to my clit. Strong fingers press against my bundle of nerves, rubbing, pinching. His hips move harder, his thumb goes deeper...

And I fucking explode.

My whole body seizes. But he doesn't let up. The fingers against my clit move faster. And I'm helpless to stop him. My legs shake. And I hear the sound of wetness dripping onto the floor below me. My eyes fly open but I'm trembling too much to make sense of what's happening.

"*Fuuuck!*" Beckett growls, giving my clit one final squeeze, "Squirting like such a good girl."

I want to be mortified, but the praise in his voice overwhelms the urge to be embarrassed.

Beckett pounds into me once more. A second time. Then he's roaring out his release holding himself as deep as he'll go for one pulse. A second. Then he pulls out, and I feel the rest of his release splash across my ass.

Chapter 56

Beckett

I STRUGGLE to remain on my feet, as I enjoy the view before me.

There's never been a more perfect sight than Elouise bent over, dress flipped up, covered in my cum, our combined mess dripping off her onto the floor. The caveman part of my brain wants to beat my chest, and the rest of my brain agrees. The sight is filthy. And hot as fuck.

If this doesn't seal my claim on her, I don't know what will.

Finally, stepping back, I remember this started as a punishment. So instead of getting something to clean her up, I slide her panties back up her legs, securing them in place, stickiness and all.

She squirms and I'm sure there's a cringe on her face, but this is the least of what she deserves for putting herself in danger.

I keep a hand on her back and bend to whisper into her ear. "You're gonna keep all the doors locked from now on. And I'm going to come over tomorrow to fix that other door." My hand trails up to give a gentle tug on her disheveled ponytail. "And I swear to fucking god, if I ever find you being unsafe again, I'll tie you down, do this all again, twice over, only next time I won't let you come." My lips press against her ear, "Nod if you understand."

She nods.

I lick up the side of her neck, then I force myself to walk away from the prettiest sight on earth.

With Elouise still bent over the couch, I leave.

Chapter 57

Elouise

When I finally blink my eyes open, the need to pee is so strong I know I've slept past my usual wake up time.

My first attempt to move out of bed has every muscle in my body singing. The delicious ache is mostly focused between my legs, but every part of me is some level of sore. I had no idea sex could leave you feeling like you did a bootcamp style workout.

I take my time getting to my feet and shuffling to the bathroom, and when I finally lower myself, my ass cheeks give a sting of protest. But I find myself smiling through the discomfort, because last night was a series of new experiences for me, and if the heat simmering under my skin at the memory is any indication, they were all experiences I'd like to do again.

Finishing my morning routine, I pull on a comfy pair of leggings and a sweater and head downstairs. Beckett said he'd be by sometime today to fix my door, but he didn't say when.

Reaching the bottom of the stairs, I glance towards the couch then turn towards the kitchen.

My cheeks are heating all over again at the memory of

wiping our mess off the floor and I find myself laughing. I feel almost proud of what happened. Maybe it should've felt degrading to be left like that, but it didn't. It was kinda hot.

The cum-soaked underwear however, was not as hot. By the time I got upstairs it was cold and sticky and I threw them in the garbage as I stripped down on my way to the shower.

I cover another yawn, as my coffee maker signals that it's done brewing. I'm pouring out my first cupful when I hear Beckett's truck rumble up the driveway.

Mug in hand, I open the front door and am surprised to see the passenger side open, followed by Beckett's nephew doing a boneless slide out of the pickup.

It's before 10:00 am on a Sunday so I understand the feeling.

Beckett smiles at me, as he comes around to close the kid's door. "Morning, Smoky."

"Good morning," with my slippered feet, I take the few steps down from the porch to the front walk.

"You remember Clint?" Beckett asks, using a hand to ruffle the kid's hair.

"I do," my heart warms seeing the two of them together. "Morning, Clint."

He mumbles something like *good mornin'*, giving me the quickest glance before looking back at the ground.

"Mind opening the garage door for us? Clint's gonna help me fix your door today, and we need to measure a few things." Beckett settles his hand on the kid's shoulder.

"I can do that," I lift my mug to my lips in an attempt to cover my face.

Just seeing him standing there is making me blush. But his smirk is the only confirmation I need that he knows exactly what I'm thinking about.

Walking through the house, I open the garage door and wait for them to join me. In the time it takes to open, a notebook and pencil have appeared in Clint's hands and Beckett is holding a tape measure.

"Thank you for doing this," I tell them both, meaning it. I hadn't really thought about that stupid door, since it's been that way for as long as I can remember, but once Beckett pointed out – rather drastically – how unsafe it was, I realized how stupid I'd been to leave it.

Beckett nudges Clint.

"You're welcome," the kid says, scuffing his shoe on the concrete floor.

Beckett rolls his eyes at Clint's shyness. He wasn't this shy when we met at the Science Fair, and I've seen him in the hallways at school a few times since then, but I'm thinking that being at my house is making him feel uncertain.

"I don't know how long it takes to fix a door, but I'd be happy to make you boys lunch." Clint's eyes dart up to me then over to Beckett. "Or something else..." I tack on.

"I promised Little Man we could do fast-food for lunch," Beckett says with a shake of his head, "but this will probably take a while. His mom is on a 12-hour shift, so if you want to make dinner we can stick around for that."

"I can do that." I think for a moment, before I ask, "Clint, what's your favorite dessert?"

"Brownies!" his exclamation is out before I even finish the question.

"Okay," I laugh, "I can make some brownies. Any requests on the entrée?"

Clint shrugs, then seems to consider it, "Pasta?"

I nod, "Pasta is good. Any preference on sauce?"

He looks up at Beckett, "What's that white stuff called?"

Beckett clears his throat before answering, and I have to bite my lips to keep from laughing. "Alfredo."

The boys have been at it for hours.

True to his word, the two of them left for a bit around lunchtime coming back with to-go drinks and white paper bags. Beckett offered to pick me up something, but I passed, opting to make a quick sandwich before heading to the grocery store to get stuff to make dinner.

The timer alerting me to strain the noodles sounds just as the door to the house opens then closes.

At first, I was surprised when I saw that Beckett bought a whole new door to replace the faulty one, but then when I thought about it, I realized I wasn't surprised at all. Just like I wasn't really surprised that he bought a wireless keypad to install for my garage door and a new deadbolt with a keypad for the front door. Ensuring I'll never be locked out even with every door firmly secured.

"Smells delicious!" Beckett herds Clint into the kitchen ahead of him.

"Hopefully it tastes good too," hoisting the strained noodles up, I dump them into the pot with the alfredo sauce. Carefully stirring it all together.

After insisting I don't need any help, the boys wash their hands at the sink, then take their seats at the table.

I plate up broccoli and roasted chicken on the side but am happily surprised when they both mix it all together and begin eating with vigor.

I ask questions about other projects they've done together,

and they both answer while clearing their plates in record time. Whatever awkwardness Clint had been feeling earlier seems to have been shattered by a pile of pasta.

He's barely finished his last bite when he turns to face me, "Can I have more?"

Beckett snorts, "This kid can eat as much as I do."

I smile, "Would you like more, too?"

"You know I do."

I purposefully don't look at him as I refill their plates. I don't know if it's just me, but I swear I'm hearing an innuendo in everything he says.

Feeling chattier, Clint tells me all about his current teacher, the kids in his class, and why he thinks math is the worst subject ever. Outwardly I tell him why math is important, but inwardly I completely agree.

With a mouth still full of noodles, Clint asks, "Did you really make brownies, too?"

"Good god," Beckett laughs, "can you at least finish swallowing before you ask for more."

My eyes snap over to Beckett's and just when I think I'm the only one with my mind in the gutter, Beckett looks up and winks.

This bastard.

Clint finishes his food, sticking his tongue out as proof, "There. Now can I have a brownie?"

Beckett sighs, "Dude, don't ask me."

Clint turns those puppy dog eyes on me.

"Yes, but we have to cook them first."

His jaw drops open, "What?!"

"I could've baked them earlier, but then you wouldn't be eating them right from the oven. And is there really anything better than a warm brownie... with ice cream?"

Clint's lips press together, then gives in, "I guess not."

After we start the oven, Beckett makes Clint help him clean up dinner, insisting that I go sit down.

When the oven chimes that it's preheated, I start to rise but Clint calls out that he'll put the pan in.

He'd been skeptical when I showed him the pan ready to bake resting in the fridge, but I'm confident I'll win him over. It's a trick I learned from Maddie after all, and she's a whizz in the kitchen.

While they bake, Clint tells me about the time he was making cupcakes with his grandma and they set the oven on fire. Beckett clarifies that his mom had forgotten to set a timer, and that it was just really smoky, but Clint ignores him, going back into elaborate details.

Thankfully we don't set my oven on fire, and a few minutes later we are loaded up with bowls of ice cream and warm chocolate brownies, and headed into the living room.

Clint claims one of the overstuffed reading chairs, and I'm silently grateful he didn't sit on the couch with us. Nothing *untoward* actually got on the couch, but it just feels wrong to have anyone other than Beckett or I near the now infamous arm rest.

I let Clint pick what we watch, and he lands on some animated superhero movie. I'm not familiar, but then again, I'm not really paying attention. I give up on my dessert after a few minutes, hitting my limit, and Beckett gladly finishes what I have left in a matter of bites.

Setting our bowls on the coffee table, Beckett leans back, pulling me into his side. His warmth and strength becoming my new version of a security blanket.

He's shown me so many sides of himself. The survivalist and teacher. The carpenter and uncle. The dirty, *dirty* man capable of bringing me to a level of bliss I wasn't even aware of and the laid back guy who wants to eat ice cream and cuddle on the couch.

He's so easy to be around. And equally easy to love.

Laying my head on his chest, his arm tightens around my shoulders, and feeling safer than I've ever felt before, I let my eyes drift close.

Chapter 58

Beckett

ELOUISE LETS out a small snuffling sound, her body soft and warm against mine.

When I realized both her and Clint were fast asleep, I turned the volume down but left the tv playing. I'd been mentally preparing myself to leave, when Natasha texted thirty minutes ago to say she'd come pick up Clint so I could stay here. My cousin likes to give me a hard time, but she understands me well. Especially after the mess at my parent's house, which my mom gladly filled her in on, Natasha has been on Team Elouise. And I like to think her stopping over here on her way home is because she wants the best for me, and not just that she wants me to fall in love so I'll move out of her house.

Headlights flash through the front window, alerting me to Natasha's arrival, so I carefully extract myself from Elouise and lay her gently onto the couch. Knowing Clint is impossible to wake, I just hoist him up into my arms and with some minor jostling, I get us outside and down the steps.

Natasha's grinning by the time I reach her car - probably because she knows how heavy this damn kid is when he's flopping around dead weight. And it only takes a little bit of maneuvering for me to deposit Clint in the backseat, stepping aside to let Natasha secure him.

Closing the door, my cousin turns to face me. And then she just stares.

"What?" I ask, feeling way too unnerved.

She waits another beat before answering, but then nods her head towards the house. "I like her."

I narrow my eyes, sensing an agenda, "I like her, too."

"Do you?" she tilts her head. "Or do you love her?"

I don't fight the grin that pulls across my lips, "I love her."

She looks surprised by my easy admission, "Oh. Good."

It's my turn to be surprised, "That's it? No lecture?"

"Here's your lecture: don't fuck it up."

I grin harder, "I'm doing my best."

She rolls her eyes, "That's comforting." She glances back at the house, "Have you told her? That you love her?"

My face sobers, "Not yet." Natasha gives me another look, one that says *you're a fucking dumbass.* "I'll tell her tomorrow."

"Smart plan," she flicks my shoulder as she starts around to the driver's side. "With any luck, you'll move out of my house and into this one by summer."

Watching her drive away, I think the idea over, and decide I should make it happen sooner.

Chapter 59

Elouise

THE SOUND of breaking glass jerks me out of a dead sleep.

"What-" I rub at my eyes and see Beckett's already on his feet. "What was that?"

"I'm gonna go see," he reaches down pulling his jeans on, "stay here." I start to climb out of bed, but he aims a finger at me. "Stay here, Elouise."

There's another round of shattering glass, and now that I'm awake it sounds like it's coming from right outside.

"I'll stay," I agree. "But I'm not gonna just lay in bed while you go investigate."

Beckett moves to the window, and pulls back the corner of the curtain, "Goddamnit."

"What? What is it?" I step up next to him and peek out, not sure what I'm looking for.

"Some asshole broke the windows on my truck."

My eyes move over to the driveway and sure enough, the windshield is covered in a spiderweb of cracks and the passenger window is smashed to bits. As we both stare, the red glow of brake lights flare from just out of view, followed by the unmistakable sound of a car driving off.

Beckett sighs, "Well that sucks."

I rest a hand on his back, feeling a little shaken up, "Why would someone do that?"

He shrugs and I see him open the keypad on his phone and type in 9-1-1, "Who knows. Probably some punk kids. Since I don't have a description, I doubt they'll catch whoever did it, but I'll need a report for the insurance."

"I'm sorry, Beckett." I lean into his side. "People are the worst."

"Thanks, Babe." He presses a kiss to the top of my head before hitting call. "Go back to bed, you've got work in the morning."

I doubt I'll be able to fall asleep now, but I have nothing helpful to add so I climb back into bed and listen to his side of the conversation while he explains what happened.

I pull the blanket up closer to my chin.

This is such a small community, and I know bad things can happen anywhere, but randomly breaking someone's car windows... It's just so weird. And pointless.

Laying back against the pillows, I close my eyes and let Beckett's voice settle around me.

I barely even remember coming to bed, there's just a foggy memory of stumbling from the couch to the bedroom. But I do remember the feeling of relief that washed through me when Beckett said he was staying the night.

A warm hand settled over the blanket against my chest and my eyes flutter open.

Beckett presses a kiss to my forehead before giving me a soft smile. "Sleep. I'll be back up to join you soon."

"Okay," I yawn halfway through the word, accepting that maybe I am tired enough to do what he's asking.

Chapter 60

Beckett

WAITING for the cops to show up, I move through the first level of Elouise's house rechecking every door and window.

I'm sure this is just some random ass bullshit but having any sort of violence this close to Elouise is stressing me out. Because what if I hadn't been here? Or if I hadn't just fixed her locks just a few hours ago? Would they have found their way into her garage? Into her house?

I drag a hand over my face, "Fuck. What a mess."

After shoving my feet into my boots, I'm just walking out the front door when a squad car pulls up. This is not how I wanted my night to go.

I lift a hand in greeting as the officer meets me in the driveway.

I'm telling him what we heard and saw when another squad car pulls up. This doesn't warrant two cops, but that's the thing about small towns with not a lot of crime you often end up with overkill.

When the new guy walks up, he looks at me and head tilts,

"Hey, aren't you the guy who almost got pancaked at the high school a couple nights ago?"

I nod, recognizing him, "Yeah, that was me."

A bystander called the cops and I had to do a whole incident report for that too. And now that I'm thinking about it, I realize I haven't even brought it up to Elouise. So she still has no idea that happened.

Elouise...

The cogs in my brain move forward, and something clicks into place. That last detail finally aligning.

New Guy whistles, "Sorry, man. Looks like someone really doesn't like you."

But that's just it, isn't it? *What if this isn't about me?*

"Fuck." My hands curl into fists as I look over my shoulder towards Elouise's bedroom.

"What is it?" First Cop asks, clearly knowing about the incident at the high school since he doesn't ask for clarification. "Do you know who could be doing this?"

I shake my head, "No. No one I can think of. I just... fuck. I don't know if it's just bad luck. Or if it's about me." I pull in a breath, hating what I'm going to say next, "Or it could be about Elouise."

"Elouise?" First Cop looks at his notes, "That your girl-friend? The one who owns the house?"

Girlfriend?

I nod, but the word is all wrong. It doesn't feel big enough.

Elouise. My Lou. My Smoky. She's so much more than just a girlfriend.

"Does she have any enemies?" New Guy asks.

I almost laugh at the thought of someone hating Elouise, "No. She's a fourth-grade teacher here in town. Maybe she's had a disgruntled parent or something, but there's been nothing..." I trail off, my mind flashing to that Shithead Adam crawling into her tent.

Could it be him? Is this someone who's obsessed with Elouise and pissed at me for being with her?

The cops are talking amongst themselves, and I bite down on the urge to tell them about the guy. I don't know Adam's last name and even if I did it's not exactly fair to point the finger at him with absolutely no evidence. Not to mention the fact that he could probably press assault charges against me for what I did to him in that bathroom.

At a loss for what else to do, I run my hands through my hair.

"Welp," First Cop shuts his notepad, sliding it back into his pocket, "we'll get this written up and let you know if we come across anything."

New Guy nods in agreement, "I've watched the security footage from the high school, but the angles weren't right, and it was too dark to make out anything useful." He drops a hand onto my shoulder. "Could be one big coincidence, but probably best to keep your eyes open."

I want to shrug his hand off, but I know I'm in a bad mood and don't need to take it out on this guy.

First Cop rocks back on his heels, "I'll drive by here a few more times before my shift is over. We have your contact info if we see anything suspicious."

I thank them both and wait for them to drive off before turning to face my truck.

The windshield is so smashed up I'll need to call a tow truck. And both the driver's and passenger's windows are shattered, pebbles of glass covering the entire interior.

I don't usually keep things of value in my truck, but since we were working on Elouise's doors today, I have a pile of tools in the backseat. I'm tempted to just leave them, but I know I'll be pissed if the perpetrator comes back and steals my shit. So, cursing under my breath, I reach in through the broken window, unlock the doors, and – making use of the new keypad I installed – start hauling all my crap into the garage.

By the time I'm done, back upstairs, and stripped for bed, it's nearly 4:00 am.

Elouise is sound asleep, curled up on her side, hugging a pillow. And the sight of her fills my chest with a mixture of exhaustion and panic. This woman – this person – means so damn much to me. And if something were to happen to her...

Not able to finish that thought, I crawl into bed and wrap myself around Elouise. She stirs slightly and I tighten my arms around her, cocooning her with my body. And only when I'm certain she won't be able to move without waking me, I allow myself to follow her into sleep.

Chapter 61

Elouise

I squeeze the excess water out of my hair, pull the shower curtain back, and yelp.

Beckett just smirks, holding out my towel.

"Jesus, Beckett!" I snag the towel and hold it in front of my body, as if he hasn't seen it all already. "Are you trying to scare me to death?"

He leans back against the vanity, "Hardly. Just trying to catch a peek." His eyes narrow as he looks at the shower I'm still standing in. "We'll need to switch that curtain with a glass door."

Doing my best to keep myself covered, I start to dry myself off. I'd love to have a real shower door, but I still ask him, "Why?"

"So I can watch you shower," Beckett leaves the *duh* implied.

"Hmm."

Swiping the towel over my face, I finally let my eyes focus on Beckett. He's nearly naked, wearing nothing but a pair of tented black boxer briefs. And the way he's leaned back against the counter makes his erection that much more noticeable. Not that that's the only part of him on display. His arms are crossed, bunching his biceps and making his chest look that much more defined. And then that trail of hair, leading my eyes back down...

"Do you always get up this early?" Beckett asks, but I can't look away. And I swear his dick twitches as I continue to stare at it. "Smoky?"

"What? Huh?" my eyes fly up to meet his.

He's smirking, "How much extra time do you have right now?"

I wet my lips, "I got up early so I could make us breakfast."

He pushes away from the counter, "Good. But I don't need you to make me breakfast."

"No?"

"No." Beckett steps forward, yanking the towel from my grasp. "I'll just eat you."

I gasp, feeling too revealed in the bright lights of the bathroom, but Beckett's gaze is scorching, telling me there's nothing on view that he doesn't like.

"On the bed," Beckett demands.

My whole body starts to throb in anticipation, and I hurry past him into the bedroom.

I've gotten both hands and one knee onto the mattress, ready to crawl to the middle, when Beckett's hands grip my hips. "Stop. Right there."

I freeze.

One hand slides down to tap the back of my leg that's still planted on the ground. "Up."

Shifting my weight, I bring that knee up to the mattress, leaving me naked, on all fours, at the edge of the bed.

Beckett's hands slide up and down the backs of my thighs,

and the soft caress sends my nerve endings into a riot. I'm so open to him. So exposed.

It's like last time, except it's completely different. There's no level of punishment here. This moment feels like pure revelry. Adoration.

"Wider," his words are a whisper, his hands moving to the inside of my knees, pressing them further apart. "That's my perfect girl."

My arms are already shaking, when I moaned, "Beckett."

"Elouise," his breath puffs across my sex and it's the only warning I have before he presses his face between my legs.

My back arches, pushing into the sensation, and I let out a cry of relief when his tongue laps over my clit.

Beckett groans against my core and I feel it everywhere. "Fuck, Baby. You taste so good."

There's another stroke of his tongue before his mouth leaves me and I whine in protest. But then a finger is pushing inside me, and my whine turns into a groan.

Another finger joins the first and my hands clench the blankets beneath my palms.

"More." I look back over my shoulder, seeing him crouched behind me, "I want more."

His fingers still inside me, Beckett stands. "Tell me." He slides his fingers in, then out. "Tell me exactly what you want."

My face heats with the rest of my body, "Your cock. I want your cock inside me."

A third finger slides in and I moan.

"I can never deny you." Beckett's fingers slip free. "On your back."

On boneless limbs, I scramble to the middle of the bed, letting my thighs fall open when I drop onto my back.

Beckett stands at the side of the bed, hand gripping the

base of his hard length. "Perfect." He murmurs, before crawling over me.

His hips lower, the bottom of his cock rocking along the length of my slit, and we both moan at the contact.

His hips press into mine harder, "You okay taking me bare again?"

I squirm, seeking the friction I need. "Yes." I hook my legs around his waist. "Please."

"In a moment," his calm voice infuriates me.

"Beckett!"

"One more thing," he rolls his hips, the head of his cock bumping over my clit, sending shockwaves up my spine.

"One more thing," I repeat on a pant, watching him watch me.

"Tell me again."

My brain is starting to short circuit, "Tell you what?"

He shifts his weight so he's braced on his elbows, not his hands. Our chests are pressed together now, and I swear I can feel his heartbeat against my skin.

Beckett leans in closer, putting our lips just inches apart, "Tell me you love me."

My heart cracks open.

"Tell me you love me, Elouise. I heard you say it. And I need to hear it again." His hips lift until the tip of his cock is pressed against my entrance. "I need to hear you say it." He presses in, just an inch. "Because I love you, too."

A sense of devotion swamps me at his admission and my eyes fill with emotion.

He presses in another inch, "I love you, Elouise."

Tears drip from the corners of my eyes, "I love you, too, Beckett."

His chest heaves and he slowly presses the rest of the way into me. My whole body tingles. The combination of physical and emotional pleasure is too much and tears continue to roll from my eyes.

"I've got you," Beckett promises quietly, as he kisses the corner of my eyes, catching the tears as they fall.

His hips continue to move in slow, shallow thrusts.

I spread my legs wider, wanting to take more of him. All of him.

"I love you," I whisper again.

There's a rumbling in Beckett's chest that feels like a purr against my skin, and I wrap my arms tightly around his neck.

Beckett thrusts into me, as deep as he'll go. His pelvis presses against my clit and I'm so close. So damn close.

"I'm yours, Baby." His hips flex, putting that pressure right where I need him. "Just as much as you're mine."

The truth of his words mixed with another roll of his hips is all I need to explode.

From one heartbeat to the next, my orgasm grips me, pulling me under the wave of sensation.

Beckett's movements become quicker, harder, deeper.

My fingers claw at him, pulling him as close as he can get. His arms circle under my back, holding me tight, as his body goes rigid, and he spills deep inside of me.

Chapter 62

Beckett

Driving Elouise to and from work these past few days has become a routine I'm rather fond of. That and sharing her bed. And dinners. And every other waking moment together.

Since my truck's been at the shop getting the windows replaced, I've just been staying at Elouise's, bringing her to work in the morning, using her car during the day and picking her up in the evening. She hasn't asked me to go back to Natasha's place and I haven't offered.

I know I can't just move in. Not yet. Probably. At least not without asking. Though it's very tempting.

Flipping on the turn signal, I pull into Darling Elementary's parking lot.

Lucking out with a spot in the front corner, I put Elouise's car into park and lay my head against the headrest.

There are lots of details we haven't discussed – like where to go on the perfect vacation, who's family we'll spend Christmas with, or the best way to torment Clint when he starts dating – but none of that matters to me. I'm pushing 40 and I don't want to waste another moment of my life waiting

Smoky Darling

for "the right time" to take our relationship to the next level. We know each other. We've known each other for nearly our whole lives, and a few more months isn't going to change how I feel about her.

Turning the car off, I suddenly don't feel so depressed about returning her vehicle.

The guy over at Axel's Bodyshop called earlier this morning, right after I dropped Elouise off at work – not 20 minutes ago – saying my truck was ready to be picked up. Part of me was tempted to delay the switch, but I have to run to my office downtown today and I don't want to strand Elouise here if I run late. Or worse yet, have her take an Uber and get a ride from some stranger.

Walking into the building, my hand flexes around the car keys.

This overwhelming need to protect Elouise has only grown since we openly admitted our love for each other. And until I figure out who's coming after me, I'm sure I'll continue to feel an increased level of paranoia.

A handful of kids are milling around the hallways and a glance at the oversized clock above the principal's door shows I have ten minutes before classes start.

There's a sign asking all visitors to sign in, but the principal herself spots me through the window into her office and waves me through. She's seen me enough by now to know why I'm here and her familiarity is one more boost to my confidence.

I belong here, in Elouise's life. And just because I'm handing her back her car keys today doesn't mean anything has to change.

Self-assured strides take me through the halls to Elouise's classroom.

She's sitting behind her desk, listening to a kid talk about something I can't hear. Not wanting to interrupt, I lean against the doorframe. The room is about half full of students, but Elouise keeps her attention on the kid in front of her. She nods along with the story, smiling and nodding, eventually ending on a laugh when the kid finishes.

Her smile is just as genuine as she is and – not for the first time – I think how lucky these students are to have her.

I wait until the kid is back at his desk then I clear my throat.

Elouise hears me over the chatter of students and her gaze snaps over. Her smile immediately morphs into something meant for only me.

The kids all carry on as Elouise stands and walks over to me, "Hi."

"Morning, Miss Hall."

She shakes her head at me and gestures towards the hall. I make room for her to pass then follow her a few steps away from the door.

"What are you doing here?" she asks, smile still in place.

I hold up her car keys, "Returning these." She opens her palm automatically and I set them in. "Just got the call my windows are done, and I need to head to the office, so I'll drive my truck."

"Guess that means our carpooling days are over," she says it like she's joking, but there's a hint of sadness in her tone.

I don't ever want her to be sad, but I'm a bit relieved to know I'm not the only one fond of our recent routine.

She left her hair down today, so I reach up and brush a lock back behind her ear. My hand pauses and she leans her cheek against my palm for a heartbeat.

"I'll be your chauffeur anytime you want, Babe."

I can feel her smile against my palm. "My knight in work boots."

My fingers itch to pull her closer so I can seal my mouth

over hers, but I'm aware we're at her place of work. Filled with children.

I heave out a breath, "Alright, I should let you get back in there before your kids tear the walls down."

"I suppose you're right," she sighs as my hand drops from her face. "Remember, I have parent teacher conferences tonight, so I'll get home late."

Home.

She says it as though there's no doubt I'll be staying there again tonight. And I want to fist pump the air. But I don't. I just nod, remembering that she told me about the conferences last night. "I might be late, too. I'll call when I'm heading back."

"Okay," she bites her lip, then pushes up to her toes and gives me the quickest kiss. "I love you."

Smugness fills my entire being, "I love you, too."

We've said it every day since that first time, but Elouise's cheeks still turn an adorable shade of pink each time I say it.

"Get back to work."

She rolls her eyes, then spins away from me and steps back into her classroom.

I'm chuckling to myself when I turn and bump shoulders with someone.

"Woah, sorry," I start to say, before I realize he's someone I know.

The blond man dips his chin, "Quite alright, Mr. Stoleman."

I feel like I should apologize for the last time I bumped into Mr. Olson, considering I did it with a door, but he's already walked away from me so I shrug it off and let my mind shift to work. If all goes well, I can wrap everything up today and spend tomorrow working out how to make living with Elouise permanent.

Chapter 63

Elouise

AFTER WALKING the kids down to the cafeteria for lunch, I drop back into the chair behind my desk.

I don't know why I've been in such a funk today. It's like when Beckett showed up and gave me back my keys, a little balloon of sadness inflated inside my chest.

It's stupid. I know it is. It's not like he was breaking up with me, he was just giving my car back since his is fixed now. But...

I press my fingers against my temples, attempting to quiet my building headache. "Stop it," I chastise myself. Beckett isn't going anywhere. Hell, he's so damn stubborn I probably couldn't kick him out of sleeping in my bed if I wanted to.

My mind is suddenly filled with a visual of me trying to drag a dead-weight Beckett out of bed and I almost laugh.

Knowing that the time is ticking away, I pull my lunch bag out of the bottom drawer of my desk.

I'm about to kick the drawer shut when a detail niggles in my mind...

Keys.

Setting my lunch bag on my desk, I bend down and push

the other items in the drawer aside. I swear I dropped the car keys in here after Beckett's visit. Opening the other drawers, I do a cursory look but don't see them. Dragging my purse out I unzip it and check inside even though I'm positive I didn't put them away properly this morning.

"What the hell..." I squeeze my eyes shut, trying to remember where I put them.

A crackling sound startles me as the intercom speaker above my door sparks to life, "Miss Hall, please come down to the office to collect a package."

My eyebrows raise and I quickly shove all my drawers shut before I hustle out of my classroom.

Usually, I'd be mad about having my precious lunch time taken up by interruptions, but I never get packages delivered so excitement wins out over annoyance.

When I step into the main office, the vice-principal makes a cooing sound as she hands me over the large bouquet of white lilies. "Look at these beautiful flowers!" She leans forward to sniff one while I hold the heavy vase, stunned. "Your boyfriend sure knows how to pick 'em."

One of the aides is eating her lunch in the office and she gives a soft laugh, "They're pretty, even if it is a classic funeral bouquet."

The vice-principal waves her off, "Oh hush, it's just a nice gesture. Not everything needs to have some sort of hidden meaning."

"Did Beckett drop these off?" I ask, thinking he should be downtown by now.

"Oh no, it was a delivery guy. Timed it nicely over your lunch break!"

At that reminder, I excuse myself and hurry back to my classroom knowing I'll have about five minutes to speed-eat my food.

Back at my desk, half a peanut butter sandwich hanging out of my mouth, I adjust the vase trying to get it just right. Wanting the biggest lily to point toward my chair, I give it one more twist, and a small envelope plops onto the desktop.

I hadn't even noticed it before. It must've been hidden beneath the large petals.

Dusting off my hands, I peel open the flap and slide a small card out. The front is blank white, but the inside has a hand-written message. *I'll always love you.* I gently run my finger over the letters. I don't think I've ever seen Beckett's writing before, and I want to memorize each slope.

The bell in the hallway rings, sounding the end of lunch, and I quickly cram the rest of my sandwich into my mouth before I pull out my phone and send off a quick text to Beckett.

Me: Thank you for the flowers.

Jerking open my desk drawer, I start to put my lunch bag back, when I notice my keys sitting right there at the bottom.

I roll my eyes at myself. Sometimes I can be so oblivious.

Chapter 64

Beckett

It's taken all my free will to stay focused on my meetings today, instead of taking my phone out to text my girlfriend.

Since I spend so much of my time working from home, I'm aware that my appearance in the office isn't taken lightly and I want to be present when I'm here. I also want my employees to see me as accessible, so I made a point to stay dressed down today. And it worked, but it might've worked too well because I feel like I've had a conversation with every-fucking-one and I just want to leave. My office manager even had the lunch-hour catered so with the exception of the times I've stood in the bathroom taking a piss, I haven't had a moment alone since stepping foot in the building.

With one final round of goodbyes, I excuse myself from the impromptu parking lot conversation and try not to run as I head toward my truck.

Work is fucking exhausting.

Unlocking my door, I admire my new windows as I slide into the driver's seat with a groan. Maybe I'll just sell this location too, and I can be a stay-at-home husband to Elouise. Packing her lunches every morning and licking her pussy every night.

Truck on, I pull my phone out of my pocket and smile at the missed text I have from Elouise.

Swiping to read the message, the smile slips off my face.

Flowers?

Ice crawls up my spine. I didn't send her any fucking flowers.

I hit the phone icon next to her name and wait for it to ring, but it clicks straight to voicemail.

I hang up and try again.

Same result.

"Fuck!" I shout the word, slamming my car into drive and peeling out of the parking lot.

I barely miss the bumper of a car as I cut across traffic, aiming for the fastest route to the freeway.

One hand on the wheel, I tap my phone again.

Silence... "Hi, sorry I missed your-"

I let it play through, taking deep breaths. She should still be doing her parent conferences, so maybe she just turned her phone off to avoid interruptions.

I force in another long inhale through my nose. It could be a simple misunderstanding. Maybe Maddie sent her flowers but didn't include a card and Elouise just assumed they were from me. But then images of my broken truck windows, a man trying to enter her tent, and cars crashed together in a parking lot fill my mind.

"-call you back."

I wait for the beep, then work to control my tone, "Babe, I'm on the way to your school now. I'll be there in..." I press the gas pedal down further, "twenty minutes. Please wait for me before you leave." I hesitate. I don't want to freak her out, but I need her to know. "I didn't send you any flowers. Just... call me when you get this. Okay? I love you."

My fingers are trembling when I hang up and I press the gas down even further.

Chapter 65

Elouise

"HAVE A GOODNIGHT!" one of the fifth-grade teachers calls to me, and I return his wave before turning the other way out the front door.

My footsteps take me to where I thought Beckett said he left my car, but I don't see it. He texted me right after dropping off my keys earlier telling me he parked it in the front corner. But I'm in the front corner and I still don't see it.

I slowly turn in a circle, but my car doesn't magically appear, so I take my keys out and hold the fob up while clicking the lock button.

Nothing.

Turning slightly, I click it again and hear my horn honk from the opposite corner of the lot.

Sighing, I start to cut between the aisles, and I try to keep my grumbling about men to a minimum. I guess if you were looking at the school from the street you might consider it the front corner, but most reasonable people would call it the back corner. And it's not that I'm lazy – which, to be fair, I am – I just don't like this part of the parking lot because it's always so dark. Especially on these late nights when I'm leaving after the sun goes down.

Approaching my car, I smile seeing that Beckett backed it in. It's a nice touch.

Clicking the fob to unlock my car, I pull open the driver's door.

I'm about to toss my purse across to the passenger seat when I remember I'd turned my phone off earlier – so I wouldn't be tempted to scroll Instagram or text Beckett between parents. Taking a second, I pull my phone out of my purse and press the button to turn it back on then drop it back into my bag.

Sliding into my car, I put my purse on the passenger seat and it takes me a few seconds to realize that the dome light didn't come on when I opened the door. Beckett must've changed some setting while he was driving my car this week. I don't have the energy to try and figure it out now. I'll make him deal with it when he gets home tonight.

Home.

I smile as I start my car. Nothing sounds nicer than being at home with Beckett.

Chapter 66

Beckett

My foot taps the break as I approach the school.

There's a herd of people still streaming from the building and my hope soars. Maybe I showed up just in time.

I want to blaze straight to the front door, but there are too many cars exiting the lot, blocking my way.

Overshooting my destination, I pull into the empty bus drop off zone. Leaving it running, I shove the gear into park and jump out. Jogging toward the building.

My feet slow as I pass the spot where I left Elouise's car this morning. Her car's not there. But the spot isn't empty either.

What the fuck?

Did she leave already?

I pull my phone out of my pocket. I tried calling a half dozen times during my drive here, the calls going right to voice-mail, but the last attempt was about ten minutes ago.

My finger is about to hit her number when dark hair catches my eye.

My head jerks up and rage tsunamis through me.

"Hey!" My yell is full of accusation and several people turn to face me. But I'm only focused on one.

I stalk towards the piece of shit, his eyes widening as he takes a couple quick steps backward, crashing into bodies.

Adam's hands go up.

I can't punch him with so many witnesses, so I just shove my finger into his chest, "Is it you? Are you the fucker messing with Elouise?"

"What!?" there's panic in his voice, "I d-didn't do anything! I swear!"

"Bullshit!" I shout, and he takes another stumbling step back, "Who else would be doing this!?"

My own panic is increasing because as much as I don't want to, I believe him.

"Fuck!" I spin away from him, hitting call again on my phone. One hand holding my phone to my ear, the other tugging on my hair, I look up just in time to catch sight of Elouise's car turning out of the parking lot.

The phone rings this time and relief sags my shoulders.

She's fine.

My girl is fine.

I'd just missed-

Then she passes under a streetlamp, illuminating the inside of her car, and my heart stops as I watch a form rise in her backseat.

Chapter 67

Elouise

My ringtone sounds through the car, and I smile as Beckett's name lights up my dashboard.

"Don't answer that."

The whispered voice behind me makes me scream.

Chapter 68

Beckett

"Elouise!"

I take three sprinting strides after her car, before I accept that I'll never catch them on foot.

Turning, I run as fast as I can to my truck, dialing 9-1-1 as I fumble with the door handle.

The call connects, "What's the nature of your emergency?"

"Someone has her- they're in the car with her!" I don't even recognize my voice.

"Sir-"

"Elouise Hall is being kidnapped," my heart shreds as the words pour out of my mouth.

My truck fishtails as I floor it out of the drop off zone.

"I don't know who-" I choke on the admission.

I don't know who has her.

I don't know who has my Smoky.

My Darling.

I spin my wheel, pulling onto the main road where I saw her last, and manage to bark out a description of her car.

"Officers are on their way. I need you to remain-"

S. J. Tilly

"South on Coastal Drive!" I shout, catching sight of Elouise's car again just before it disappears around a turn.

The road she's on now leads out of town. The road is windy and narrow as it follows the edge of the lake, and it's secluded.

I blow through a red light.

I can't see her.

If they get far enough ahead of me, whoever has her could make her turn down a side road and... and...

My breaths are heaving in and out of my chest.

I can't see her.

"Sir, please don't pursue -"

I hang up the call, and dial Elouise again.

Chapter 69

Elouise

My chest hurts and I try to keep breathing, but the knife keeps nicking at the side of my neck.

"Please..." my words cut off into a sob.

"Shut up!" Mr. Olson snaps, leaning his body forward between the front seats. "Just drive!"

I don't know what to do. I know you're not supposed to drive to a second location with a kidnapper. *I know that.* But I don't know how to get out of this. I don't know how to stop my car and escape while a madman has a knife pressed to my throat.

I take my foot off the gas, hoping to buy some time, but Mr. Olson jabs the tip of the blade against my skin, "Faster!"

My whole body shakes as I grip the wheel in both hands, "Why are you doing this? What did I do?"

His laugh sounds completely unhinged. "You didn't do anything! That's exactly the point!" The knife presses harder. "I gave you time, Elouise. I gave you so much time to accept the idea."

S. J. Tilly

"To accept what?" I croak, not sure if keeping him talking is good or bad.

"That I love you!" he screams. "But you had to be a stupid little slut. Fucking *Beckett!*" he spits the name. "Letting him take what should have been mine! You're just like the rest of them!"

"Ri-Richard, I'm sorry!"

"No!" his voice is a wail. "No! You don't get to call me that! Not now!"

Tears stream down my cheeks.

The last time I cried, it was because Beckett made me feel so loved. So cherished.

He called me perfect.

Panic that I'll never see him again claws at my throat, making it even harder to breathe.

The road turns again, bringing us to a short straight away. The ground dropping away on my right, the water below looking black under the night sky.

My ringtone ripples through air, as Beckett tries to call me again.

"Don't answer that!" Mr. Olson screeches.

Blinking through my tears, I know what I have to do.

Letting the knife bite into my neck, I dart my hand forward and slap Accept Call.

"Elouise!" Beckett's panicked voice fills the car.

Mr. Olson lunges between the seats, jabbing at the dashboard with his knife, letting out inhuman shrieks.

"Lou! Baby! Can you hear me?!" The worry in Beckett's tone gouges my heart.

"I-" my grip tightens on the wheel, "I love you, Beckett."

I tell him my truth.

Then I jerk the wheel to the side.

304

Chapter 70

Beckett

"NO!" I roar.

Coldness fills me as I watch Elouise's car flip off the edge of the road. Her lights illuminate each roll until they vanish into the water.

"No! No no no!" I speed the last hundred yards then skid to a stop where her car disappeared.

I leave my truck angled across the road as I run on numb legs.

"Elouise!" I shout her name, skidding across the gravel at the edge of the road.

The ground gives way to a steep muddy slope, and I slip, dropping onto my ass as I slide down towards the lake. I come to a stop at the edge of the water and I frantically kick my boots off.

Her headlights are still lit under the water, telling me exactly where I need to go. But it looks impossibly far away. The momentum of the roll threw her further away from me.

Sloshing through the first few steps, I dive into the freezing water, the bottom of the lake dropping out beneath me.

I swim until I'm right above the vehicle and my heart seizes when I see that the car is upside down.

Taking one deep breath, I dive under the surface, just as the headlights go out.

Chapter 71

Elouise

THE WATER FEELS LIKE A CAGE. Holding me suspended in nothingness. The freezing cold is endless around me.

My fingers fumble again, trying to undo my seatbelt. But I can't get the button to work. Or maybe it's my hands.

The water is so cold.

One of the windows shattered during the violent roll down the hill. Maybe mine. Maybe all of them.

The water was immediate. Rushing through the window openings, flooding my existence.

My lungs scream.

How long has it been since my last breath?

Seconds?

It must have only been seconds.

My throat clutches at nothing.

I blink through the dim light.

I need to get out.

I need to get out!

And then everything goes black.

Pure darkness surrounds me.

I need to inhale.

I just want to inhale.

It burns.

My fingers try the seat belt again.

I can't!

I squeeze my eyes closed. Shutting out the horror of my situation.

FOCUS!

My fingers slip and I want to scream. I want to cry!

I need to breathe!

Click.

My seatbelt gives way but I hardly move, my body stuck floating in the same position.

I blink. But there's nothing to see.

Which way?

I have to breathe!

Which way is out?!

I NEED TO BREATHE!

My eyes burn along with my lungs.

I'm crying.

I'm crying because I know-

Hands grip mine. Pulling me free.

Beckett.

Strong arms close around me.

I know it's Beckett.

I want to sob.

But I need to breathe.

I can't...

My mouth opens, my lungs forcing me to pull in air that I know isn't there.

My mind tries to scream at my body to stop, but my body doesn't listen.

My lungs expand. And pain explodes through my chest as...

Oxygen.

Oxygen fills my lungs.

"It's okay. You're okay." Beckett sounds like he's crying. "Please be okay."

I want to tell him I am. That he saved me. But I'm coughing. Trying to learn how to breathe again.

My hands clutch at Beckett's warm body.

"Elouise, talk to me. Baby, please talk to me."

My numb fingers grip him tighter, and I can feel him pulling me through the water. Then my feet drag against something, and there's ground beneath me.

Our legs are still in the water, but Beckett's gotten us to the shore, our limbs are in a tangle as he lays me on my side.

His hands touch me everywhere. "Elouise. Baby."

I swallow, taking in a less painful breath, "I'm okay."

Beckett pulls me into him, his hug almost too tight.

"Elouise." He keeps whispering my name, I can feel his body shuddering.

"Thank you," I whisper between my own sobs. "You saved me."

He shakes his head as he presses his face into the side of my neck. "You were gonna get out." His hold tightens. "You would've gotten out."

We both know his words aren't true. But I still nod my head.

Chapter 72

Beckett

"I'm okay," she says it again, knowing I need to hear it.

But I continue to hold her against me, needing to feel her heartbeat against my own.

Covered in mud, soaked through with lake water, the cold hasn't quite caught up to me yet, the adrenaline still coursing through my blood.

"He-" her voice hitches, "He's still in there."

"Good." I whisper back. Knowing exactly what it means that he hasn't surfaced.

I caught enough glimpses of him through the back window while I was chasing after them that I was able to recognize the man as Mr. Olson. And fury thunders through my veins.

She starts to tremble, "He had a knife."

I pull myself back just enough to look at her. Flashing lights of arriving emergency vehicles streak through the night, but it's not enough to illuminate her face completely.

"Did he hurt you?"

She shakes her head.

"Elouise."

Her trembling fingers reach up to touch the side of her neck, "Just a little bit."

My teeth grind, and when she starts to cry again, I pull her back into my chest.

"It's over now." I glare at the lake. "It's over now."

The motherfucker is surely dead by now. And I don't feel the least bit sorry. If he were to break through the surface of the water now, I'd swim out there and drown him myself for what he put Elouise through. For whatever he was planning to do.

I press my lips to the top of Elouise's head.

The flashing lights are right on top of us now, and someone calls down from the road. After tucking Elouise's head into my body, so I'm not shouting into her ear, I yell up to let them know we're okay.

The slope is too steep and we're too wet and muddy to climb up on our own. So I wrap my woman in my arms, giving her as much body heat as I can, while we wait for help.

When the first responders reach us, I have to force my arms to unlock from around Elouise so they can bring her up before me.

She tries to put up a fight when they tell her they'll bring her up on the stretcher, but when I say please, she gives in.

The few minutes she's out of my sight, my anxiety flares back to life.

Gripping the lowered safety rope with my frozen hands, I frantically scramble up the bank.

But I don't have to search for Elouise. Because the stubborn woman is standing, arguing with a paramedic who is trying to get her into the back of an ambulance.

"Babe, you need to get checked out."

Elouise turns at the sound of my voice and the look on her face breaks my heart all over again.

I open my arms and in two steps she's colliding with my chest.

"I want to go home," her words are quiet and I hug her tighter.

"I need you to get looked at. I won't be able to settle down until you do."

Her chest heaves against mine, and I know she'll agree because I asked her.

I look over her head to the medic, "Can you treat her here?"

I can tell he wants to argue, but he nods.

Cupping Elouise's cheek, I give her a nudge until she looks up at me, "He'll look you over in the ambulance. But if he says you need to go to the hospital, then we're going."

She blinks up at me, "Okay."

Someone hands over a jug of water, and we use it to clean the worst of the mud off. The room temperature liquid feels almost warm cutting through our current chill. And I know we need to get out of the elements soon or else we'll end up with hypothermia.

There's a commotion on the hill leading down to the lake.

Elouise starts to turn towards the sound, but I catch her by the shoulders and turn her towards me.

Her lip wobbles and I don't know if it's from cold or emotion, "Is it him?"

I slide my hands up until I'm holding her face still, then move my eyes over her shoulder.

A handful of first responders crest the edge of the road, pulling a stretcher up with them. Once they're all up, they lift the stretcher and carry it to the back of the other ambulance. A few emergency flood lights have been set up, making it easy to see the hilt of the knife protruding from the dead man's chest.

Some part of my brain is telling me I should be repulsed by the sight, but the knife sticking out of his heart is the same knife that threatened Elouise's life. And if it wouldn't land me in cuffs, I'd jerk that blade free just to stab him all over again.

I press my lips to her forehead, holding them there until the ambulance doors close on Mr. Olson's corpse.

"He's gone."

She shakes her head, "I don't get it. He always seemed nice..."

I kiss her again, "Later."

Guiding her into the ambulance, I follow her in and sit down next to her. The heated air swirls around us as the medic checks vitals, asking Elouise questions and cleaning the cuts on her neck.

With no signs of a concussion and no need for stitches he reluctantly lets us go.

Of course, the cops stop us, needing questions answered.

With Elouise visibly shivering, I'm able to convince them to follow us to her house, so we can shower off the rest of the mud and warm up.

I help Elouise up into my truck and reach across to buckle her seatbelt. I wish there was a way to get her home without putting her right back into a vehicle, but there's no other option.

She shivers, and I adjust the air vents so they're blowing their hot air directly at her. "Sorry Babe, I wish I had another blanket in here for you."

She holds her hand out over the vent, "It's okay we'll-" she cuts off and looks over at the lake, "Your sleeping bags!"

"Uh," I glance out to where her eyes are pointing. "What?"

Her eyes hold far too much sadness when she looks up at me, "Your sleeping bags are still in my trunk." She sniffles. "I meant to give them back to you. I'm so sorry."

The tears break loose again and I almost laugh at the ridiculousness of it all.

"Smoky," I kiss the salty streaks off her cheeks, "I can buy more sleeping bags."

"But-"

I shake my head, "No buts." My thumb runs over her skin again and I want to see her smile so badly. "I can buy a whole store of sleeping bags. I'm rich. Remember, Baby?"

Instead of smiling she just nods like I'm being serious, "I remember."

Pressing a soft kiss to her mouth, I decide I'll only make it through the rest of the night if I focus on one task at a time.

And right now, it's getting us home.

Chapter 73

Elouise

MY EYES BLINK OPEN, and I snuggle further into Beckett's side, soaking in more of his steady strength.

Beckett held me up. All night.

After saving my life, he brought me back here. Stripping the clothes from my numbing body, he helped me into the shower, following me in and washing every inch of my skin. Then we stood together under the hot stream of water, and he held me while I cried. And cried.

And when the cops showed up, he held my hand while I retold every detail. From the flowers, to the car that was apparently moved, to the things Mr. Olson shouted before I ultimately ended his life.

Beckett got furious when I worded it like that. Claiming Mr. Olson killed himself with his actions, and I saved myself with mine.

He's right. I know he's right.

Then when the cops finally left, Beckett carried me all the way up to bed. I wasn't sure he'd be able to do it – I'm not light and it was a whole flight of stairs – but when I told him I could walk, he told me to stop talking.

I smile against his side and inhale his scent, letting it calm me further.

Last night was truly awful. The absolute worst. But if it had to happen, there's no one I'd rather have at my side. Not last night. Not right now. Not tomorrow.

The thought of him leaving, of Beckett eventually buying his own house and starting to sleep there, makes my shoulders tense with worry.

"What's wrong?" Beckett's voice rumbles against my ear, and he sounds like he's been awake for a while.

I tip my head back so I can look up at him, "I don't want you to leave."

His brows knit together and the arm around my back tightens, "I'm not going anywhere."

"I know. I..." my fingers trace a pattern on his chest and his free hand closes over mine, pressing my palm flat over his heart.

"What is it?"

I consider backtracking but then decide just to ask it. Life is too short. "Will you move in? With me?" His eyes hold mine. "Here?"

The side of his mouth pulls up, a hint of a smile, "You sure you're okay with that?"

I nod.

"Good. Because I was already planning on it."

My own lips form the smallest smile, the first I've felt since before everything went to hell last night. "Well, that was easier that I thought."

"Being with you is the easiest thing I've ever done."

My heart swells, "I love you so much."

That cocky smile is back, "Good," he repeats, and I roll my eyes. "Now it's time to get up."

"What? Why?" I groan, knowing I don't have to go to work.

Someone got ahold of the principal last night, and they've canceled all the classes at Darling Elementary today. Giving everyone a long weekend to decide how we're all going to deal with Mr. Olson's death.

Through some sort of phone call chain, the principal called Beckett's phone – when the cops were still here asking questions – to make sure I was okay. And when Beckett got off the call, he informed me I'd be off the entirety of next week too. Some sort of paid leave that I didn't really want to take, but I think he needs the time together as much as I do.

Plus, I'll use that time to start therapy. It doesn't take a genius to know that I'm going to need it after all of this.

"I have to go get a few things," is the reason Beckett gives me.

At his obvious vagueness I narrow my eyes, "What sort of things? And why do I need to be out of bed for it?"

"You'll see. And I'm not leaving you home alone, not today, so don't even ask." I sigh but don't argue. "Plus, you need to get up and move around. You're gonna be sore and the best thing for it is movement."

I know he's right about that, too, because the tiny motions I've made since waking up have my muscles straining in protest.

"Fine..." I drag the word out.

"Good girl," the arm around my back loosens and he swats my ass.

Even with my body aching, a lightness settles over my shoulders, and I make my way out of bed and into the shower.

There's coffee, toast and pain killers waiting for me on the edge of the sink when I turn off the water. And by the time Beckett walks me out of the house, I feel mostly human.

I don't know when he got the mud out of his truck, but the

seats are clean, and I take his help getting up into the vehicle.

"Here," Beckett holds out my phone and my eyes widen.

I tap the screen and am shocked when it lights up.

Someone had rescued my purse from the car last night and when Beckett took it from the cop who brought it over, I was certain it'd never work again.

"Well I'll be damned," I whisper, scrolling through all the missed notifications. I know Beckett talked to my mother early this morning, and that they're on their way back to Darling Lake – arriving in a day or two – so I don't need to worry about calling them back.

I ignore everything else and tuck my phone into my pocket as Beckett turns on the truck and starts driving. He still hasn't told me the plan for today, so I'm shocked when he pulls up outside of Maddie's little townhouse a few minutes later.

"What are we doing here?" I ask, as he helps me onto the sidewalk.

"*You* are spending time with Maddie. I'll be back in a few hours."

My lips part to ask more questions, but then Maddie's front door flies open and she comes running down the steps towards me.

"Lou!" Maddie's already sobbing, and just like that my eyes fill with tears all over again.

She's still a few feet away when Beckett holds up a hand, "Careful!"

Maddie instantly slows, Beckett's warning reminding her that my body is sore all over.

Maddie and I hug for a long time on the sidewalk, before Beckett insists we go inside and lock the door.

The next few hours pass in a blur of calories and crying.

Time with my best friend was exactly what I needed today, but I'm still happy when Beckett calls to say he's here.

I take the steps down to the sidewalk carefully and stop a few feet away from where Beckett is standing with a serious look on his face.

"What-" I look behind him, "Where's your truck? How'd you get here?"

Reaching back, he pats the hood of the massive, brand new, over-the-fucking-top expensive SUV, "I drove your new car."

"You..." My eyes widen, "I'm sorry, what did you say?"

"Your new car," he tilts his head towards the vehicle, like the answer is obvious.

"I can't accept that! Look at it!"

He actually looks at it and I roll my eyes.

"It's just a car, Elouise. You need a car."

"That's not *just* a car. It's... it's... a freaking bus! And it's expensive as hell!"

"So?" Beckett steps away from the curb, closing the distance between us.

"So, I can't accept that sort of gift from my... boyfriend."

He nods, then pulls a small box out of his pocket, "What about your husband?"

A small squeak leaves my lips as Beckett lowers to one knee before me.

"Elouise Hall, you are not just my girlfriend. You're my everything. My happiness. My sanity. My home. And I can't stand for another goddamn day to go by without my ring on your finger." He gently opens the velvet box, pulling out a giant sapphire attached to a sparking ring of diamonds. "Smoky Darling, I love you with every inch of my soul. And I need you to be by my side from now until forever. Will you please marry me?"

My heart is racing, and tears are streaking down my cheeks, but I don't need a single second to think about my answer.

"Of course, I will."

Epilogue

Elouise

"BECKETT!" his mom calls out across the lawn for the second time, and I snicker.

He heaves out a sigh, "Laugh it up Smoky, she'll be your mother soon, too."

"Compared to mine, your mom is a walk in the park."

Beckett snorts but doesn't deny my claim. And as if on cue, my mom's laughter cuts across the party making us both roll our eyes.

Watching him walk away, I lift my beer bottle, pressing the cold glass against my temple.

"Cooling yourself off from the view or the weather?" Maddie teases but does the same thing with her can of hard cider.

"Both," I laugh, then groan, "it really is hot as hell today. Whose idea was it to have an outdoor engagement party in June?"

School ended last week, and our summer is already packed with plans. Not to mention a continuous series of remodel

320

projects that Beckett's been chipping away at since he officially moved in the day we got engaged.

True to his word, the first thing Beckett changed was the en suite bathroom. Not only did he encase the shower in clear glass, he also managed to rearrange all the fixtures so the shower is now big enough to easily accommodate two.

And even though he's also updated the guest bathrooms, my parents surprised the crap out of me when they said they'd no longer park their RV in our driveway. Claiming that since I no longer live alone, I needed the privacy. *As though privacy for a single person is unnecessary.* So now when my parents come to town, they park in Beckett's parent's driveway.

I don't bother looking towards the front of the house. I know it's there.

It really shouldn't be a shock that our moms rekindled their friendship. Nor should it be a shock that the two of them insisted on hosting an engagement party for us.

They really did do a good job coordinating guests and food, even if the heat didn't cooperate. James has gotten over his attitude about Beckett and I being together. And with Tony, Beckett's brother, back in town for the party, there's no telling what sort of trouble those two will get into before the day is done. There are also some teachers from my school, some of Beckett's employees, and of course a whole slew of our moms' friends in attendance.

From across the yard, Beckett waves to catch my attention and I head over to join him.

With his arm around my shoulders, he holds up his drink, and the crowd quiets. "First off, thank you all for coming. It's so nice to have our friends and family in one place." People lift their drinks up in agreement. "And thank you to our parents for putting this all together." A small round of applause sounds and the moms both give little curtsies. Beckett gives me a quick grin before continuing, "And we can't wait to see you all again next month."

There's a beat of silence before my mom asks, "Next month? What's next month?"

I copy Beckett's grin, "Our wedding."

Beckett and I clink out bottles together then take long drinks as our mother's lose their shit.

Score one for Team Stoleman.

Epilogue II

Maddie

TAKING another sip of my iced mocha, I glare at my phone as it sits on the counter mocking me.

Another Saturday night spent working alone because it seems that every one of my employees has more of a life than I do.

"Fine!" I slam my cup down and pick up my phone. My finger hovers over the screen, but I hesitate. "Gah! What am I doing?!" I set the phone back down.

I'm not gonna cry. *I'm not gonna cry*!

Closing my eyes, I take a slow inhale through my nose, letting the coffee-scented air calm me.

Another slow breath in. *Find my happy place.*

I know why I'm doing this. I'm doing this because I'm lonely. Because I want to have someone special in my life. Someone to care about me. And hug me. And maybe even touch my vagina. With their face.

And I'm doing this because after that engagement party last weekend I now have barely a month to find a date for my best friend's wedding.

Blowing out my exhale, I open my eyes – and before I can second-guess myself, for the hundredth time – I pick my phone back up and click the button. Activating my dating profile.

Panic swamps over me.

Oh god. Oh god.

I drop the phone back on the counter and begin to pace.

What was I thinking?! I'm not prepared for dating apps!

Ding

Hands clenched in front of my chest, I lean over the phone, reading the notification at the top of my screen.

You have a match.

Bonus Epilogue

Elouise

"But what if someone's out there?" I whisper.

"No one is out there," Beckett replies, unzipping the cover over the screen window.

"But how do you know?" I glance past him towards the dark forest.

Beckett shrugs as he drags the zipper the rest of the way down, making one side of the tent see-through to the outdoors. "I just know."

"You can't possibly know!" My tone is still quiet.

Beckett stops what he's doing and slowly turns his head to look at me, "Babe, why are you whispering?"

Sitting back on the little inflatable mattress I throw my hands up, "Because I don't want anyone to hear me!" Then I gesture to the open tent window. "And now anyone could just look right in and see us naked!" I hiss.

We're still fully clothed, but we both know it's only a matter of time.

He glances outside, taking in the darkness for himself. "If

we don't open these, we'll pass out from heatstroke long before any voyeur is able to film and sell our sex-tape to the tabloids."

This isn't our first time camping since that trip back in the spring, but it is the first time we've gone since the weather turned this hot and sticky. And the fact that I'm already starting to sweat proves that we need the fresh air.

But I still feel weird thinking someone might've set up their tent nearby without us knowing, and they'll unwittingly walk by on their way to the bathroom only to get an eyeful of something they didn't ask for.

I'm busy imagining the worst when my handsome fiancé sighs, "Would you like me to take a walk around the campsite to prove that it's empty?"

I don't even hesitate. "Yes, please."

I'm sure he was only offering to be nice, but the fact that he doesn't complain makes me love him even more.

"Alright, Smoky, I'll make you a deal."

I'm already nodding, agreeing before he lays out the stipulation.

"I'll go check the perimeter, while you open the other flaps and get naked."

I snicker at the word *flaps* but keep nodding my head.

As Beckett climbs out of the tent, I let my gaze linger on his ass for a moment before I scoot over to unzip the next window.

I'm securing the flap when I hear my phone buzz.

With the full effects of the cross breeze cooling the interior of the tent, I crawl back towards my bag to check my texts.

We're trying to have a romantic and rustic evening, but Maddie's on a date tonight, for the first time in forever, and I told her to keep me updated. And I don't want to miss her texts in case she's asking for a fake emergency call so she can bail.

Opening my messages, instead of seeing a plea for help, I'm

greeted with a slightly blurry photo of an expensive looking black car.

"Damn, girl," I murmur to myself.

I don't know much about cars, but good for Maddie that her date drives something nice. And smart of Maddie to include the license plate in the photo.

He must be driving her home. Maybe she'll even get some dick tonight.

Then I see she sent a photo a little while ago of the guy's drivers license. I click on it, zooming in.

"Damn, girl!" This time my voice is louder, my eyes widening at her date's mugshot. He's fucking hot.

"I'm starting to feel jealous, and that doesn't bode well for you." Beckett's voice next to my ear startles a scream out of me.

He tsks, grabbing the phone from my hands and tossing it into the corner of the tent.

"So distracted, you didn't even hear me coming." Teeth drag down the side of my neck and despite the heat, a shiver rolls through my body.

"Is the c-coast clear?" I stammer, rotating my body towards Beckett.

"Completely." He grips my shoulders and topples us over, trapping me beneath him. "No one out there to hear you coming either."

THE END...

Acknowledgments

With every book I write, this list just gets longer and longer.

First and foremost, I need everyone to stand – go on, get the fuck up – and clap your hands for my mom, Karen. She does everything for me when it comes to these books... alpha reader, beta reader, editor, promoter... and of course, she does this without pay or accolades, which is so like her.

Next, my bestie Mandi- You get the sneak peeks and you know why I love you.

To the rest of my family, both born and chosen, thank you for all of your support. All the time. For every book.

Gigantic thank you to my cover designer, James Adkinson. You are a mother freaking genius and you can never stop designing my covers, or all the other things you've designed for me. I will literally grab you by the ankles and cling to you if you try to leave me.

Thank you to Brittni for agreeing to edit this book for me. You're amazing and I love you and I can't wait to go on more smutty adventures with you. (P.S. Everyone go search for The Smuthood and join the fun!)

Thank you Kerissa, I freaking love you and your guidance so much. You've held my hand, walked me through the Book World- and perfect example, you led me straight to Brittni, the editor for Smoky Darling. #bestdayever

Thank you, Shani Haim, my Mornight bestie. You've talked me off so many ledges and helped me to keep my sanity so many times- for that I can not thank you enough. I love you and I think everyone needs to read your books.

Thank you to my Sprint Ladies – Cat Wynn, Gabby Marie, Elaine Reed, S. L. Astor and Beatrix Sawad, I feel like most of this book was written on our Zoom calls (between snacks, discussions about snacks, and planning for our next snacks).

Thank you to my Banshees in the BeanBag. You got the dedication, but that's not nearly enough to tell you how much I appreciate all of your love and support. There's too many of you to name individually, but if you're in my group, then yes, I'm talking about YOU. I heard once that being an author is a lonely profession. But that's not even close to the fucking truth for me. You all are with me every step of the way and I see you. I feel you. And I couldn't do it without you.

Thank you to my bookstagrammers and booktokers. If you've shared anything about my books, I owe you a debt of gratitude that I'll never be able to repay. You make a world of difference and don't ever believe otherwise.

Extra thank you to Eloise for letting me steal your name. It was perfect.

Thank you to the J/P Group (iykyk), The Smuthood and all the other book groups out there that let people be themselves. As you allow members to share their favorite books and request new ones, you provide a safe space for so many readers and authors. Because of that, I have been introduced to new and amazing friends. (Looking at you A. Hall, hope you enjoyed your namesake.)

And a special thank you to teachers everywhere. These last few years have been absolute shit and you've been on the front lines helping the next generation move forward. It's truly inspiring work.

About the Author

Hi, I'm S.J. Tilly! Thank you so much for reading, it means the damn world to me and I appreciate each and every one of you!

A little about me, I live in Minnesota with my handsome husband and our small herd of rescue Boxers. When I'm not busy with them, or my books, or reading other people's books, I can probably be found in one of my gardens. Unless it's the winter half of the year... because then I'm for sure sitting with my face in a book.

But there's lots more to come, so stick around and follow me on any/all the social media platforms. Easiest way to find the links is through my website https://sjtilly.com/

Books By This Author

Sin Series
Romantic Suspense

Mr. Sin

I should have run the other way. Paid my tab and gone back to my room. But he was there. And he was... everything. I figured what's the harm in letting passion rule my decisions for one night? So what if he looks like the Devil in a suit. I'd be leaving in the morning. Flying home, back to my pleasant but predictable life. I'd never see him again.

Except I do. In the last place I expected. And now everything I've worked so hard for is in jeopardy.

We can't stop what we've started, but this is bigger than the two of us.

And when his past comes back to haunt him, love might not be enough to save me.

Sin Too

Beth

It started with tragedy.

And secrets.

Hidden truths that refused to stay buried have come out to chase me. Now I'm on the run, living under a blanket of constant fear, pretending to be someone I'm not. And if I'm not really me, how am I supposed to know what's real?

Angelo

Watch the girl.

It was supposed to be a simple assignment. But like everything else in this family, there's nothing simple about it. Not my task. Not her fake name. And not my feelings for her.

But Beth is mine now.

So when the monsters from her past come out to play, they'll have to get through me first.

Miss Sin

I'm so sick of watching the world spin by. Of letting people think I'm plain and boring, too afraid to just be myself.

Then I see *him.*

John.

He's strength and fury, and unapologetic.

He's everything I want. And everything I wish I was.

He won't want me, but that doesn't matter. The sight of him is all the inspiration I need to finally shatter this glass house I've build around myself.

Only he does want me. And when our worlds collide, details we can't see become tangled, twisting together, ensnaring us in an invisible trap.

When it all goes wrong, I don't know if I'll be able to break free of the chains binding us, or if I'll suffocate in the process.

Sleet Series

Romantic Comedy

Sleet Kitten

There are a few things that life doesn't prepare you for. Like what to do when a super-hot guy catches you sneaking around in his basement. Or what to do when a mysterious package shows up with tickets to a hockey game, because apparently, he's a professional athlete. Or how to handle it when you get to the game and realize he's freaking famous since half of the 20,000 people in the stands are wearing his jersey.

I thought I was a well-adjusted adult, reasonably prepared for life. But one date with Jackson Wilder, a viral video, and a "I didn't know she was your mom" incident, and I'm suddenly questioning everything I thought I knew.

But he's fun. And great. And I think I might be falling for him. But I don't know if he's falling for me too, or if he's as much of a player off the ice as on.

Sleet Sugar

My friends have convinced me. No more hockey players.

335

With a dad who is the Head Coach for the Minnesota Sleet, it seemed like an easy decision.

My friends have also convinced me that the best way to boost my fragile self-esteem is through a one-night stand.

A dating App. A hotel bar. A sexy-as-hell man, who's sweet, and funny, and did I mention, sexy-as-hell... I fortified my courage and invited myself up to his room.

Assumptions. There's a rule about them.

I assumed he was passing through town. I assumed he was a businessman, or maybe an investor, or accountant, or literally anything other than a professional hockey player. I assumed I'd never see him again.

I assumed wrong.

Sleet Banshee

Mother-freaking hockey players. My friends found their happily-ever-afters with a couple of sweet, doting, over-the-top in-love athletes. They got nicknames like *Kitten* and *Sugar*. But me? I got stuck with a dickhead who riles me up on purpose and calls me *Banshee*. Yeah, he might have a voice made specifically for wet dreams. And he might have a body and face carved by the gods. And he might have a level of Alpha-hole that gets me all hot and bothered.

But when he presses my buttons, he presses ALL of my buttons. And I'm not the type of girl who takes things sitting down. And I only got caught on my knees that one time. In the museum.

But when one of my decisions get one of my friends hurt... I can't stop blaming myself. And him.

Except he can't take a hint. And I can't keep my panties on.

Darling Series

Contemporary Small Town Romance

Smoky Darling

Elouise

I fell in love with Beckett when I was 7.

He broke my heart when I was 15.

When I was 18, I promised myself I'd forget about him.

And I did. For a dozen years.

But now he's back home. Here. In Darling Lake. And I don't know if I should give in to the temptation swirling between us or run the other way.

Beckett

She had a crush on me when she was a kid. But she was my brother's best friend's little sister. I didn't see her like that. And even if I had, she was too young. Our age difference was too great.

But now I'm back home. And she's here. And she's all the way grown up.

It wouldn't have worked back then. But I'll be damned if I won't get a taste of her now.

Latte Darling

I have a nice life - living in my hometown, owning the coffee shop I've worked at since I was 16.

It's comfortable.

On paper.

But I'm tired of doing everything by myself. Tired of being in charge of every decision in my life.

I want someone to lean on. Someone to spend time with. Sit with. Hug.

And I really don't want to go to my best friend's wedding alone.

So, I signed up for a dating app, and agreed to meet with the first guy that messaged me.

And now here I am, at the bar.

Only it's not my date that just sat down in the chair across from me. It's his dad.

And holy hell, he's the definition of Silver Fox. If a Silver Fox can be thick as a house, have piercing blue eyes and tattoos from his neck down to his fingertips.

He's giving me Big Bad Wolf vibes. Only instead of running, I'm blushing. And he looks like he might just want to eat me whole.

Tilly World Holiday Novellas

Second Bite

When a holiday baking competition goes incredibly wrong. Or right...

Michael -

I'm starting to think I've been doing this for too long. The screaming fans. The constant media attention. The fat paychecks. None of it brings me the happiness I yearn for.

Yet here I am. Another year. Another holiday special. Another Christmas spent alone in a hotel room.

But then the lights go up. And I see *her*.

Alice -

It's an honor to be a contestant, I know that. But right now it feels a little like punishment. Because any second Chef Michael Kesso, the man I've been in love with for years, the man who doesn't even know I exist, is going to walk onto the set, and it will be a miracle if I don't pass out at the sight of him.

But the time for doubts is over. Because Second Bite is about to start - "in three... two... one..."

Made in United States
North Haven, CT
31 May 2025